ALSO BY KARISSA KNIGHT

THE CLIENT,
Mina's Choice Book One

PRAISE FOR THE CLIENT

"**Sexy Suspense!** Love the main character-an in-control-professional law-yer, mixed with a thrill-seeking cliff diver who has other steamy secrets. The author puts this intriguing character in the middle of a perfectly twist-y psychological thriller, creating a delicious beginning to a series that will have readers anxious for the next book. (I know I can't wait.)" Valerie Biel, Author of the Circle of Nine Series

"**Sizzling!** A titillating tale [THE CLIENT] moves at a heart-racing clip as a steamy love-can-hurt-so-good courtship unfolds. The author deftly blends a provocative story with a thriller plot that builds from a nice slow burn with plenty of sizzle to a climactic explosion." –Laurie Buchanan, author of The Sean McPherson Thrillers

"**Intriguing mystery with hot sex.** When high profile attorney Wilhelmina Green takes on a handsome billionaire client, she gets more than she bargained for—or exactly what she wants. You'll need a fan and a cold glass of water close by when you read this one." Sheila Lowe, author of the Claudia Rose Mysteries

"**Riveting plot!** Meet Wilhelmina Green: This high-powered defense at-torney to the notorious is conflicted by her success. No wonder she's a divided self: Wil to her family and friends, loyal and fun-loving. Mina in the shadows-a stranger even to herself. With her reputation for success in the court, she should easily be in charge and control. But some con-tracts are binding in more ways than one. Enter the client, a person of interest connected to a string of murders who proves to be a dangerous distraction for Wilhelmina. This novel is more than a walk on the wild side: prepare to dive from a cliff and gasp for breath again and again in this first thriller by Karissa Knight." –Joy Ann Ribar, Wisconsin Author

"**More than a sexy romance.** Give yourself over to this gripping tale, and you'll be flipping pages into the night. More than a sexy romance, [THE CLIENT] is an entrée into the mind's secret places. Knight's debut is sure to be a break-out-success. Saralyn Richard, author of Bad Blood Sisters

"LOVED this. The settings, the atmosphere, the clever use of physical danger in more than the obvious... I'm inspired and want more novels with this kind of plotting. When will #2 be available???" Gisele Vezelay, author of Pride and Prejudice fan fiction books.

THE CONTRACT

THE CONTRACT

Book Two

Mina's Choice

— Karissa Knight —

GENRE: Romantic Suspense

THE CONTRACT

Published in the United States by 3 Elements Publishing

ISBN (ebook): 978-1-7368524-3-9

ISBN (paperback): 978-1-7368524-4-6

Edited by Stacey Donovan at Book Editing Associates

Cover Design by Tatiana Villa of Vila Designs

Cover image and internal images licensed with Adobe Stock Images

First Edition: August 2022

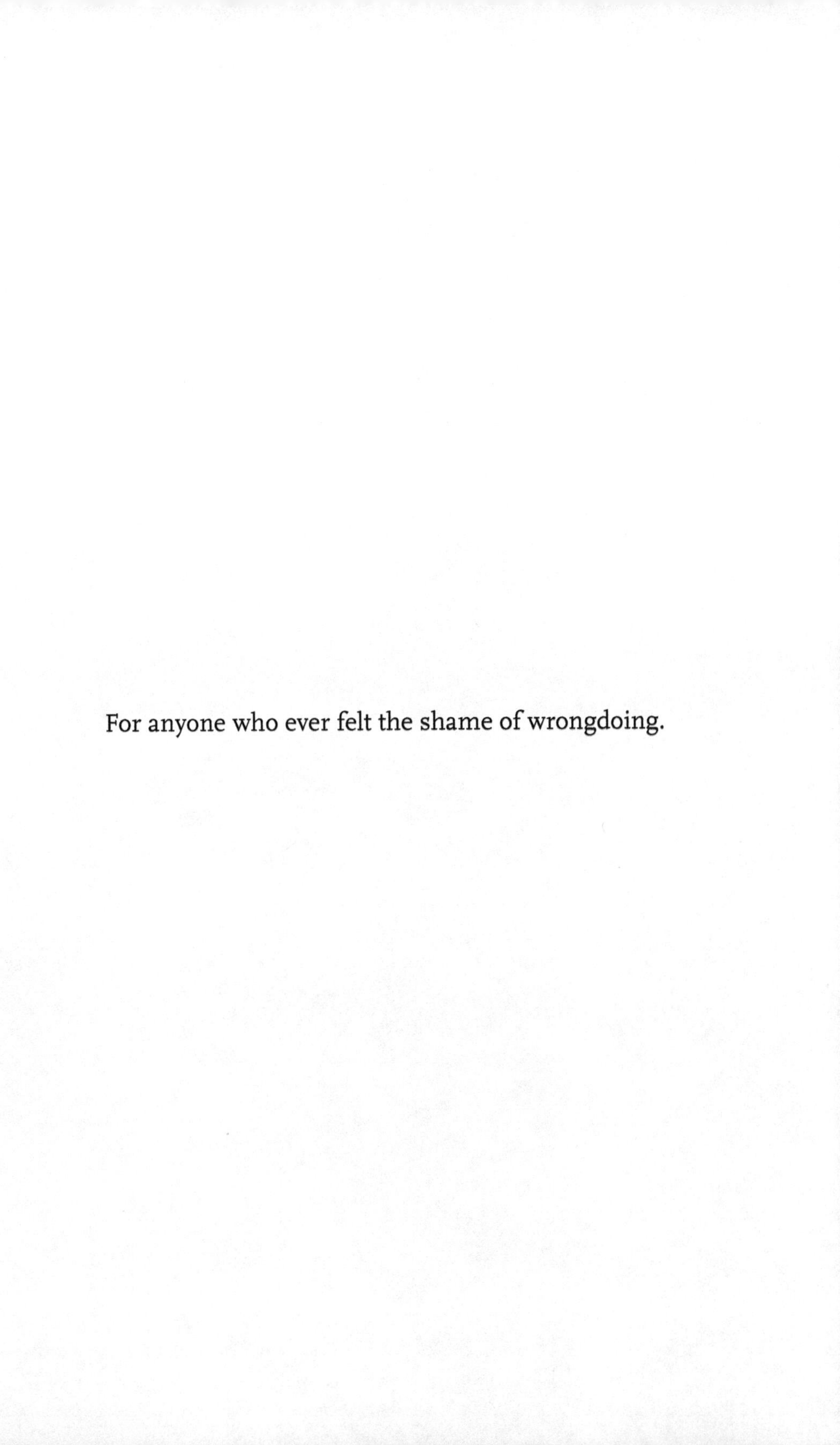

For anyone who ever felt the shame of wrongdoing.

A Word from the Author

(On the dark matter within these pages)

Self-abuse and self-harm are very real mental illnesses. If you are strug-gling with emotional distress and thinking of hurting yourself, know that there is help. Emotional support is available. (Though self-harm is not the same as attempted suicide, according to the National Alliance of Mental Illness, it can lead to an increased risk of suicidal tendencies. Suicide was the twelfth leading cause of death the US in 2020 with 45,979 American individuals taking their own lives.) Before consider-ing self-harm or suicide, please reach out to your health care provider for more information or to learn more, here's a list of resources:

National Alliance of Mental Health (NAMI): https://www.nami.org/About-Mental-Illness/Common-with-Mental-Illness/Self-harm

Mental Health America: https://www.mhanational.org/conditions/self-injury-cutting-self-harm-or-self-mutilation

MentalHealth.gov: https://www.mentalhealth.gov/what-to-look-for/self-harm

Suicide prevention helpline: 1-800-273-8255

Human trafficking helpline: 1- 888-373-7888

"As I jumped from that cliff into the black abyss below there was no way to know what I would find at the bottom. Perhaps it was my destiny. For whatever reason, I rode that wave as if my life depended on it. What I eventually discovered surprised everyone who thought they knew me. Though mostly, it surprised me."

— Wilhelmina Green

"I'm yours," she said at length . . . "I'll be whatever you want me to be."
— Pauline Reage

PROLOGUE

ONE YEAR AGO:

From heights of sixty to eighty feet, it takes up to three and a half seconds to hit the water. In that brief moment of time, a thousand thoughts, images, or feelings rush through my mind. Sometimes during the fall, I'd worry I'd forgotten how. The air would rush past my body, but I'd keep my eye on the landing—growing closer each fraction of a second—as I'd tuck and somersault or straighten into an arrow. With three seconds to freefall, you enter at such a force that if any part of your body is out of line, it will break. But I'd trained for this. My body knew exactly what to do. When I hit the water, profound silence—as near to death as I could imagine—allowed me to forget what I'd done.

I had a suitcase packed and ready under the defense table in the courtroom. The prosecutor Aaron Stroheim and I gave our closing speeches, and the jurors filed out to deliberate. They didn't take long to come up with a verdict, my case was solid. My client was acquitted.

As soon as the foreperson read the verdict, I lowered my head and began to gather my things. I wanted to get as far away from Cook County Courthouse as I could. I alone knew Martin Liebert was guilty of raping his young associate.

"Thank you, Miss Green." Martin's congratulatory tone sickened me. He opened his arms.

I avoided his embrace, nodded, and politely congratulated him. Then I turned my back on the courtroom and dove through the crowded hallway. Reporters shoved microphones into my space as I dodged one question after another. The security guards cleared the way for me. Four officers escorted me through the crowd of journalists and female protesters throwing hateful words like stones. I felt shamed like Cersei Lannister in later episodes of *Game of Thrones*.

I ducked into the nearest cab. "O'Hare, please. Delta departures." A week of vacation was exactly what I needed to put my head back on straight.

Martin Liebert, aka Slippery Marty as the media nicknamed him, was an investment broker. He had been arrested and charged with raping Leeann Reigns. Other victims had accused him of inappropriate conduct and assault in the workplace. It was his fourth offense like this, the first to go to trial.

I didn't like him from the start, but I was a young attorney working for a big firm. Allegedly, Slippery Marty had gotten in an argument with Leeann about an investment client, a local politician. Leeann had given this politician financial advice and subsequently "stole" him away from Liebert. As a result, Marty lost hundreds of thousands in projected income.

He threatened Leanne in front of her eight-year-old daughter, then took Leanne to her bedroom and raped her. In my defense arguments, I discounted the child's witness testimony and maintained that Leeann had wanted Marty's job. I painted her as a power-hungry, ladder-climbing bitch. I told the jury she led him on. That her nuances couldn't be understood by an eight-year-old. The jury sided with me, a female defense attorney. No wonder Milton, Wallace & Edwards appointed me.

Marty confessed to me. He would have confessed to God if he believed in such a thing. I tried to refuse him the opportunity, but not quickly enough. He told me how he'd pinned her to the bed and unzipped her pants while she squirmed.

I'd helped exonerate him. His sins became mine.

After my earlier success defending other sexual predators, Milton, Wallace, & Edwards assigned to me the most high-profile rape and sexual misconduct cases. I didn't get to choose. I took these controversial cases with the promise of a long and successful career. So far, I was on a winning streak and my upcoming twenty-ninth birthday would be a milestone to remember. My reputation for acquitting bad men was growing. And now, I had seven days to consider my sins against humanity. Seven days alone with my cell phone turned off. Seven days to escape the hell in my mind.

The only people who knew I was traveling were my boss Jim Milton and my paralegal, Christina. They had no idea where, and I told Christina I'd be someplace with no service. Toting a small carry-on filled with essentials—a sundress, bathing suit, toiletries, and athletic shoes—I checked in at the airline kiosk. In line for TSA, I avoided people's gazes and kept my eyes on the floor. Once through security, I put my shoes back on and caught my breath before heading to my departure gate.

Anonymous, I wandered the streets of Dubrovnik and admired the quaint and beautiful ancient coastal city in Croatia. Centuries-old buildings with red tiled roofs and cathedrals from bygone eras lined the streets. No one here knew me. Bright sunshine washed away the storm cloud of post-trial negativity. With no commitments and no cellphone, I could breathe. On these cobblestone streets I was simply one of a thousand tourists with a *Game of Thrones* guidebook. Long lines of visitors filed into Fort Lovrijenac, the home of King's Landing, made famous by the book and subsequent HBO series. Though these sites thrilled me, recalling the magnificent cinematography of the popular series wasn't why I'd come.

During the nearly direct flight to Croatia, I killed time researching my tombstoning jump site. After placing third in the National Diving Championships in college, I'd discovered a way to cleanse my soul—metaphorically—by jumping into the arms of God and into water several dozen meters below. Tombstoning, as it was called, freed me from mental torture, chains I wrapped around myself after each trial.

The rocky coasts surrounding this region jutted over clear, azure water. The private tour guide and his translator drove me in a speed boat around numerous Croatian islands where I searched for an ideal diving location. From the water, I looked up at the tortuous cliffs surrounding

Stiniva Beach and the Blue Cave. Uninhabited rocky outcrops, like the peaks of a sunken mountain range, dotted the Adriatic Sea. During the day trip, we finally anchored near Mana Island. Here, I climbed the pale, square rock formations and dove a dozen meters into the green-blue sea. My audience of two gave me a standing ovation. I tipped them a thousand euros because their applause didn't feel earned. I wanted a higher cliff. Something more dangerous.

At Dugi Otok Island, a wall of tan and orange rock met the sea. This location provided the tallest cliffs, some reaching 160 meters above the ocean waves. My crew reluctantly stood lookout while I climbed the face to a tiny ledge. Twenty meters above the turquoise water, I faced the wall. With just enough room to bend my knees in preparation, I sprang backward.

The rock crumbled beneath my toes as I pushed off, diminishing the force of my kickoff. Because of the weak launch, I had no time to arch my back and entered the water feet first at an angle. The crooked entry snapped my left ankle to the side, tearing the extensor tendons on the top of my foot. Disheartened, I swam slowly back to the boat.

For the rest of my trip, I wrapped my foot and babied it. I applied heat and ice every few hours and massaged it with medicated salve I'd found in a local drug store.

Late on my fifth day I dined at a five-star restaurant overlooking the Adriatic Sea. A pair of gentlemen flirted with me from across the patio. On their way out, they sent a bottle of champagne to my table. I didn't finish even one glass, so before I left, I gave the bottle to a couple who seemed to be enjoying the night and each other. I had no idea those two gentlemen would play a greater part in my life the following year.

By taxi, I returned to the hotel, donned my bathing suit, and wrapped my foot in supportive, waterproof Coban. I gathered a few tools and walked from the hotel to the pier. My tour guide and I left Pile Bay at midnight. His translator assured me this was not the best time to see the area, but I didn't want a visual spectacle. I wanted to be alone when I dove.

On the south side of the Island of Vis, Stiniva Beach offered the best opportunity for my dangerous mission. The populated island where soaring white cliffs protected a pristine, white sand beach, was a tourist attraction frequented by beachgoers and boaters. An array of lounge chairs lay in wait for the next wave of sunbathers. In the cove, my guide dropped anchor about thirty feet from shore, away from a half dozen boats floating beside buoys. I paid my drivers double their rate and tipped them another thousand euros then told them to leave me. Money in hand, they reluctantly agreed. I slipped into the salty ocean and swam to the beach.

I'm not a solo climber but I had practiced at a climbing gym. I gripped the wall tentatively as dull pain throbbed in my ankle. Despite it, I maintained the kind of control that eventually beats a person down. I convinced myself—just as I had convinced the jury—that there was no doubt, no pain, and nothing wrong. I craved having that control taken away. I wanted to be punished for playing God with another person's life.

When I reached the peak, the fragrant smell of rosemary growing wild among these rocks bloomed as I hiked through the knee-high plants. The piney scent filled the air. A sliver of moon rose to the east. Uneven footing jostled my swollen ankle. A loose pile of rocks collapsed under my weight, causing me to fall on my butt and slide about ten feet. I caught myself but scraped the heels of both hands as dislodged stones tumbled down the cliff. I pressed onward.

Adrenaline made me impervious to the pain in my bleeding palms. If I could locate it, the ideal jump site dropped straight into the undulating water below. Where I approached the point, the sky turned from black to cerulean blue over the sea. Dark shadow enveloped the rocky wall all the way to the water below. During daylight, I had found the deepest water to safely plunge into but hadn't anticipated how black the sea would be at night.

While checking the stability of the stones beneath my feet I stepped out on the ledge. Visibility increased with the light of dawn. Quickening my forward progress, I finally reached the edge and looked into the black waves below. In the daytime, the water was so clear that rocks beneath the surface were apparent. Their location obvious. I recalled that I needed to propel outward about fifteen feet to avoid collision.

Salty breezes whipped my hair into my mouth. Dark water splashed below promising to wash away my sins. Euphoria, fear, excitement, all mixed together in my personal brand of escapism. In the time it took to hit the water, I would have no control. My burdens would remain on this ledge. And then. . . quiet forgiveness would silence my mind.

My arms rested at my sides. I curled my toes over the edge of the stony cliff and looked downward. Three seconds of freefall. It was enough. I looked toward the horizon where black water met purple sky, then closed my eyes. I inhaled deeply, bent my knees, swung my arms, and propelled outward, away from the rocky ledge.

The launch was a perfect 6.0. In flight, I twisted into a somersault then hit the cool water feet first with minimal splash. As I went under, something tore at my leg.

I'd misjudged.

The force of the impact told me what my senses could not. I didn't feel the gash as I should have, as I kicked away from the unseen rock and rose to the surface. My fingers found the side of my thigh where sharp coral had torn my leg wide open. But cool water and cortisol denied me the onset of pain.

Winded, I floated on my back and gently kicked my way toward shore. In the shallow water, I limped to the beach. I needed to sit but couldn't afford to get any sand in the wound. In the dark night, I couldn't see the extent of it. Air stung the bleeding gash and now pain registered in my nervous system. I collapsed on a beach lounger and groaned. My vision clouded, and I knew I was losing a lot of blood. As darkness threatened my consciousness, I pulled from my belt bag the Ziplock baggie protecting my cellphone and called my translator.

In the dim light of the streetlamp, a bloody trail connected me to the sea.

— 1 —

The orange Chicago skyline glowed like fires burning in the distance. The sun hadn't yet gone down on the sizzling summer evening. In Jonathon Heun's Lake Forest mansion, I closed the floor-to-ceiling curtains of the luxurious first-floor bedroom windows then lit two candles. I dabbed on tinted lip-gloss and stripped off every bit of clothing, then fastened tightly around my neck the diamond-studded collar that Jonathon, my lover, had given me weeks ago.

Earlier, I'd printed out the document written by Jonathon: the Elements of Submission contract which described the relationship I was about to dive into with him. I'd taken two days to read it. Two days to read my lover.

The contract outlined consensual sex play between a dominant and submissive. It listed sadistic pleasures to be given or received, including the acts of piercing and tattooing, caning, and nipple torture. Invasive devices—gags and anal plugs—were among the toys listed in the contract. Jonathon asked me to check off items and label them as hard or soft limits.

Until a week ago, Jonathon had been my client. I was his criminal lawyer in a case where he—it later turned out—had been nothing more than a person of interest. He'd hired me because he had the money to do so. As the CEO for a top-ten Forbes-listed software company, he needed to protect himself and his assets.

As the case progressed, my role as Jonathon's criminal lawyer became moot. We helped investigators work to solve the murder cases and after the killer came for me, our contract dissolved.

Yet during that time, our interests in each other had bloomed.

Afterward, Jonathon brought me to his mansion in Lake Forest,

Illinois, because—I thought—he wanted to pursue a relationship with me. At first, I'd taken his offer of the contract as a power play. But I realized I'd read him wrong. This new contract defined our roles. It allowed me to give or deny consent to certain activities related to sex play. By signing it, I gained power, too. It gave me the ability to define the activities we would explore together. Most importantly, it gave me what I'd ultimately wanted. Punishment.

By now I'd read the contract dozens of times. I knew it as well as the legal documents I wrote for my clients. With Jonathon as my dominant partner, he would have control in the bedroom. His job would include decisions to deliver pleasure and pain by various means. I would be his submissive, the recipient of his rulings. By signing the contract, I gave him the right to bind my ankles and wrists. I gave him the right to whip me or pour hot wax on me. I gave him the right to control my orgasms.

When I signed the contract, I set no limits and repealed none of the suggested activities. I wanted to try them all. My safeword *tombstone* gave me an out if I needed it. Otherwise, Jonathon would have unlimited domination over me, and that was *my* choice. I wanted Jonathon to master me and loved the pain as much as the pleasure. I needed to lose control.

I placed the contract on the foot of the bed in front of me then positioned myself kneeling with my knees spread wide, wearing nothing but his diamond-studded collar. When Jonathan entered the room, I held my breath.

Black hair framed intense blue eyes above his straight nose and chiseled jaw. From across the room his powerful energy fluttered my heart. His tall muscular body could shield and protect or overpower and conquer me. Tonight, I chose the conqueror.

He closed the door. His eyes may have needed to adjust to the dim candlelight because he took time to soak up the ambience. Slowly, a wicked smile spread across his lips. "What mischief are you up to?"

I nodded to indicate the contract lying at the foot of the bed.

Jonathon picked up the paper. "Elements of Submission?" he said, flipping to the second page. "You've signed it."

"I have."

Jonathon regarded me carefully and then frowned. He set the contract down on a table, took off his suit jacket and loosened his blood-red tie. He paused and looked over the pages. "You've set no limits of play."

"I'll use a safeword if I need to."

Am I reading him wrong? Is he uncomfortable with this?

He said, "I hope you've made a conscientious decision, Mina. With a contract in place, I'll expect more from you. If you don't comply with the rules, punishments will be severe. Do you understand?"

"Yes." The tingling thrill of submitting to him cascaded down my back. I smiled.

He took a deep breath and picked up the pen. "Are you absolutely certain, Mina? BDSM is an intense lifestyle, one that I take seriously."

"Yes, Jonathon. I've thought it over carefully."

"As dominant, I reserve the right to make changes to this document based on your good behavior and/or transgressions. Once I've signed it, I reserve the right to make decisions for you regarding this document. This will not change how you behave in the real world, or how you do your job, but it changes things between you and me to a large degree."

"I'm aware of that, Mr. Huen. I like rules."

His smile and chuckle broke through thick air. "My expectations of your behavior will also change. Having signed this, you'll need to follow the rules, Ms. Green, or pay the consequences."

I nodded. "Aren't rules made for breaking?"

"I don't think you would have said that a month ago." His white teeth flashed behind his grin.

I shrugged. "Things have changed."

Jonathon seemed to think it over. Heavy regard for the situation drew lines around his mouth. We both understood the ramifications of a signed contract. He waited; I think he expected me to back down, so I stared into his eyes without faltering.

He took a slow breath, and a distinct change came over him—so subtle that I couldn't identify it—and he leaned over the table and signed. "Now you are mine. I control your pleasure and your pain. I am your Master."

Just as some people become addicted to extreme sports or tattooing, I longed for this. I savored the anxiety mingled with excitement that sent my blood racing for what would come next. Adrenaline flooded my veins. Three seconds of free fall. Three seconds to wonder if I'd made the right choice . . . *splash*. I was ready for this. I was ready to submit to Jonathon.

His hand came down hard on the bed as he leaned toward me. He whispered the command, "Put your head down and extend your arms out in front of you with your wrists crossed, Mina."

In yoga it's called Child's Pose. It's a vulnerable posture. I lowered my head in a submissive manner. My naked butt raised up in the air, exposed. I heard him unbuttoning his shirt and longed to look up at his strong physique. Instead, I waited for his instructions.

Jonathon tied my wrists together with something soft. He stood beside the bed and caressed my shoulders, gently stroking downward. I tingled at his touch. Though I wanted it, I'd asked for it, we hadn't had rough sex since Jonathon brought me to his house in Lake Forest.

"Your skin is soft and smooth," he said.

"And your hand is warm and gentle." I turned to see his face. As his gaze met mine, something like doubt crossed his features. It seemed fleeting. But I wondered, was he as hesitant and uncertain about this as I?

His blood-red necktie encircled my wrists. Jonathon helped me rise and I lifted my bound-together hands to his chest. His arms. His broad shoulders.

I asked, "What do you want, Jonathon?"

"I want to please you. I want you to be happy, Mina. And if this is how you want it, how you want me—"

"I thought you wanted it, too."

He dropped his chin and for a moment, Jonathan looked down at our feet. He said, "I realize what a big step this is in our relationship. This contract will simply clarify our roles. That's important to me." His sexy, silky voice hummed. "If you want me to take control—if that's what pleases you—then I'll do as you wish. The submissive—"

"—has all the power. You've said that before." I held out my wrists to him. "Take control, Jonathon. Punish me."

He gave a slight nod and looked into my eyes. The hungry look on his face, like a tiger observing his prey, made me want to kiss him.

He said, "I did not give you permission to look at me. Keep your eyes down."

I dropped my gaze and smiled. The red tie looped around my wrists reminded me of *Fifty Shades of Grey*. The irony didn't get past me.

Jonathon stepped closer and lifted my chin in a rough manner. "Is something funny? Tell me what's funny."

I tried not to look at him and replied, "Why? Does it bother you that I'm smiling? Don't you want to spank me?"

The corners of Jonathon's lips curled upward. In one swift movement, he tossed me over his knee. Aware of his overpowering strength, I didn't fight. I wanted the reprimand. With his flat hand, he gave me just what I'd asked for. Repeated blows left no time to recover in between. I gasped and cried out with the fiery burn of his slaps. As my skin heated, sharp pain caused my mound to warm. On instinct, I struggled to get away.

Jonathon released me. "Is that punishment enough? Or do you want more?"

I sat on the bed, on my hot ass, and looked him in the eye. "It's sufficient punishment for now." Indeed, the heat radiated to my pussy. Aroused, I moaned and touched myself.

His muscles rippled, firm and powerful as he removed his black trousers and freed his erection. He lifted me up by my waist and cupped my bottom with his strong hands. I pressed my hips against his and curled my legs tightly around his waist as he eased me onto his hard penis. I lifted my bound arms over his head and rested them on his strong shoulders.

Jonathon carried me to the wall nearest the bed and pinned me against it. He took advantage of the leverage he gained and plunged into me. Waves of pleasure flowed through me. I bit into his neck, and Jonathon groaned and pulled away.

Kissing me hard on the mouth, he swung me back to the bed. He lowered his lips to my belly, my swollen sex, his hot breath against my pussy, his tongue dipped into my folds, flicking, burning. Desire engulfed me, and I writhed beneath him. Cruel hands stilled me . . . and he began again.

Jonathon kissed my hips, my breasts. He thrust deeply into my tight opening, and I reached a peak—a cliff—and my body spasmed with euphoria.

He unbound my wrists. Grateful for freedom, I wrapped my arms around his muscular back. I stroked his taut shoulders and arms. In beat with his rhythmic movements, my hips met his pelvis—again, again, again. Our thrusts matched, together building speed and intensity. And then, in that instant of twisting, sublime pain, we cried out in unison.

When finally we collapsed, our arms and legs entwined.

We were quiet for many long minutes before Jonathon delicately traced my features with his fingertip. His steely gaze eased and met mine with unexpected softness and understanding that I'd never had from anyone before. We were equals in so many ways.

Could a relationship like ours last?

I kissed his fingertips, and he rolled to his side facing me. "You surprised me tonight, Mina," he said. His features had relaxed. His lips slightly parted as he stroked my hip.

"How?"

"I didn't think you'd sign another contract." He was referring to our previous legal contract as his criminal lawyer. Two women close to him were murdered.

I kissed his rough, stubbly cheek. "I want this contract and I want you, Jonathon." My words hung in the air like the exhalation from a cigarette.

After a bit, he whispered, "We're a perfect match."

Did he doubt it?

I did. I'd entered this relationship with one selfish purpose in mind. Jonathon was a self-proclaimed dominant, and I wanted—no, needed— his discipline.

"You don't sound so sure," I said.

"I'm not sure I can give the proper amount of time to this relationship right now. I want you here, and I love your company. But I'll be traveling again, soon."

Jonathon had offered me the contract early in our relationship. Had he meant to scare me away? To tease me? In previous relationships, men in my life had been needy. They had wanted more than I could give. So this—Jonathon's reluctance to spend time—turned the tables. Unsure how to react, I said, "I only have two weeks of vacation, and then I'm going back to Chicago. I won't get in your way if that's what you're worried about."

"You could never get in my way. I'll give you what you want—"

"—spankings?"

"Whipping, caning, you name it." He pushed up on his elbow and gazed down at me. "While you're here, let me take care of you and spoil you—"

"As per contractual terms—"

He touched my hair. "At least until you return to Chicago," he said.

"What we do in the bedroom stays here, in my opinion. If I'm to remain your submissive, it will have nothing to do with my professional life."

Jonathon smiled and rested a hand on my waist. "Now you sound like the woman I hired. The woman I admire."

There was something else he was going to say, I sensed he held back. Jonathon had teased and captivated my curiosity about this lifestyle. I wondered what he was keeping from me. If he was having second thoughts . . . Well, I had them too, but it was too soon to voice them.

He shifted to his side and raised up onto an elbow, taking a lock of my long brown hair and twirling it in his fingers. His eyes sparkled in the dim light, but there was something else, something dark in his look that I didn't recognize.

~ 2 ~

Not a deep sleeper like me, Jonathon didn't stay in bed long. He eased under the covers and curled around me in the middle of the night, then he was up again at the crack of dawn.

My bedroom at his mansion was just for me. He had another somewhere upstairs—I hadn't seen it yet—where he did private things, collected his thoughts, and dressed in his beautifully cut suits and jackets, dark jewel-toned shirts with cufflinks, and high-priced Italian leather shoes.

Used to living alone, I didn't mind the privacy. I slid my arms and legs into a pair of black-satin pajamas. I splashed water on my face and gave my long oak-brown hair a brush. Then I dabbed on lip gloss and went to the kitchen in search of coffee.

Grant, Jonathon's cook, and casual butler was preparing a meal that filled the house with tempting aromas. He stopped what he was doing to smile at me. With a style all his own, he wore a black apron over orange slacks and a red button-up shirt with a bowtie. "I made a fresh pot of coffee. May I pour you a cup?"

"Yes, thank you."

Grant filled a black mug and added the right amount of half and half.

A bowl on the counter held shiny, dark-red cherries. I popped one into my mouth, bit it in half, and discreetly spit the pit into my napkin. "I might get spoiled living here."

"That is the plan, Ms. Green."

A flat-screen television on the wall drew my attention. The news anchor discussed local politics, but my eye caught the news feed scrolling across the bottom of the screen.

Travis King, the man charged with accessory to kidnapping Chicago Defense Attorney Wilhelmina Green, has been released to the witness protection program. King is a person of interest in the ongoing investigation of two murders. The victims were both known associates of billionaire Jonathan Heun.

I sipped the hot coffee to ward off the chill spreading up the back of my arms. A few months ago, after someone killed Jonathon's personal assistant Kymani Zhao, Jonathon hired me to represent him. Jonathon then assigned his own bodyguard Travis King to protect me after the murder of a second victim, another female friend of Jonathon's. For weeks Travis escorted me everywhere while Jonathon and I helped police with the investigation.

I never questioned why Jonathon would need a bodyguard. Since the onset of COVID-19, Prevail Software Systems sales had soared and as CEO, Jonathon's net-worth was in the stratosphere. These days, every clinic and hospital needed the easiest access to pharmaceuticals. PPS made the network software that connected doctors within health care systems and beyond. By securing each patients' records and making communication between specialists easy, PPS had risen above similar software systems, connecting doctors to pharmacists and pharmacists to suppliers across the globe. In an industry where communication was imperative to an individual's health, PPS software was by far one of the best in the industry.

Travis King's Chinese connection stole the key software designs from PPS and gave them to the Chinese government. It was still unknown whether King assisted in the murders, but one thing was clear. He consorted with the Chinese to undermine Jonathon's control of his multimillion-dollar business by framing Jonathon for murder. When I nearly became the third victim, King's betrayal hit home. After he and his cohort attacked me, they were arrested and charged with kidnapping and accessory to the murders. King traded valuable information about the Chinese in exchange for his freedom.

Fortunately, my client Jonathon, was never truly suspected of the crimes. He was guilty of nothing but trust and loyalty to his bodyguard. In my humble opinion, he trusted people too much.

I turned away from the television. "Is Jonathon around?"

"He's upstairs in the Kendo room."

I hopped off the stool. "Thanks, Grant. Let me know if they say anything interesting."

"I'll keep you apprised, Ms. Green."

I took my coffee and went looking for my lover. The spiral staircase in the entryway contrasted with the light marble floor. Luxurious, chocolate-brown hardwood stretched the length of the second-floor hallway, which overlooked the front door. I climbed the stairs in my bare feet. The high ceiling supported a dark metal chandelier—suggestive of a gothic castle—that matched the black wrought-iron railing. Scattered Persian rugs added splashes of red, orange, and blue.

At the top of the stairs, Jonathan's voice boomed on the other side of a set of walnut double doors. Another man cried out, and I heard a loud thump as if someone had fallen.

I knocked softly, then opened the door. In the center of the room stood Jonathon with a black cage mask over his face and wearing a black skirted robe and protective padding. In his hands, a shiny metal sword flashed in the light. The other man lay on the padded floor. Jonathon stood over him with the advantage.

Behind the protective mask, Erik Edwards, Jonathon's new head of security said, "Good shot. I should have seen that coming. Maybe someday my skills at kendo will match yours. For now, I'm still your humble student."

Jonathon pulled Erik to his feet. They bowed to each other, speaking Japanese words. Then Jonathon removed his face protection. "Good morning, Mina. Please, join us."

"Hi, Mina," Erik said. He took off his face cage and began removing the other gear.

Jonathon sheathed his sword and removed his shoulder pads. "You did well this morning, Erik. We are all students of the art. I haven't trained in a few months, so you challenged me today. Excellent work."

A collection of swords hung on the far wall between windows overlooking Lake Michigan. About twenty sheathed and unsheathed swords gleamed in the sunlit room. I inspected one sword with red gemstones embedded in the hilt. "You have quite a collection here," I said.

Jonathon said, "They are Katanas, Japanese samurai swords." He pointed to the one I'd admired. "That one is about five hundred years old."

After he removed his gear, Jonathon joined me by the window and put his arm around my waist. "Did you sleep well?" He nuzzled his unshaven face into my neck and hair.

His rough beard tickled, and my shoulder inadvertently crept to my ear. "Yes, I did." I wrapped my arms around his warm body and gave him a kiss. The heady odor of his perspiration aroused me.

"All of Jonathon's swords are weapons grade," Erik said. "Which means they can kill you."

"They're beautiful, but I wouldn't want to be caught on the other side of that," I said, noticing the razor-like edge of the blade.

"Jonathon could teach you some practical self-defense. He's a good fighter," Erik said.

"Mina can defend herself," Jonathon said.

"I'm a first degree Aikido black belt," I said. Indeed, I had trained for about ten years.

"Then maybe you'll give us a run for our money." Erik laughed and removed his chest shield. His slick, blue Under Armour t-shirt brightly contrasted his coffee-colored skin.

Jonathon remained serious. "You two ought to train together. It would be good practice for you both. It always helps to be prepared."

"True," I said, recalling the day Travis attacked me and nearly bested me.

Erik stowed his gear in a tall wooden wardrobe on the right side of the room. "I'm going to hit the shower before lunch if you don't mind. See you soon."

I followed Jonathon to the door, and we watched Erik walk down the hall to his rooms. "After the attack last week, I see how my skills need improvement."

"I'm happy to help. What are you worried about?"

"Nothing, really. Travis King is in a witness protection program. They'll relocate him to another city," I said.

"Travis." Jonathon grunted and his jaw muscles tightened. "That will never happen again, Mina."

He took my hand and kissed it. "The weekend is coming, and I'll be home. Is there anything you'd like to do?"

Funny he asked. I'd been thinking about my best friend, Traci. This year we'd grown closer than ever. Weekends were usually our time together, but I'd skipped out on several luncheons and bar-crawls with her, having spent the last month completely devoted to Jonathon.

I turned in his arms and said, "I miss my friend, Traci."

"Invite her." Jonathan's smile brightened his eyes.

Jonathon's statement rocked me backward. "Here?"

"Of course." His impish grin was contagious.

My smile widened, too. "But I thought you never invited anyone to your house." He'd said as much when we drove here a week ago. He'd told me that only his dad had come here. His mom had passed away before he bought the mansion.

His eyes twinkled. "I've never met anyone like you, Mina."

—3—

Traci, I found out, was also busy. She had finally met a guy and her calendar was full until the following week when he went out of town. We agreed to tell each other everything when we got together then.

In the meantime, unproductive summer days grew long and lazy. Empty hours filled with meditative reverie. Most days, Jonathon drove to Chicago to work and returned home around seven. While I slept, Jonathon worked in his study. He rarely spent the night in bed with me and was usually gone from the house before I woke in the morning.

During the day, I swam in his pool or lay in the sun on his pool-house patio overlooking Lake Michigan. At night, we talked about our childhoods or explored some of the things in the contract. He seemed to have an endless supply of gags and rope with which to tie me. And he proved to be an expert in the art of eliciting and then extending a woman's orgasm.

With Jonathon's case closed, I used my leave of absence to figure things out. Was I ready to get back in the game? I had needed this retreat and savored each moment. Court proceedings, meetings, and deadlines—the fast attorney's pace that I'd grown used to—quickly became a distant memory.

And yet . . . after ten days, I was more than ready to go back to work. Emails from my paralegal, Christina, poured in with new cases to profile. I vowed never to represent men like Senator Peterson again, not after he savored telling me that he brutally raped his assistant.

As if I could forgive him. In a way, I'd absolved him by helping get his acquittal. I couldn't even forgive myself.

Until recently, I'd let Milton, Wallace, & Edwards dictate my assignments while they battered and fucked my self-esteem. As I scrolled through my emails under a canopy of great oaks and maple trees, the glass-top table wobbled slightly on the paved stone patio. A cool northern breeze indicated there might be showers later today, so I wanted to stay outside as long as possible.

One of the emails from Christina highlighted a case in which a Chicago investment broker was recently charged with solicitation and money laundering. Bohdi Michaels had been calling and emailing my office for over a week. I didn't want to work with the predatory types interested in my brand of representation. However, I had a high-priced condo in Lincoln Park to pay for. I needed the money.

My attention drifted to the last part of Christina's email, where she wrote that the Lake Shore Women's Shelter sought volunteers. They needed role models from the community to become mentor *Sisters* who could befriend battered women.

I typed the name of the shelter into the search bar. LSWS offered a full array of services to mistreated women, including legal advice and police protection. They offered counseling for women and children, victims of domestic abuse. The website had links to local hospitals and safe houses, and a bright blue button with the beckoning words, Volunteer Now.

Wind rustled the leaves above. Behind me, the sliding door opened.

"Good morning," Jonathon said.

I sat back in the wrought-iron chair and stretched my arms over my head. "Hello, Jonathon. You're home from Chicago early today."

"I haven't left yet." He set a fresh cup of coffee in front of me. "What are you working on?"

"I'm figuring out my next dive."

Unease scribbled lines on his forehead as he smoothed his slacks and sat in the chair next to me. "You don't mean that literally." Jonathon was the only person who knew about my secret tombstoning trips. I was sure he didn't approve.

"Not literally. Christina sent a couple opportunities my way. A man charged with money laundering wants my representation. He's left numerous emails, apparently. It would be a switch from the sexual predators I normally work for. And it might be exciting to work in the federal court system for a change. I'll study the case notes to see if I want to take it." I closed the lid on my laptop and let my fingers rest on the coffee cup.

"Let me know if there's anything I can do." He leaned forward and rested a hand on my thigh.

Jonathon had already helped to focus my career. I covered his hand with mine. The day we met in the conference room at Milton, Wallace, & Edwards, Jonathon's good looks and charm had flustered me. I laughed about that now. "Do you have any idea how much things have changed since the day you hired me, Jonathon?"

"I might." He gave me a knowing glance.

"I'm more confident than ever before." I sat forward and touched Jonathon's knee.

"You seemed plenty confident when I hired you."

"There are things you still don't know about me," I said.

"And things you don't know about me." Doubt—or was it worry—puckered his eyelids. It was the same look that crossed his face after I signed his contract. Jonathon stared at the stone pavers under his brandy-colored, bespoke Italian leather shoes.

I said, "We have time. I hope we have the chance to get to know each other better." I slid over to sit on his lap and traced my fingers down the row of buttons on his shirt.

Jonathon took my hand and held it. "I look forward to more experimentation with your dark desires."

"You tease." I kissed him, hoping to interest him with a sexy diversion. "I was hoping for a little bondage-play today."

"All in good time."

I could tell his thoughts were elsewhere. "You seem to have a lot on your mind." I said.

He nodded. "Work has been crazy lately. Not only that—" His gaze darted from one of my eyes to the other.

"What's wrong?" I brushed a lock of his wavy black hair away from his ear.

"An old associate from overseas has reached out and asked to stop by," Jonathon said.

"Stopping by . . . as in, coming to the house?"

"Yes."

Since Jonathon never brought anyone to his home, I immediately knew something was different about this *associate.* "Is he visiting or here on business?"

"I don't know." His gaze moved miles away to the sparkling surface of Lake Michigan.

My hair whipped into my eyes, and I combed it away with my fingers. I hadn't seen him like this since the murder of his assistant, Kymani Zhao. "You don't like him, do you?" I said.

"That overseas associate is no friend."

— 4 —

With the two-week leave of absence over, Erik drove me to my office at Milton, Wallace, & Edward's in Chicago's West Loop. Christina welcomed me with open arms. She looked happier than I remembered and shot a flirty glance at Troy Milton, son of the senior partner, as he came by to say hello.

I had missed working, though I didn't miss my clients. Today, that was going to change. When Milton Sr. knocked on my door with a list of new cases he wanted me to take, some had committed crimes against women. A few had murdered their spouses or companions. I told him I was through representing men who abused women.

"From now on, I'll pick the cases right for me," I said.

Milton shifted uneasily and seemed to bite his tongue. "Do what's right for you, Wil."

It was a step in the right direction.

Christina brought me up to speed with the two cases we had been working on, and I busied myself with research in my office until around lunchtime when I heard a bold knock on my door.

Charlotte—aka Charlie—Reid, my colleague, and a hard-nosed bitch in the courtroom, poked her long face inside the door. "Hey stranger. Got some time to join me for lunch?"

When I'd first started working at the firm, I admired Charlie. She was the kind of star defense attorney I'd always wanted to be. I welcomed her in and saved my work on the computer. "I do. In fact my stomach is growling."

"Great!" She pushed the door open. Charlie wore a perfectly fitted black skirt-suit, probably Prada or Louis Vuitton, with a pinstripe white blouse open to her brassiere. A long strand of opalescent pearls hung to her waist. Next in line to have her name on the list of partners, Charlie had been a defense attorney for almost thirty years. Her salary tripled mine. Her go-for-the-kill courtroom style put fear into every prosecuting attorney in the Midwest.

"I've got a table reserved at Ever for one o'clock," she said. Years of smoking cigarettes had deepened her husky voice.

"I thought Ever wasn't open for lunch."

"They aren't," she said. "Unless you know the chef. I've made him my personal friend, so he lets me stop by occasionally. I've been meaning to take you out for some time, Wil. Where've you been lately?"

We walked to the elevator together. I hadn't spent much time with Charlie, who was as intimidating in the office as in the courtroom.

"I'm staying in Lake Forest these days."

"Oh, right. You're with that billionaire. What's his name? Heun?"

As if she didn't know. She made everyone's personal business her own. That's how she got ahead. "Yes. Jonathon."

"Seems like a good match for you. Where you're headed career-wise, you ought to be with someone very rich and powerful. Like him." I let her enter the elevator first.

"So tell me. I heard you told off Old Jim Milton before you left. I want all the blood spatter and gore. Don't leave anything out." Charlie dug into her huge Gucci bag searching for something until her bony, wrinkled hand came out with a pack of cigarettes.

I watched the elevator's numbered lights counting down. "There's not really much to tell. I told Milton I didn't want the client he assigned to me. Perry Ward was a womanizing bastard and his company Runway Review victimized Anna Fiske."

The elevator door opened, and Charlie led the way with a cigarette between her fingers. "Just like Senator Peterson. So? What happened, Wil? Are you going soft?"

Charlie had tried to mentor me from the start. It was only lately that I had doubts about my choice of careers. "I don't know what you mean," I lied.

"Oh, yes you do. Quit the bullshit," she said. She held the outer building door for me then took off at a fast clip. Her high heels hit the pavement like the gavel striking a judge's desk. "You've had a number of courtroom wins and made a name for yourself. Do you think you can get out of the business now?"

My longer legs kept even stride with her quick steps. "I'm not trying to get out."

"The hell you aren't. Hold on a minute." She stopped in the middle of the sidewalk to light her cigarette. Cupping her hand around the lighter and cig, she inhaled deeply then blew out smoke and started walking again. "You can't fool me. I see what's happening."

My tight lips curled upward in a grin. "Why don't you tell me, then."

"Sure. You're afraid of the backlash against you from all this #MeToo movement. You feel guilty for letting those bastards back into society. And you think you can change careers now that you've made a name for yourself as one of the best defense attorneys in Chicago. Am I right?" She tilted her head and looked up at me with a satisfied smile.

"Yes and no, Charlie." She was old enough to be my mother. Early in our relationship I accepted her attempts to nurture my career, to mother me, because my mother passed away when I was very young. Things changed about a year ago when I decided that I never wanted to become a cold, hardened bitch like Charlie Reid.

I said, "I think you believed you could change directions once. But you didn't when you learned it was much easier to fit in. Your revenge for not getting what you truly wanted was to become exceptionally good at what you do."

"Those are valid insights, Counselor."

"But now, the world is a much different place. Women have power. *I* have the power to do whatever I choose. If I want to, I can defend victims of the system. I can stand up for people who were misrepresented by the law and victimized by corporate America."

Charlie threw her head back and with a great big gaping mouth, she cackled out loud like the witch she was. "You're certainly young enough to believe that. Girl, we need to talk."

My own words echoed in my head. I didn't want to help acquit the guilty. I wanted to incarcerate them. I wanted to defend those who were subjugated by a fixed system. The beginnings of a picture—the new me—formed in my mind.

She took my arm with her free hand as if to guide me.

I respected Charlie's knowledge and years of experience, so I wanted to hear her advice and decide if it was right for me. But it seemed the years had jaded her—pitted her—against any actual freedom within the legal community. She wanted me to follow in her shoes because she had no one else. In her quest for power, she had lost sight of what really mattered.

I pulled my arm from hers as we walked the length of the block in silence. Approaching Ever, a man called my name from behind.

"Ms. Green?"

I turned but didn't recognize him. "Who wants to know?"

The out-of-breath man about Charlie's age, put one foot in front of the other and lumbered toward me with his gaze on the dirty sidewalk. His red silk tie choked the thick folds under his chin as he huffed to catch up to us. "My associate has been trying to reach you. He wants you to call him."

There was something strange about his accent. I might have identified him as Eastern European, but his speech was thick, and he spoke slowly. As if he'd worked very hard to erase any accent he had.

I opened the restaurant door for Charlie. "I'll meet you inside," I said to her.

"Are you sure?" Her gaze dropped to his shoes and rose to his face again. "Cheap suit. Cheap shoes. Someone doesn't pay him enough," she said under her breath.

I let the door to Ever close behind Charlie and faced the man on the sidewalk. "Who is your associate?"

He pulled aside the lapel of his suit jacket and slid one hand into the inner pocket. "Bohdi Michaels."

"Bohdi was charged with money-laundering, not my usual type," I said. "I'm not sure I want the case."

The man held out a black business card. "Mr. Michaels isn't a criminal. He's an honest businessman," he said.

"That doesn't mean anything to me."

"He sent me to beg for your help."

"Beg?"

"He'll pay twice your fee." He pushed the black card toward me.

"I don't except bribes."

"Mr. Michaels is a victim, Ms. Green. He needs your help."

Victim. It was the new criteria I had for clients. I took the titanium card, and its sharp corner pricked my finger. I'd rarely seen cards like this. Only the elite minority could afford them. The face of the card was blank except for an etched phone number with an area code I didn't recognize.

"Enjoy your lunch, Ms. Green," he said. "Call the number on the card when you are through. He'll be expecting it."

~5~

After lunch, I took another look at the charges against Bohdi Michaels. The spelling of his first name was odd. I was familiar with the Hindi name, Bodhi, which meant *enlightened one*. I double-checked the spelling and meaning with Google before continuing my search. The definition that showed up most often said awakening or enlightenment.

Despite the odd spelling, given my desire to change the path of my career, his name was as good a reason as any to research the case. It turned out he was a banker by trade and worked for a Fortune 500 company, Houghton Chambers Investment Bank. He made close to seven figures a year.

The solicitation and money laundering charges brought against Michaels were related to the recent police sting involving a prostitution ring at Red Lace Escort Services. The business advertised young women, and others—genderqueer, transsexual, or gay people—for hire as arm-candy for ritzy events and parties. Under the umbrella of Red Lace Escorts LLC, the individuals hired performed any number of private services for the customers.

Angelique Sartre, the owner, made more than a "living" from her employee's sex acts. She was charged with solicitation after an undercover investigator posed as a wealthy john visiting from Texas. The charges were reduced to a warning when Angelique gave up Bohdi Michaels as her associate. She claimed to have known Michaels for many years.

Video caught Bohdi Michaels taking a hand-off, a briefcase full of illegal earnings, from Angelique Sartre. He then deposited the money in small sums over an extended period of time into the accounts and private funds he managed at Houghton Chambers Investment Bank.

Curious, I dug into the history of Houghton Chambers Investment

Bank and their clients, the wealthiest aristocrats in the world. HCIB held accounts owned by sheiks and oil moguls. Top CEOs and descendants of royalty placed their money in the care of that company, according to a ten-year-old *Forbes* magazine article. Bohdi Michaels had been a certified investment broker for decades. It made me wonder why he had strayed from the straight and narrow.

Bohdi had helped Angelique by depositing the illegal income from Red Lace Escort Services and he—according to police—knowingly laundered it through the largest and most lucrative investment firm in the world. Bohdi, the arresting officer claimed, was Angelique's *smurf*—the person hired to make the deposits. Over time, the small transactions, gains from illegal activities were layered between multiple accounts owned by various fictional people. None of those *people* existed but the accounts all lead back to Sartre and Michaels managed them all. Hence, Bohdi was charged with a federal crime.

A man of his stature ought to have the connections to get all charges reversed. At the very least, he would have a lawyer on retainer. But Bohdi Michaels had not secured an attorney before his initial appearance and arraignment. The court-appointed lawyer had spoken with the federal prosecutor—a man who presided over all of Cook County's federal cases—but had been unsuccessful in bargaining lower charges. Michaels posted bail. He was released and placed under house arrest.

I tossed the titanium card onto my desk, and it landed with a tinny clatter. I dialed the number.

"Michaels's residence," a male voice announced.

"Wilhelmina Green here. May I speak with Bohdi Michaels?"

"One moment," the man said.

"Ms. Green," Bohdi answered with a surprised tone. Once again, I couldn't quite place his accent. His thick speech sounded Eastern European, like the man who gave me the business card.

"You were expecting my call."

"I was. Thank you very much for obliging."

"Mr. Michaels, I'm not accepting clients at this time." Indeed, I had decided not to take Michaels' case. He didn't quite fit the profile of the types of men whom I wanted to represent at this time. And from my experience, the proof of his guilt was in his desperation. He needed me too badly.

"Please don't say that." His frantic response was followed by a ragged inhale. "I'm sure you've done the research. Those misguided and foolish officers have charged *me* with money laundering."

"Yes, but I don't understand why a man like you couldn't secure an attorney before the arraignment."

"That's not your concern."

"You're charged with a crime for which, if you are found guilty, you could face up to twenty years in prison."

"Yes, but, this case should never go to trial. Please focus on that, Ms. Green. Someone is using me as a scapegoat, and I need you to get those charges reversed and expunged from my record." That panicky quality still colored his tone.

I sat back in my leather desk chair and swiveled it to the side. "You seem well connected. Why doesn't a man like you have a single judge or defense attorney on your side?"

"I never thought I'd need one. Don't you understand? I have committed no illegal acts. I've never met that woman before in my life. They said I deposited her money, and that I made hundreds of thousands off her investments. It's not true," Michaels said with a desperate whine. "Please, Ms. Green. I need to get out of here. I'm restricted from trading, from my work, and I want to go home. To my country. I want to see my family one last time." He sounded desperate.

Could he actually be a victim? If Michaels wasn't guilty, then how were the police so sure he was involved? He clearly had the money to hire me, or an attorney like me.

I said, "My fees are very high."

"Please. I'm a respected businessman. Just write up the engagement papers. I'll wire the money directly to your bank account."

– 6 –

The next step in my redemption path was volunteer work. We drove to Bridgeport, south of the river, and Erik waited for me in the strip mall parking lot outside the Lake Shore Women's Shelter while I went inside.

The quiet waiting room had a green couch and coffee table. Several blue and gold striped chairs circled the room. I approached the front desk, where a woman was speaking into the phone.

"Send donations to LSWS. The address is on our website. We're happy you could help." The woman's long dark curls shook as she nodded her head. She clicked off her Bluetooth headset and jotted something down before looking up, in no hurry to help me.

"I hear you're looking for volunteers, and I'd like to sign up to be a *sister*." I said.

"That's right, we always need help." The receptionist sat back and eyed me up and down. "Wait. You look familiar."

I had a feeling I wouldn't have to introduce myself. In the past few months, the news media had plastered my face all over local channels. Senator Peterson's trial was filmed for Court TV. After that, I represented the *most eligible bachelor* in Chicago. My fame had grown.

"I'm Wilhelmina Green." I reached across the desk for a handshake.

"I know who you are. What're you doing *here?*" The receptionist's upper lip curled as she tucked her hands under her armpits.

"I saw that you're looking for volunteers. I want to help however I can."

"We've filled those positions."

Her frosty stare sent a shiver down my back. "Are you turning me away?"

"I'm saying we don't want your kind of help." She pressed her palms into the armrests of the chair, elevating her body to standing position. Over her shoulder, she called, "Avril? Can you come out here?"

A woman dressed in jeans and a pink sweater that hung to her knees entered from the back hallway. "What's up, Wendy?" When she saw me, she stopped short and straightened her back. "Oh."

The corners of Wendy's lips pinched. "I *asked* her to leave."

Trying to understand, I said, "Can you tell me what's going on?"

Avril asked, "Wilhelmina Green, right? You defended Martin Liebert, didn't you?"

"Yes." Heat rose to my cheeks. Now I knew where this was going.

Avril said, "After the trial—after you got the jury to declare him not guilty—Liebert raped six more women."

"He's back in jail," I said.

Wendy hissed, "No thanks to you."

"Two of those girls ended up here after the community hospital treated them for their injuries."

"Are they okay?" I asked.

"What do you care?" Wendy said.

Avril stepped up beside her coworker. "The point is *you* represented him. You're on the wrong side of the battlefront. None of our women would want your help."

Wendy pretended to spit to her right.

"I get it. I thought—"

Avril sneered. "Go home."

~ 7 ~

With my tail between my legs, I returned to Lake Forest. The encounter at LSWS singed my ego. I had been labeled.

During the drive, I looked up the LSWS website and found their *Donate Now* button. I pulled five-thousand dollars from my retirement account and sent the payment. Money—in the form of an anonymous donation—was one way for me to help those women. I set up a monthly reminder to continue the trend for the rest of the year. It was the least I could do.

Still, my reputation as a defense attorney for sexual predators stuck to me like tar and feathers. Escape was my next thought. I needed to get away from the world. I needed to dive. Right after Martin Liebert's trial, I fled Chicago. The Croatian cliffs punished me in unexpected ways. The cuts on my hands and knees had left lasting scars.

I turned my palms and looked at them. Could Jonathon take the feeling of guilt away? Could he draw the pain out of me and replace it with the sting of a whip or deep rope marks on my legs? The kind of pain that heals.

I texted Jonathon,

I need you tonight.

Grant met me at the door with a message from Jonathon. At five he would meet me in the basement bar.

"There's a bar in the basement?" I asked.

Grant nodded. "Fully stocked."

"Thank you, Grant. I'll freshen up first."

It occurred to me that I hadn't seen half of this mansion that my lover called home. After changing into a comfortable sundress, I had half an hour to kill, so I wandered to the foyer where a hidden door beneath the curved staircase stood open. On the dark red walls, I found a light switch. Electric torches at shoulder level dimly illuminated carpeted stairs. I descended into the semi-darkness below and entered an entertainment room with tables, a bar, and a big-screen TV mounted on the wall.

Sets of double doors on either side of the room piqued my curiosity. The deadbolt and electronic keypad above the door handles especially intrigued me. What could be so private? To my surprise, I found the first set of doors unlocked. Storage shelves stretched along on both sides of the long dark room. The acrid smell of wine hinted at the contents. The cellar extended back into the depths of the house, with wine bottles organized by year and country, Spain, South Africa, and Peru and dozens of others. The wine cellar was a fitting investment for someone of Heun's wealth. I backed out of the cool dark room and quietly closed the doors.

Still curious, I crossed the room to the doors on the other side and found this set locked. I played with a deadbolt and keypad with no success.

"Looking for something?"

"Jonathon." I spun toward the stairs. "You scared me."

"I didn't mean to." He crossed the room in four strides and pulled me into his arms. "How was Chicago?"

I tilted my head and tried to shrug off the rejection from the women's shelter that still simmered in the forefront of my mind.

Jonathon's black tie was loosened about his neck, and the top two buttons of his dark gray shirt were undone. He seemed to sense my disappointment. His blue eyes roamed my face. "Something happened."

I carried that indignity and humiliation like a scarlet letter. "I don't want to discuss it."

"But . . ." he pressed. He traced the shoulder strap of my sundress and tucked his finger underneath.

I didn't want to talk about my shame. When I thought about the embarrassment and disgrace, my heart thudded in my throat as my knees weakened. I needed a distraction. I needed punishment to get me through it. I kissed his firm lips then quickly changed the subject, my voice shaky. "I peeked into your wine cellar. For someone who doesn't drink, you've amassed quite a collection."

"I've put aside an Italian red for you, if you'd like a glass."

We moved in sync, Jonathon leading with his arm around my waist, to a leather bar stool. I sat, and he went behind the bar and pulled a glass from the rack.

"I love your style," I said, admiring the fixtures.

He poured dark red liquid into the glass, then handed it to me. "I saw the torches in a cigar bar in New Orleans and decided I had to have them. They're hand blown by a specialty company that makes movie sets for Paramount." He waited for me to sip.

The dry, fruity red warmed my core. "Delicious, thank you."

He poured a Perrier and added sliced lime from a container in the mini-fridge. "I'll bet your cat-like curiosity has you wondering what's behind door number two." Jonathon smiled like he was up to something.

I played along and glanced at the locked door. "Maybe."

"Come." Like an excited kid, Jonathon strode to the door and punched a quick series of numbers onto the keypad. The bolt slid to the side. He opened the door and reached inside to flick the light switch on.

I entered the room with my wine glass held close. Adrenaline and longing replaced all questions about whether Jonathon could be the one to fulfill my desires. And some healthy amount of fear cascaded down my spine and onto the backs of arms, replacing the humiliation from earlier.

Similar design and color schemes of the outer entertainment room flowed into this one. In the center, a king-sized bed with carved mahogany pillars, covered by a dark red bedspread and pillows, took central stage. It begged the question, dungeon?

"Exactly like a book I read," I said.

"Not exactly, I hope."

How far is he willing to go?

Behind the bed, a tall narrow cage had a deadbolt attached to the door. In one corner, an elaborate X-rack stood vacant—expectant—with straps and belts for tying someone down. A swinging apparatus hung near tall dressers with many narrow drawers. Instruments of pleasure and pain—whips, ropes, paddles—hung on the walls in strategic locations all around the room. Many tools were unfamiliar.

"Full disclosure would have been apropos," I said. Had I known how my lover fully invested in the dom-sub lifestyle, would I have signed the contract?

Yes. The answer was yes.

Sporting a thin smile, Jonathon clearly enjoyed my reaction and yet he seemed slightly nervous. His shoulders and neck stiffened.

I strolled to the bed and sat down with the wine glass firmly in my grip. "Were you saving this for a special occasion? Or do you bring all your girlfriends down here?"

"You don't need to worry. I've only had one other relationship like ours."

Could that explain his nervousness?

I teased, "With all this apparatus I was thinking maybe you ran a business."

He looked away. I sensed that Jonathon was uncomfortable. "No, Mina. I like to collect things."

Near my feet, steel rings fastened to the floor on each side of the bed. I bent over to pull on the secured metal ring. I raised one eyebrow and asked, "When can *we* play in this room?"

Jonathon smiled, "I should've brought you down here blindfolded and handcuffed."

"You tease."

"You've known that I'm a dominant, Mina, and you know I like to play with pain. I've collected these . . . for some time now." In his sky blue eyes I saw a flash of something endearing. Jonathon was seeking my approval. He was looking to me to take the first step.

Jonathon sat on the bed next to me and gazed around the room. I felt a little overwhelmed by the torture devices, cages, and variety of whips. Many times I had imagined ropes binding me.

Anticipation played like heat lightning across my skin. I looked my lover in the eye and said, "Let's play."

— 8 —

Crow's feet crinkled the corners of his eyes. With a smile, Jonathon crossed the room to close the door. The sound of a deadbolt sliding affirmed my fate. Here, I was at my master's mercy.

"Kneel on the bed, Mina."

My heart rate quickened. *This is what I came here for.* I set my wineglass on the nearest dresser. The mattress was higher than most. I climbed up on it like a child might, one knee then the other, ungracefully plopping onto my rear. I scooted, situating myself in the center of the crimson bedspread. In yoga, it's called Virasana or Hero Pose. Except that here with Jonathon, I spread my knees wide.

Jonathon wandered around the room resting his hand on a whip, or a set of handcuffs. "Tell me about your darkest fantasy."

Like a kid in a candy store my eyes grew wide, and I smiled. Suddenly the possibilities were endless.

He asked, "Ropes? Chains? How about something new?"

Laughter exploded from my mouth. "Everything is new with you, Jonathon."

His gaze flew to a tall red candle. "Wax play?"

My smile faded.

"The pain of the hot wax fades quickly," he said.

"I'll take your word."

"Manacles? The X-rack? What would you like?"

"I'll let you decide. If I'm uncomfortable, my safeword is tombstone, remember?"

Jonathon had come up with the word before our first bondage exploration. I loved how it related to my diving expeditions. "And you'll recall, I asked for this."

"Well, then, let the games begin."

Jonathon opened a drawer in one of the tall dressers. He took out a black box and turned to face me again. Something changed in him, like someone flipped a switch. I'd only seen glimpses of this side of Jonathon. This person, whom I didn't quite know, was coming into a spotlight.

"Ben Wah balls are an old Asian tool for strengthening your muscles. Try to keep them inside while we choose a few toys. Place your hands and face down on the bed."

As he walked toward me, the box rang like a bell. I stretched my arms out and lowered my cheek to the bed. The red bedspread was cool and silky smooth on my face. I turned my head to the side and glimpsed two gold balls, about the size of ping pong balls, gleaming in Jonathon's hand. He pulled my panties aside, then parted my slit with his fingers. The two cool balls slid easily into my moist, wet opening. I moaned.

"You may sit up now."

I adjusted my panties and then took Jonathon's hand. As I stood, I squeezed my pelvic floor muscles. Gripping tightly to keep the balls in place, I walked with him to the dresser. The balls moved inside me, releasing my nectar.

Jonathon opened a drawer that contained an array of short paddles. Long ones and short fat ones all looked able to deliver plenty of pain.

"You may choose something from here. Or—" he opened the drawer above it, "—from here."

I studied the contents with fascination. The second drawer displayed several thin switches and reeds, the type that would whistle in the air if you flicked them fast enough. I knew immediately how those would sting against flesh. The instrument that caught my eye was made of light-colored wood like bamboo and had Japanese lettering on the handle. It was about eighteen inches long with a handle wrapped in red silk ribbons.

Unconsciously, I reached for it to admire it more closely. Jonathon quickly stopped my hand. His eye followed mine to the Japanese switch.

"Well chosen, Mina." His voice wrapped around me like the silk ribbon on the device. He picked it up with only his thumb and forefinger as though it was light as a feather. The artfully designed reed whistled like I'd expected as he swished it through the air. I cringed with hope and expectation.

"You're not wearing your collar today," he said.

His comment took me off guard. Did he expect me to wear it every day? I'd never asked. The promise of punishment over it fed my thirst for his dominance. "I was hoping you'd punish me if I didn't."

I took a step toward him, and a Ben Wah ball slipped out of my panties. It hit the floor and rang like a bell.

Jonathon forced a laugh. "Hmm. Pick up the ball and get back on the bed."

As I bent down for it, the second ball fell out with a ping.

"Mina!"

I couldn't restrain the giggle that escaped my lips. I picked up the balls and held them out to Jonathon. Inlaid with colorful flowers, the heavy gold balls dripped with my moisture.

He took them from me and pointed to the bed. "Take off your clothes."

As he instructed, I let my sundress pool at my feet. I stepped out of it and my panties and kneeled on the bed, placing my hands on my thighs.

Jonathon crossed the room and dimmed the lights. He busied himself with a panel on the wall and in a moment, the room came to life with low, solemn classical music. Resolute, Jonathon crossed the room to the foot of the bed.

Knowing full well what was in store—what I wanted—I took a deep breath and lay on my belly. I needed what Jonathon could deliver. From behind, I heard the reed whistle through the air. And though I expected the sting that followed, the sheer pain still alarmed me. I gasped, then cried out. How could such a small object cause such a divine burning feeling?

Jonathon massaged and rubbed out the pain. Another whistle and sting followed his gentle massaging hand. He repeated these actions— striking my ass in a different place each time then stroking the spot with a cool hand—until my entire backside was on fire. The spicy heat radiated and warmed my sex.

When Jonathon slid his fingers into my wet folds, I moaned with pleasure. His teasing fingers took the focus away from my warm buttocks. The whip, his fingers, and the intensifying music played me. They brought me to a climax where desire and pain flooded my body with the pulsing rhythm of orgasm. I panted with my mouth open wide.

"Turn over," he said.

I'd do anything he asked. Propped on my elbows, I watched him.

Jonathon removed his shirt, revealing ripped, muscular shoulders and abdominals. He eyed me and walked slowly around the bed as if scheming his next move.

"Place your arms above your head and leave them there."

I reached for the carved bed post and held on with both hands.

Jonathon circled the bed once more, then the red ribbon flashed. The sting of the switch burned my sensitive inner thigh. Heat rose from my flesh, and I sank into the sensation and moaned. I let it overcome me. Jonathon's rhythm became my own. The stinging burn followed his cooling palm. His soft caress and the explosion of heat. This was what I wanted. This is what I deserved. Sensation was all I knew until—

Searing pain shot through the inner arch of my foot, and I screamed. My eyes watered.

"Do you want to use your safeword?" Jonathon's voice lifted me from the abyss.

Tombstone. I couldn't breathe. I gripped the bed post and waited for his next strike. Jonathon held my foot and what happened next shocked me more than the sting of his Japanese reed. He kissed the soul of my foot. With his thumbs and strong fingers, Jonathon massaged the sting out of my foot and then kissed my legs.

Tears dripped down the side of my face onto the red bedspread. He crawled beside me on the bed. His arms offered solace. Forgiveness. I buried my face in his neck as Jonathon soothed the pain away. Absolving me.

Jonathon pressed his lips deeply into mine. With his powerful hands, he lifted my hips to meet his own. His erection sought my opening, and I longed for the encounter. I guided him into me and gasped as our rhythm, our songs, became one. Jonathon grew inside me, and I let go. Ecstasy, the eternal compulsion of flesh, became my master.

Our thrusts increased in tempo and intensity. His back arched as his entire body stiffened. Finally, he cried out, "Mina!"

I matched his vocal intensity used his final thrusts to bring myself to the summit. As he slowed, the orgasm flowered inside me. I pumped my hips against his, not wanting it to end. He quivered. I gasped. When it was over, I curled into his arms and wept.

— 9 —

Jonathon traveled to Tokyo the next day, but the sublime strike of his reed remained in my memory. Despite his absence, I longed for my fix. The seed of desire—for punishment, for pain—was blooming, and its thorny tendrils held me by the ankles. While sitting at my desk, the simple pressure of the chair cushion caused my sex to weep for more.

With Jonathon traveling for work, there was no reason for me to stay in Lake Forest and my new client demanded my attention. So I went home to my apartment in Chicago where fewer distractions allowed me to focus on work for the rest of the week. Later that day I was sitting at my desk when I received notice of an incoming, encrypted video call. I answered, but without turning my video camera on.

The man in the screen had shaggy brown hair with silver streaks at his temples. He was shaved to a polish and his intensely blackish-brown irises were rimmed with heavy gray circles.

"Who's calling?" I asked.

"Bohdi Michaels. Turn on your camera, Ms. Green. I want to see you." Bohdi sat close to his screen in front of mahogany bookshelves lined with what appeared to be red encyclopedias.

I studied his surroundings in my video feed then did as he asked.

"Have I caught you at a good time of day?" he asked.

I checked my watch. "It's fine. I wanted to share my research with you, anyway."

"Please. Tell me what you've found." His face remained so near the camera I could see each pore on his cheeks and nose.

I went to my Google documents and opened the file with his name. "Mr. Michaels, you've been charged with a federal offense, money laundering. It doesn't matter that you've worked for Houghton Chambers

Investment Bank for fourteen years. Or that you worked in the Paris office then you moved to Chicago and became head of corporate investment accounts. If the prosecution can prove that you knowingly deposited and invested money that came from proceeds of criminal activity, if they can prove that you turned a blind eye, or didn't ask where the money came from, then you will be convicted."

"I am innocent."

"I understand. You didn't know where the money came from. The prosecution claims you've been involved with Red Lace Escort Services, for eight or nine years. Is that true?"

"I know *my* history, Ms. Green. Please." Bohdi's wiry eyebrows fluttered with worry. "Tell me how you're working to remove the charges."

"It's not as easy as you think. Since it's a federal crime to launder money, you're facing twenty years in prison and fines that could be double the earnings you made in that time. The prosecution has built a solid case, indicating that your extended time hiding the illegal funds has made you and your associates quite wealthy."

"My associates? They aren't my friends. Those people threatened me. I was forced to make those deposits." His gray-rimmed irises flicked back and forth.

"That's not what the prosecution says. You've been laundering money since you arrived in the US. The prosecution maintains that you and Angelique Sartre, the owner of Red Lace, have known each other since you both arrived in the United States eighteen years ago. She's been soliciting since then, under the guise of 'escort services.' The truth is all her employees bring her a percentage of the extra income they make. In fact, right up until you went into business with Angelique, you were a regular john at Red Lace. They've got her computer records with the proof, and they've built a serious case against you."

"They don't have proof. They're manufacturing the evidence out of thin air. That's what they do! The truth is they needed someone to take the fall. And you know what? Here I am." The flesh beneath his chin jiggled as he spoke. The whites of his eyes were slightly yellow from prolonged alcohol use. He seemed barely able to hold his fear at bay.

I edged my seat forward toward my desk. Michaels didn't fit the usual profile of my clients—guilty and confident—and I thought he was truly afraid of something or someone. "I'm telling you that I've done my research. I don't think their facts are skewed, Mr. Michaels. Investigators have been trying to bring you in for over five years."

"That's irrelevant! They don't want me in jail. They want me dead. I need to go home before it's too late!" He pushed his chair several feet away from his monitor. "See this?" With some difficulty, Bohdi lifted his leg to show me the locked ankle bracelet. "I'm a sitting target. Help me, please! I need to get out of here!"

"A sitting target to whom?" I softened my tone to soothe his frenzied speech. "Who wants to kill you, Mr. Michaels?"

"The ones who framed me!"

"Who is that, exactly?"

He shook his head. "I'm not sure. I'm in a deadly position here, Ms. Green. I'm not comfortable talking about that over the—this." He waved at the computer screen. "Help me. Please!"

"I can't prove your innocence unless I know their angle. The fact that you have no prior convictions will come into play. The best I can do is try to convince the US attorney you made a mistake."

"I didn't make any mistakes. I did everything they asked. Please. You must convince the prosecutor that I'm innocent."

"Mr. Michaels—"

"I'm a dead man if you don't do this for me." Michaels' head bowed over his keyboard. "Please."

~10~

Charlie's lasting words from our two-martini lunch lingered in my mind, *"Whatever you decide, Wil, just make sure you give 'em hell."*

Bohdi Michaels, a scapegoat? It teased my lawyer brain in a way that made me want to represent him. Who would try to frame a powerful financial officer HCIB, the largest investment firm in the world?

My thoughts drifted to Jonathon. I had no idea what my lover was worth financially or who managed his money. Now, I wondered if he had an account with HCIB.

As if on psychic cue, he called.

"How is Japan?" I asked.

"I miss you. I'm taking the red-eye home because we're done. Will you meet me in Lake Forest?"

"Yes. Remember you said I could invite Traci? I planned to spend time with her this weekend."

"That's fine. Invite her."

"Are you sure?"

"Absolutely. Listen, I wanted to tell you Janko Vorobiev, the colleague I spoke of, is coming to Lake Forest, too. He'll join us for dinner one night. It would be good to have Traci there, because, Mina, I don't trust him."

"Then why invite him to your house?"

"I prefer to keep my enemies close."

"Tell me why you don't trust him."

The connection crackled as Jonathon answered. "We met years ago at a celebration. The Austrian International Business Bureau hosted a gala to welcome new businesses to the area. I was sealing a contract with the Vienna Hospital, and a colleague introduced us. Janko made a point to meet me. He invited me to share a meal with his family and discuss a business deal with the Dubrovnik General Hospital Clinics in Croatia. He worked for Dubrovnik Health, but I didn't have time for him. I was scheduled to fly out the next day. I thought taking a rain check would suffice and promised to be in touch."

A fly flirted with the sun's reflection off my glass coffee table on the ceiling. The fly landed, then circled and landed again.

He continued, "We played phone tag for a few months, but I couldn't solidify a deal with him. Janko caught up with me again last summer—desperate to sign a contract. I was extremely busy, and our deal got put on hold for another six months. In that time, Janko was fired from Dubrovnik Health. The government found suspicious emails on his computer and accused him of working with terrorists. I did my research and found out they were right. Janko consorts with the Russian mafia." Jonathon took a breath. "Afterward, I heard a rumor through my European connections that Janko was smearing my name. He threatened to ruin me. I took those threats seriously."

"Do you need anything from me?" I asked.

"Find out why Janko Vorobiev is in Chicago if you can."

"Whatever you need."

The line crackled again, and I lost the signal. I tried calling Jonathon back but couldn't get through.

Christina brought me the fresh cup of coffee I asked for. I thanked her and glanced at my emails. The Lake Shore Women's Shelter thanked me for my generous donation. It gave me only small comfort to know I could help victims of crime.

It never occurred to me that I could become a victim too.

With the fresh cup of coffee beside my type-pad I entered Janko Vorobiev's name into the search bar. From the small country of Slovenia, sandwiched between Austria to the north and Croatia to the south, Janko was fluent in Slovene, Croatian, German, Arabic, and English. He'd worked in communications and human resources at clinics and hospitals across Croatia.

I had an uncanny memory for faces, and Janko was a striking man. In photos, age had drawn hard lines on his face, though I suspected that he was only in his fifties. His dark, suntanned skin tone and gray-flecked hair made him both handsome and intimidating and for some reason, he looked familiar. I was certain that I'd met him before.

His two brothers owned Vorobiev Exports with a staff of twenty driving trucks and flying four small planes across southern Europe, Turkey, Germany, Italy, and Croatia. They exported to the Republic of Georgia, Poland, and Czechia. I could only find information on one, Marco Vorobiev, a retired Croatian war hero.

Out of habit, I called Gary Underwood, the detective who worked for me at Milton, Wallace, & Edwards.

"Ms. Green, what an unexpected pleasure."

"Hi, Gary. Got a minute?"

"I've got all day for you, babe."

"Be careful whom you call babe, Gary. Some girl's going to take it the wrong way." Although Gary's harmless flirtation was endearing, the news was filled with stories of people fighting back against perceived slights. #Metoo hadn't ended, and the events, shootings, and riots of 2020 had amplified all minority's battles against discrimination. No one put up with anything sketchy anymore.

"Yeah, you're right. My old-school ways sometimes get me slapped in the face."

"As well they should."

"What's up?"

"I'm working a side-case on my own, and I need the dirt on someone." I downed the last of my coffee.

"Shoot."

"Janko Vorobiev. A citizen of Croatia, an HR specialist who worked with the hospitals and health clinics in . . . Dubrovnik." I paused. That city was a trigger for me. I thought back to my dives from the cliffs in Croatia. "Anyway, Janko's coming to Chicago to see Jonathon. We both need to know why he's here."

"Branching out and contracting international criminals?"

"No. He's Jonathon's frenemy. He was fired from Dubrovnik Health, and now works with his brothers' shipping business. I'll send you links to everything I've found. See if you can find out more about Vorobiev Exports. . . " My voice trailed and I stopped talking. There was something about Vorobiev's image on my screen that made my skin crawl, and I couldn't put my finger on it.

Dubrovnik? I'd been there.

Then I remembered meeting Janko before. And *Jonathon* was there.

"And?"

"It's nothing."

"Nothing is *always* something," Gary said.

I dropped my shoulders and looked at the computer monitor, but my eyes were out of focus and my heart pounding in my chest.

Jonathon and I had met before.

I traveled to Croatia after a particularly difficult court case when I represented the sexual predator Martin Liebert, a slimeball of the worst kind. Yet I was able to get him acquitted of raping his junior associate. And then I needed to dive from a cliff.

I had been dressed in a black sleeveless dress and had taken myself out to an expensive restaurant for dinner. A treat, a celebration of freedom from self-imposed condemnation. The five-star restaurant overlooked Pile Bay on the western shore of Dubrovnik. White elegant linen sharply contrasted with the eternally rugged stone walls. I imagined diving from there and mentally prepared myself, visualizing my toes curled over the stony cliff.

The tall, blond sommelier interrupted my preparation with a bottle of champagne. He was mistaken. I had ordered a glass of the house white wine. He nodded toward the opposite end of the terrace. I gazed past four tables to where two dark-haired men sat. Though I didn't know it at the time, they were Jonathon Thomas Heun and Janko Vorobiev.

The sommelier had popped the cork neatly into his hand and poured fizzy liquid into a glass in front of me. Jonathon approached first. Something about his eyes, even in the dark, weakened my knees. I should have known who he was—a semi-celebrity—yet I didn't place him in the usual context of Chicago news.

I wasn't in the habit of accepting drinks from unknown men, let alone a whole bottle. Jonathon introduced himself with a handshake—one that I now distinctly recalled as feeling sensual and familiar—when I met him again in Chicago. When he introduced me to Janko, a little warning flag had gone up in the back of my mind. Janko had held eye contact with me daring me to turn away until I finally faltered.

"And?" Gary pressed.

"Janko threatened Jonathon behind his back. I want to know if he has the means to follow through. And Gary?"

"Yes?"

"Tell me how Jonathon and Janko really know each other."

"Give me a few days."

"Thanks, Gary."

I kicked myself internally for forgetting I met Jonathon in Dubrovnik. In the courtroom, I prided myself on my ability to recall the smallest details and use them against the prosecution. Possibly because the dive I took later that very night nearly killed me—I'd lost a lot of blood—I'd forgotten. Or maybe it didn't think it was significant. Either way, when I met Jonathon earlier this summer, I should have remembered him.

Several questions remained unanswered about our brief, yet significant meeting. Did Jonathon recall it too? Did he reach out to me this summer because we had already met? Why didn't he mention Croatia? Why *didn't* he mention we'd met?

My trust in Jonathon stood on a very rocky precipice.

-11-

Traci arrived Saturday in her cerulean blue Toyota hybrid, parking in the brick, circular driveway. She crawled out of the car as I ran outside to greet her. Her head tilted upward; her gaze drawn to the eight triangular gables on the roofline of Jonathon's house. "Wow."

"Hello to you, too," I said. Paying no attention to her gaping mouth, I hugged her until at last, she dropped the act and embraced me.

"Missed you, girl! And I have so much to tell you," she said.

I gave her a short tour of the mansion and Grant showed Traci to her room down a long hall on the second floor, a wing of the house I hadn't been in before. When I'd first arrived in Lake Forest, Jonathon had given me the lower level bedroom to stay in. A suite fit for a king—or queen. He didn't often sleep in the bed with me, especially if he had work to catch up on.

I asked Grant, "Does Jonathon sleep up here, too?"

"Since you arrived, Mr. Heun sleeps in the guest room at the other end of the hall. He typically works very early in the morning and doesn't like to disturb you," Grant said. His unconventional uniform consisted of slim-fitting slacks in unusual colors like pale blue, mauve and harvest gold. His untucked, neatly pressed shirts were always topped with a sharp-looking button-up vest or bowtie. Today his purple pants offset a cream-colored shirt and black vest with royal blue piping.

He led the way into Traci's room and opened the curtains to show off a splendid view of the forested shoreline.

"How many bedrooms are there?" Traci was a buyer for a small Chicago clothing boutique and lived in a brownstone near Northwestern University on a beautiful tree-lined street.

"Seven," Grant said.

Traci raised an eyebrow at me as she carried her overnight bag into the room. "He sleeps in a different room?"

My best friend worried about me way too much. I whispered, "We'll talk later."

Grant, moved to the door. "I'll leave you ladies to get caught up."

"Thank you, Grant." I closed the door.

Traci sat on the bed and looked up at me. "I've been dying to tell you something."

"What?" I sat down and scooted beside her, just like when we were in college.

"Do you remember David?" Traci asked.

"Didn't you date him for a couple years?"

"I kept breaking up with him, but he kept coming back for sex."

"That was your fault. You kept giving it to him."

She laughed. "He was a lot of fun, and *man*! When he put his pout on, I couldn't turn him away. Wil—" Traci grew thoughtful. "David's back."

"What do you mean, back?"

"As in, we're dating again."

Eager to hear more, I looked into her mossy, hazel eyes. "You look happy about it." Indeed, she looked absolutely smitten.

"David and I have only gone on a couple dates." She tapped on her cell phone. "He got his hair cut and grew this cute little beard. I have pictures, Wil. Isn't he handsome?" She waved the phone in front of me. Traci looking content and happy, stood beside smiling David with the Ferris Wheel on Navy Pier looming behind them.

"His eyelashes are gorgeous. I'm jealous," Traci said. "And the sex—"

"Don't tell me." I stood, drawing the line at her sex-capades. For the past few years, the most important quality Traci sought in a man was his performance in bed.

Traci said, "No, I mean it. He has me trying things I have never done before."

I turned to face her and crossed my arms. "There can't be anything that *you* haven't done." I'd never told her about my secret desires, my fantasies about ropes and whipping. I was curious, though. "Like what?"

Traci said, "The first time we did it was pretty normal."

"Not sure what *normal* is for you . . ." When Traci and our friends went out together, she was the one who ended up with the guy. It never lasted, but that's what she seemed to like about those flings.

"The second time, he asked if I would tie him up."

"During sex?" I pretended the idea shocked me.

"Yes, during sex."

"Did you go all *Fifty Shades of Grey*?"

"Yes." She said the word slowly. "I never thought I'd enjoy doing that, but it was intense. At first, I was a little nervous."

I imagined Traci with a crop in her hand. "You'd make a sexy dominatrix."

Her cheeks colored, and she looked at the floor. I'd known Traci for eight years and in all that time, I'd never seen her blush. "Next time, we're going to switch," she said.

"What do you mean, switch?"

"He wants to tie my wrists to the head of the bed."

I suddenly worried about my friend's choice of lover. Perhaps it was because I was now in that very position, worrying about who Jonathon was. What was he hiding from me? What secrets did he keep? What were my lover's motives?

"Traci, how long have you known this guy? I mean, do you feel safe?"

The blush left Traci's cheeks. "Ok, *Mom,* he works at Northwestern University. He's a history professor, and he's drafting a book about modern warfare. David is thirty-seven years old and has never married." She leaned back on her elbows and grinned. "He's . . . I mean . . ."

"What? Is he mean to you?"

"No! Will, I think I'm in love!"

My jaw fell, but I swooped to the bed and sat beside Traci. "Really?"

"He's been so kind. He does things for me that I never asked for. The brakes went out in my car, and I couldn't drive. He showed up the next morning to drive me to the city."

"Aw, that's sweet." My lips puckered as I tipped my head to one side.

"He offered to do that every day while my car was in the shop. He likes to walk along the shore and wants to take me up north to his family's summer cabin in Wisconsin. And all I can think about is settling down with him."

"I'm so happy for you." I was. But the seething tendrils of jealousy wrapped around my heart. I wanted to feel the way she did.

Did I love Jonathon?

In all honesty, no. I entered the relationship with one thing in mind. My selfish need for punishment. He gave me what I needed, and I went for it with the same determination I defended my clients in the courtroom.

I pointed at her with a scolding finger. "With all that talk of ropes, I had to make sure you're not dating a sociopath."

"Sociopath? I swear you are the biggest prude," Traci said.

"I am not a prude. Traci, you have no idea—"

"—Seriously," she interrupted.

"No. *Seriously.*" I sat on the bed with my ankles crisscross, or Easy Pose in yoga and gazed into her eyes.

"Oh my god. Have you—"

"I have. We've tried bondage and spanking—"

"And did you like it?" She leaned forward, eager to learn more.

Could I tell her about Jonathon's playroom? "It's . . . amazing. I've never had better orgasms in my life." I told her about my love of bondage and sexual submission. I explained that losing control, giving him the power gave me more freedom to embrace the sensuous, erotic feelings and to let go. The combination of pain mixed with the pleasure added spice—like hot sauce—to the experience. I didn't delve into my personal need for punishment. Traci knew I struggled with ethics of acquitting evil men and women.

I said, "He never hurts me enough to cause bruising, just enough to get my attention. To draw heat from my skin. By morning, the red marks are all gone."

"Something to remember when I'm holding the whip," Traci said. She took my hand. "Are you happy with him?"

"I'm very happy." I was relieved that Traci didn't ask if I was in love. Because I knew that I was not. As much as I tried, I couldn't imagine a future with Jonathon beyond our current contractual agreement.

~12~

Traci and I changed into bathing suits and spent the rest of the day on the deck perched on the rocky ledge of the Lake Michigan shore. We swam in Jonathon's indoor swimming pool, where a diving board silently waited for the splash down. Three sets of sliding doors faced the lake. Our laughter echoed off the high vaulted ceiling where a half dozen blown-glass light fixtures dangled over the water. A stairway led to a boathouse on Lake Michigan where Jonathon's big cabin cruiser and smaller, water-ski craft were docked.

After our swim, we ate dinner on the patio outside the living room. Grant, now wearing an embroidered black vest and slim-fitting dark blue jeans with a crisp white shirt, brought platters to the table and poured a wine from Portugal then quietly left us to our discussion.

We recalled tales from our college days, Traci's numerous boyfriends, and all the parties. She told me how David spoiled her with flowers, and I told her about the expensive eateries Jonathon had taken me to. She asked about bondage and submission, and I shared a time that Jonathon bound my breasts with a long length of rope. First he draped it over my neck, one half the length on either side of me, then wound it around my chest like a tight fitting corset. My nipples were left free to tease and torture. Letting him take control of my orgasm gave me a sublime sense of fear and anticipation. It drew my attention exquisitely to my sex and to every tactile sensation.

For a change, I was the one sharing sex-capades to her engrossed, unwavering gaze.

"If he can deliver an orgasm like that, he sounds like a keeper, Wil." She finished her wine and pushed away from the table.

"Not staying for dessert?" I asked.

Traci waved her cell phone. "I have a virtual date with David in a few minutes. He texted me three times today to tell me he missed me."

With a knowing smile, I said, "Tell him I said he better take care of you, or I'll come after him." I meant it.

Traci laughed. "Thank you for dinner. I'll see you in the morning."

I retired to my suite on the first floor and Traci to her bedroom. Jonathon hadn't returned. He'd texted to apologize for not being here to meet Traci. I lay awake wondering why he'd never mentioned meeting in Croatia.

What is he afraid of?

Unable to close my eyes, I threw on a black satin robe and tiptoed to the foyer. The darkened house hummed as light rain pattered on the roof. My gaze was drawn up the grand stairway to the second floor. I wanted to see where Jonathon was sleeping. My research into Jonathon's past hadn't revealed any secrets. But I would dig deeper.

Light shone from under Traci's door, I went the opposite direction, where the hall angled right. At the end of the hall I pushed open a closed door, and the stark simplicity immobilized me. Had I thought Jonathon occupied a similar, or perhaps grander, bedroom?

I had assumed wrong. He had put distance between us from the start. The contract was just another means to keep intimacy at bay.

This ordinary guest room had an unmade queen-sized bed and side table. An old-fashioned wooden dresser—so unlike his style—held a bottle of expensive cologne, two pairs of cufflinks and a comb. The closet contained his suits and pants, neatly arranged on hangers spaced about three fingers apart.

The one focal point of the room, a large gray and white drawing hung on the wall across from the dresser. Renowned artist Miguel Endara's piece used to hang in the Art Institute of Chicago. I recognized it at once. Both the stipple technique and the ultra-realistic content of this artistic work were stamped into my memory. *Benjamin Kyle.*

I stared into Benjamin Kyle's eyes.

The subject of Endara's drawing had had severe amnesia when he was found near a dumpster in Georgia. The man was naked and without any wallet or identification. He adopted the name Benjamin Kyle until identified by family more than ten years later.

How is the painting significant to Jonathon? Why is he putting so much distance between us? There's so much I don't know about him.

Questions bounced like superballs in my head as I backed out of the room and right into Jonathan's arms.

"Mina."

"Jonathon?" I peeled his arms off me and faced him head on. "I have so many questions."

Stars twinkled above the trees on the western shore. Stifling, end-of-summer humidity bathed us in its heavy atmosphere. Jonathon and I stood on the patio outside the kitchen. He pulled out a chair for me, and though I was tired, I didn't sit.

"I always connected with the Benjamin Kyle painting," Jonathon said. "He was lost and alone. Not even *he* knew who he was."

"Why do you keep it locked away in that bedroom?"

"It's a very personal reminder. I never want to be that person. I *never* want to lose myself."

I said, "So you stay in control of everything. You don't even drink or let your guard down for a moment."

"I can't."

"Can't or won't?" I finally sat in the cold, wrought iron chair.

"That's not fair." He eased into the chair next to mine.

I put my courtroom voice away. "Sorry."

Jonathon smiled and leaned toward me, putting a hand on my thigh. In the dim light, his eyes glistened. "I missed you, Mina."

"And I missed you." I took his hand in mine. "Traci returns to Chicago on Sunday. I hope you don't mind her staying the weekend."

"I don't mind at all. Janko Vorobiev will be here for dinner tomorrow. Traci's presence will lighten the conversation and give you something to do. Janko and I have some business to discuss after dinner."

The night air chilled me. Gary Underwood had left a message while Traci and I ate. I hadn't listened to it yet. After recalling the night in Croatia where Jonathon and I first met, I wanted to see if Jonathon would bring it up. "You're worried about Janko coming."

Jonathon gazed out at the distant boat lights on the water. "Since you have a sixth sense about people, I'd like to see what you think of him."

But we've met already.

I pushed. "Tell me how you know Janko."

"We met in Europe years ago."

"You told me that before." Irritation that he was hiding something from me welled up.

"True," he said. "One of the first international contracts that PPS obtained was with a hospital in Munich. Prevail software was so well received there that other clinics throughout Germany purchased it. That was five years ago. In those days I frequently traveled to Italy, Hungary, and Austria. I met Janko there." He acted as if he didn't recall the night he and Janko sent champagne to my table.

"In Austria?" I heard it in my voice and knew I couldn't be pleasant anymore. I needed to find out what Jonathon was hiding and why he had never mentioned meeting me in Dubrovnik. I sat up and pulled my robe around my shoulders.

"In Zagreb." He put an arm around me and rubbed my shoulder. "Do you want to go inside?"

"No." I lifted his arm off my shoulder and turned to face him. "Jonathon, I've met Janko before."

Muscles in Jonathon's neck tightened long before he turned his gaze on me. "Where?"

"I thought you would remember. *You* were there."

"Mina—"

"No, Jonathon. We met long before Kymani Zhao was murdered. Why didn't you just say so?"

In the dark, his gaze darted back and forth, searching for something in my face, in my eyes. He finally said, "It was last year in Croatia. I sent a bottle of champagne to your table at the oceanside restaurant on the fortress wall."

"Did you think I wouldn't remember? Eventually?" Anger heated my cheeks. I stopped rubbing my arms.

Jonathon shifted on the chair. He made a short, choked sound like a laugh yet so unlike a laugh at the same time. He was withholding something from me. "I hadn't really thought about it. I chalked it up to some crazy kismet or something."

"*Kismet?*" I pushed his hand off my leg. The strangeness of meeting Jonathon a year ago tied my gut in knots. Had he planned it? Had he bided his time? "Why didn't you say something when we met again?"

"If I told you I'd forgotten, would you believe me?" Jonathon was playing a game. I hadn't yet figured out which chess piece *I* was.

"No. Would you say under oath that you'd forgotten?"

"I did remember you, Mina. You are unforgettable."

"That's bullshit and you know it." I stood.

Shifting forward, he placed his elbows on his knees, acting way too comfortable. As usual, Jonathon had control of the room. But I wouldn't let this slide. "What are you playing at, Jonathon?"

"It never came up. We are two high-profile people. You can't expect that someone like you—working newsworthy trials—wouldn't get recognized. Even if it was in Europe."

"Now . . . *Now* I remember it like it was yesterday," I said. "My tombstoning adventure that night nearly killed me. I was lucky that my translator and the boat driver didn't leave me as I'd asked. They found me and put pressure on the gash as they drove me back to Pile Bay. You've seen the scar." I touched my thigh where the bumpy scar would never let me forget that night. "The EMTs clamped the ruptured vein and gave me a blood transfusion. I was lucky, but the trauma made me forget about you. What's your excuse?"

"It wasn't important, Mina. It was over a year ago. What's important is that we're here now. We're together."

For a moment, my anger seemed unfounded while I let his statement sink in. Was he was missing the point? Or was it really *nothing* as I'd said to Gary.

Nothing is always something.

I didn't want Jonathon to know I had doubts about him. "You're right," I said. But it was a concession. I was giving in.

"I'm surprised that you didn't remember the meeting sooner. I thought that *I* was unforgettable." Jonathon's hand grazed the hem of my robe near the raised diving scar. His boyish smile didn't warm me this time.

It wasn't the first time I'd given in and let him win. And it wouldn't be the last. But the conversation left a sour taste in my mouth. From now on, I'd watch Jonathon closely.

~13~

Along with Janko's mugshot, Gary Underwood sent a short article translated from Croatian. The author suspected there was more behind the Dubrovnik General Hospital's firing Janko than was on paper. Janko was suspected of stealing drugs from their supply rooms. A photo of him with known organized crime boss, Artur Protsenko, was featured in the header.

Gary Underwood's brief text asked:

How does Jonathon know this gem? Is he working with PPS?

I replied:

Not with PPS. Keep digging. He's visiting the States for unknown reasons. I want an excuse to get him arrested or sent back home.

Gary replied later:

Sure thing, Ms. Green.

Gary had learned the hard way to never divulge his research over the phone. I let him know I wasn't available for a few more days. His simple reply felt like an ice cube down my shirt.

Be careful.

We didn't see Jonathon until that evening, and he greeted Traci with a friendly embrace. "I'm so happy to meet you, Traci."

Traci said, "It's nice to finally meet you, too. I might have read every article about you I could find. Thanks for letting me stay."

"Happy to have you here." Jonathon looked my way. Tonight I wore a shimmering slate-blue summer dress that matched Jonathon's eyes. He put a hand on the small of my back and drew me closer to him. I kissed him on the lips, but he pulled away. Our conversation last night had put distance between us.

Grant, in dark red pants and a black vest with red buttons, appeared in the doorway and announced Janko, then ushered the man I recalled from last year into the living room.

"How have you been, old friend?" Jonathon shook hands with Janko and pulled him in for a manly embrace. Their chummy cordiality belied what he'd told me, that Janko was *no friend.*

Janko vigorously patted Jonathon's back. "Good, good, it has been too long."

"There's scotch on the bar if you like. Can I get you a glass?" Jonathon said.

Janko looked exactly like his photos. Suntanned and fit, he had the hard, rugged appearance of someone who had been to war. His gaze had an edge when he turned it on me and locked onto the glittering collar around my neck.

Traci and I were sitting on the forest green Art Deco couch, glasses of red wine in our hands. Jonathon introduced us.

"We have met before," Janko said. He tipped his head to the side while appraising me.

I stood to greet him and looked upward. Janko was a few inches taller than Jonathon. In my high heels, I stretched my spine longer and shook his hand. They say there's a lot you can assess from a handshake. Janko's grip was tight, yet cold and damp. I instantly didn't like him. "We have met." I said. "Last year in Croatia. I'm Wilhelmina Green."

Janko seemed taken aback. "Jonathon, you didn't tell me. Is this the lawyer we met beside the Pile Sea?"

Even Janko remembered details about our first meeting. Jonathon put his hands in his pants pockets and said, "She is. I hired Mina a few months ago."

"What kind of law do you practice?" Janko asked.

I already knew that he was the kind of man Jim Milton would ask me to represent in court. He exuded hypermasculinity. At once, I knew he was a misogynist and an anti-feminist bastard. He was the type of man who didn't see women for their value to society, only for their bodies.

"*Criminal* law." I hoped to intimidate him.

Janko continued to study me with narrowed eyes.

I introduced Traci to change the subject. "This is my friend, Traci Lambert."

He took Traci's hand and his gaze darted back and forth between us. "You two could be sisters."

With a playful dig meant for me, she said, "I'm taller, but we get that a lot." Without sharing what I learned about Jonathon's frenemy, I'd prompted Traci with the brief story Jonathon told me and let her know we were wary of this man. "Nice to meet you," she said politely.

I said, "Traci and I have been friends since our first college days. We were roommates, so we got to know each other quickly."

"In other words, I tolerated her," Traci teased.

"Oh, you should talk!" I quickly replied with a big smile.

Janko poured scotch over ice and Jonathon refilled his Perrier with lime. The men sat in royal blue damask wingback chairs on the other side of a marble-topped coffee table from Traci and me.

Janko said, "It's been too long, Jon."

"It has," Jonathon said.

"Only a year," I said. "You were together in Dubrovnik last summer."

"A lifetime has passed since then." Janko's closed smile masked a darker emotion, one I couldn't identify.

Jonathon sent a sidelong glance in my direction. His gaze shifted up my legs to my breasts and latched onto the collar around my neck. He seemed to be holding his breath before he asked, "What brings you to Chicago, Janko?"

The older man shrugged, "A little of this, a little of that. You know, business."

"What business are you in?" Traci leaned back on the couch with her legs crossed. Her black patent-leather high-heeled sandal hung half off her foot, and her toenails were painted black to match.

Janko hesitated before saying, "I'm in exports, now. My brothers and I ship rare products, items that are hard to come by."

Jonathon leaned forward with his Perrier in one hand, his elbow on a knee. "Janko used to work with the Dubrovnik hospitals. In Croatia, medical research is innovative in the fields of organ transplants and new drug technologies. Government-provided health insurance is offered nationwide in Croatia. It's mandatory for residents."

"That's true," said Janko. "The cost of medical procedures in Croatia is often up to seventy percent lower than in Western countries."

"A woman I know went to Croatia for a kidney transplant that her doctors wouldn't perform," Traci said. "She was very sick and desperate. The surgery was less than half the cost and although she paid out of pocket for it, she regained her health. She's much better now, thanks to the doctors in Croatia."

"This is why many Americans come to my country. Our doctors are the best." His thin lips tightened over his teeth. "Our most recent shipping contract is with the resorts on the island of Hvar. They require the latest, most beneficial products in health care and wellness."

My research about Janko had led me there, too. I said, "People visit Hvar to cleanse and replenish their bodies. Their spas and wellness centers are some of the best in the world."

Traci said, "Sounds like my kind of vacation."

Janko lit up. "The pristine Adriatic seawater and cerulean sky is perfect for cleansing your soul. Have you traveled to that part of Europe?" He directed the question to Traci.

She said, "Last year I visited London and Amsterdam. I was there for almost three weeks."

"Cloudy. Not as beautiful as my homeland," Janko said.

"How long are you staying in the States?" Jonathon asked.

Janko's mouth curled into a smile that didn't reach his eyes. "Not sure, my friend. As long as it takes. I came to Chicago to meet with you, Jon. You have connections, you know?" He waved his glass and sipped while looking at me.

"Connections in the medical field, you mean," Jonathon said.

"Yes of course." Janko didn't elaborate. "I want to hear about you, Mina. Tell me what brought you and my old friend together?"

Jonathon shot me a furtive glance. The less I told Janko, the better. I briefly explained the case of Jonathon's murdered assistant, how he was cleared of any suspicion, and soon it was time for our meal.

We ate dinner in the dining room, a meal of blood orange salad vinaigrette, juicy Cornish game hens, and roasted baby carrots. The stilted discussion moved between travel and politics. I shared some of my adventures, without discussing my addiction to dangerous tombstoning.

"I didn't know you've been so many places," Traci said. "Take me with you next time you go . . . Please?" She didn't make the connection that each location I mentioned was famous for its cliffs.

"I'd love to," I said. The thought of including my friend on a trip made tension of the evening melt away.

After dinner, Jonathon and Janko went to the patio to discuss—as they put it—personal matters. Traci and I decided to sit on the deck beside the pool. I returned to the kitchen for the half-empty bottle of wine.

Jonathon's low, deep voice caught my attention. "Has the transition been smooth?"

Jonathon and Janko sat on the patio with their backs to me. Through the open French doors, I heard them clearly. Janko said, "Not smooth at all. In fact, my situation has changed dramatically. I need your help with something, Jonathon. I have a proposition for you, and I'll wager that you won't be able to refuse."

"What do you mean?" Jonathon shifted in his seat.

I listened from the dark living room.

"Payback is a bitch, isn't that what they say?"

A hint of anger colored Jonathon's response. "You can't blame me for the Dubrovnik GH firing you."

Janko said, "I offered you kindness and a chance to do business with hundreds of clients. You responded with unkept promises. Your delays cost me my job. The Dubrovnik GH was buried in paperwork, and I had a chance to help them and become rich."

"We didn't have a contract." As Jonathon stood, the metal chair grated against the stone pavers. When Janko stood, too, I backed into a dark corner. I couldn't risk them seeing me.

Janko's voice grew in volume and intensity. "The point is your delay cost me."

"You were caught consorting with the Russian Mafia," Jonathon said.

Jonathon knew. I inhaled sharply through my nose. Gary had uncovered photos of Janko with a known Russian mafia leader. No wonder Jonathon didn't trust Janko. And it might explain why he didn't remind me about our first meeting.

Janko said, "You don't know anything. I lost respect. Dubrovnik GH would have paid me handsomely, but you didn't meet the contract deadline." He drilled his pointer finger into Jonathon's chest.

Jonathon swatted Janko's hand away and even in the low light, his eyes glowered like hot coals. "You can't blame me."

"But I do. In return, I want something of yours that will be impossible for you not to give."

"This is extortion."

"It's the cost of business. You will give me fifty million dollars as payback."

"Not a chance."

"You *will* give me the money. The men I work for are very dangerous. We also have connections here in Chicago—that's why I've come."

Jonathon lowered his voice to a near whisper. "Who are your associates?"

"You know who I work for."

"The Russians."

Janko swirled the ice in his glass. "I will get the money from you regardless."

In the darkened living room, I clutched the wine bottle to my chest. Their voices grew soft, and I strained to hear the end of the conversation. I didn't catch their drift until Janko asked, "Are you in love with her?"

Jonathon nearly choked on his sparkling water. "Don't bring Mina into this."

The mention of my name sent a shockwave through my nervous system.

Janko laughed. "I see."

"You don't see a thing, Janko. You can't threaten me."

Janko took a big swallow from his glass and the sound of ice clinking echoed off the stone patio and the brick siding of the house. "Be mindful of your things, Jon."

"What are you saying?"

"Give me what I want in one week, and your woman is safe."

Blood drained from my face, weakening my knees.

Had I become a bargaining chip in this extortion plot?

"There you are!" Traci came up behind me. Her loud, sing-song voice exposed me in the darkened living room. Jonathon and Janko looked through the screen.

"I was looking for the opened bottle of wine," I said. "Oh, here it is!" As I turned to go with Traci, I glimpsed the whites of Jonathon's stormy eyes through the sliding screen door.

-14-

Traci and I stayed up late, watching clouds pass in front of the moon and talking about how far we'd come and where we saw ourselves in the future. Despite her loose ways all through our twenties, Traci had changed. Both of us would turn thirty before the end of the year. She wanted to settle down. She wanted a family. On the other hand, I couldn't see myself with a family in any future. Especially in light of the conversation I'd overheard between Jonathon and Janko.

After Traci'd gone to bed, I went to the kitchen for a glass of water. There, I found Jonathon standing over the sink, his head lowered. He had removed his blazer and his sleeves were rolled up.

I put my hand between his shoulder blades. "What's wrong?" I asked.

Jonathon turned in my arms. "Mina." He held me for a moment then looked past me, his gaze introspective. He said, "I've made some good choices in my life, and I've made some bad ones. Befriending Janko was a bad one."

"He reminds me of men like Senator Peterson."

Jonathon nodded. "He'll do anything to get ahead, and now he thinks he can blackmail me into giving him money. He has no idea who he's dealing with."

I didn't want to admit what I'd heard. Not yet. "Do you want to talk about it?"

Jonathon nodded and hugged me once more. "Let me get us both glasses of water."

It was well past one in the morning when we took our water glasses to the sofa in my bedroom. Jonathon lit a candle, and I watched the jaw muscles on his face pulse to some internal beat. He stared into the flame.

Somehow, this was different. Jonathon's level of distress and angst felt much higher. His silence regarding Janko unnerved me more than anything that we'd been through. Together, we had sorted through the list of possible vengeance-seeking enemies. Together, we had proven his innocence. Together, we'd faced a killer.

I tucked my feet underneath my bottom and curled up near my lover. I placed a hand on his shoulder and massaged his tense muscles with my thumb.

Jonathon's hand and his gaze floated to the scar on my thigh. To my shoulder. He put an arm around me.

I said, "I heard part of your conversation. I'm sorry for eavesdropping, but I'm very concerned. Why does he want so much money?"

Jonathon took a deep breath. "He's blaming me for his current situation, and he's involved with terrorists."

"I don't know what he's threatened you with, but in Illinois, the penalty for extortion is six years in prison. If it goes to the federal courts, he faces up to twenty years in a penitentiary. Report him to the police. No matter what, no matter who he is or who he thinks he is, he can't get away with that." I touched the hair above Jonathon's ear and caressed his head and neck.

"This isn't something a lawsuit can fix, Mina. He's well connected to Russian organized crime. I believe he won't stop until I give him what he wants." Jonathon took my hand in his. "And I can't let that happen."

"When you were out on the patio with him, I heard my name. How is he dragging me into this?"

The muscles in his jaw flexed.

"I need to know."

He turned toward me on the sofa. His soft, worried gaze wrinkled the crease between his eyebrows.

"Long before I met you, Janko and I met in Austria." Jonathon's blue eyes flicked back and forth over my face. "He wanted to purchase PPS Software for the healthcare systems in Dubrovnik. At the time, we were scheduling out at least six months for initial contracts and training. Before that, before we were able to deliver the initial paperwork, he lost his job. A journalist took photos of him with Artur Protsenko, known leader of a Russian terrorist group. Janko was accused of working with the terrorists and fired."

"You knew about this and still invited him to dinner?"

"I needed to know his game. In martial arts, you fight an opponent by getting very close to them. It throws them off guard."

"I know," I said. I understood the correlation now. "Was he still working with the healthcare systems when I met you in Dubrovnik?"

Jonathon leaned forward and rested his elbows on his thighs as he looked up at me. "Yes. You explained why you didn't remember our initial meeting, now let me explain my point of view. I, like you, had an experience that distracted from the memory of our encounter.

"The night I first saw you in Dubrovnik, Janko and I were discussing business, scheduling meetings, arranging for the payment. Afterward, Janko took me to a private, exclusive event. He said we'd be rubbing shoulders with government officials, doctors, and clinic managers from the area. I thought he planned to introduce me to the hospital manager, the person who would purchase our software. I was mistaken."

"What happened?"

"When we arrived at the location, I knew something was wrong. We were far from the tourist sights, the *Game of Thrones* movie sets, and the ocean. In the hills beyond the city, armed guards stood outside a property with razor wire on the walls. As we approached the building, soldiers with assault rifles flanked the doors and each corner of the building. It appeared to be a government fortress."

I dropped my feet to the floor and sat up while swallowing some of my angst. I needed to hear the truth. "What kind of party has military-level security?"

"It struck me that way, too. But Janko kept me in good spirits. I dismissed the knot in my stomach because he didn't acknowledge the heavy weaponry. As we entered, we were patted down then handed black masks—the kind you would wear at a Halloween gala. Janko said, 'Protocols, you know? We better do as they ask.' By now I'd started to worry. I wondered why we were here and where Janko had taken me. It wasn't the first time I suspected he was involved with crooked people."

Jonathon stood and smoothed out his slacks. He paced in front of the unlit gas fireplace. A long slow breath expanded his ribcage. "Mina, what I'm about to tell you stays between us. It was my presence at this event that Janko holds over my head."

I looked out the window. In the dark evening sky, Chicago city lights illuminated fast-moving clouds. "What did they do there?"

He said, "We were ushered into an upper floor ballroom that over-looked a circular stage. Lights were dim, but about fifty men and women milled about, conversing with each other in hushed voices. They all wore the same masks to disguise their faces. Still, I recognized a US Armed Forces General, two US Congressmen, and a senator from Georgia. I asked Janko, 'What is this?' He said, 'You'll see.'

A naked girl that couldn't be old enough to drink alcohol passed by with a tray of champagne glasses. And soon enough, music announced that a show was starting. We were invited to observe from the balcony. People moved to the edge and leaned over a wooden rail."

"What kind of performance was it? Did they have illegal endangered animals?"

"No. The soldiers closed the outer doors and guarded them with au-tomatic weapons. Below us on the stage, a woman in black disguised by an elaborate mask directed a parade of soldiers carrying large trunks. They set them down all around her and opened them one by one. Each case was filled with bags of white powder. Enough fentanyl to kill mil-lions of people."

I pictured the horrifying scene in my mind. I whispered, "And she was selling it?"

"She said that each case was to be distributed to American cities. Her plan was to infiltrate the illegal drug industry and threaten the American way of life. She asked for help destroying our freedom by weakening the infrastructure and giving power to the communists. A man near me called out thirty thousand. Bidders shouted higher and higher figures. The first case sold for fifty thousand dollars. The street value of that amount of fentanyl would be ten times that amount. Do you understand what I'm telling you, Mina? These are the people Janko is involved with. They are communist supporters and terrorists."

My stomach had grown queasy. "Did the US officials know? Were they blackmailed, too?"

"I believe most attended of their own free will." A tempestuous ridge ran across Jonathon's brow. He choked on fury and outrage.

"He's got proof that you were there. What else does he have on you?"

"I believe he's manufacturing evidence that I purchased a case and brought it back to Chicago."

"If the media were to find out . . . it would be your career. You would lose everything."

"Yes. Secret photos were taken of each person in attendance as they entered the building. Cameras placed around the venue recorded the entire event. It's how the people operating it keep everyone in their grip. And that's only part of what Janko is holding over my head."

How could there be more? My legal mind was trying to figure out how Jonathon could be implicated in an international trafficking ring and how I could defend him if he were charged.

Jonathon didn't turn to look at me, but I felt his shame as it poured off him like smoke from a charred piece of meat.

"A few years ago, Janko and I made a silly wager about finding the perfect woman. When we saw you at the restaurant in Dubrovnik, you became part of that wager."

That explained why Janko had seemed so interested in me at dinner tonight. And why he asked so many questions about the two of us. I leaned forward to meet Jonathon's gaze locked somewhere on the floor near the fireplace.

"Janko sees women as objects. As I've said, he's connected to some of the most ruthless people in the world. And he wants to hurt me." Jonathon sat beside me and put an arm around me. He looked me in the eye. "He knows I've fallen for you, Mina."

"You have?" I took a breath as if about to plunge my head under water. It was my turn to feel the shame of wrongdoing. I had approached the relationship with my personal needs at the forefront. Where Jonathan had come to me out of love.

"In every way." He stroked my hair.

"Jonathon, I don't know what to say." I linked my fingers behind his neck. I wanted to kiss him if it weren't for the heartbreaking look on his face.

Jonathon then told me what I already knew from my eavesdropping. "If I don't give him fifty million dollars, he promises to come for you."

~15~

$\mathcal{J}$ onathon was a sensuous, attuned lover, mindful and meticulously attending to my needs. At times, I resisted his touch, climbing on top of him and taking him in my mouth. Giving pleasure to him satisfied a deep need to return his kindness. I submitted to the exquisite feeling of his weight on top of me and the pressure of his mouth against mine. He put my pleasure first. He quenched my thirst before mounting me. His driving thrusts both tender and cruel.

After our lovemaking, Jonathon didn't sleep with me, or like me, he didn't sleep, but in the morning, he quietly entered the bedroom. He padded across the floor to my bed and eased himself down as if trying not to disturb me.

While lying in bed, I looked long and hard at our relationship dynamics. Though we were bound previously by the elements of engagement—our legal contract—and now the dominant/submissive contract, Jonathon had kept me at a distance. The knowledge that we met a year ago—that he'd kept that history from me—built a wall of distrust in my heart that crumbled with his admission that he loved me.

Jonathon had given me nothing but space since the day we met. The thought twined its deadly tendrils around me. And last night, my lover admitted that he'd fallen for me. A bright red bloom at the end of the prickly vine.

"Good morning," he whispered. Shirtless, and wearing only gray silk pajama pants, he leaned in toward me.

My body still hummed from sex last night. I rolled over sleepily. "What time is it?"

"It's early . . . but I brought you a cup of coffee." He held the cup out to me. "Cream, no sugar, right?"

"Thank you." Lately, I slept wearing only panties. I sat up, pulled the sheet up to my armpits then took the coffee from him.

Jonathon's solemn expression showed me he was not in a flirtatious mood, but neither was I. Studying him, I carefully sipped the too-hot coffee.

He said, "Traci's in the kitchen and asking if you're up. I thought you'd like to spend the day with her."

Traci could wait. I had things on my mind to discuss with Jonathon. "I was awake for a long time last night thinking about Janko. What he's doing to you is extortion. He can't get away with that. Tig Wallace, one of the partners at my firm, is an excellent defense attorney who is well-versed in extortion law. If you give him the facts, I'm sure he can help you. At the very least, Janko will be forced to go home to Croatia."

Jonathon nodded and placed his hand on the covers over the scar on my thigh. "I'd expect nothing less from my lawyer." He took my hand and kissed it. "But this goes way beyond a lawsuit. I can't convey enough, Janko is a merciless, bloodthirsty criminal. And he fraternizes with terrorists."

"You're scared of him?"

"No. But I see no other way than to play his game."

I set the cup on the night table and swung my feet over the side with the sheet clutched to my chest. "How?"

He cupped my chin in his hand. "I'll do everything in my power to protect you. I'll hire—"

"—Another body guard? No. Not this again."

"Your life is in danger. I need to be sure that you're safe."

"I *am* safe. I'm here with you—"

"A team is on the way," Jonathon said. "My friend Greg Hauser is one of the best. When you go to Chicago, he and his team will meet you at your apartment."

I wouldn't have it. "My Lincoln Park condo has added surveillance cameras on every floor. Guards are stationed at each doorway, and they require ID for entrance. I'm not afraid of Janko. Don't you understand? His threat means nothing to me."

"He'll take your life."

"He wants your money."

"He's not getting it. This is where I draw the line, Mina. I refuse to give him what he asks for. And he's not taking you."

"I see. It's just. . .." I reached for the black satin robe on the foot of the bed.

"What?"

"How did I become part of a wager between you and Janko?"

Jonathon stood beside me and took my hand. "He knows I have a weakness for you. I never saw this coming. You must believe me."

"You're under no obligation to hire security for me." I pulled the robe over my shoulders and stood.

"Mina, I feel . . . responsible for you."

Jonathon had indirectly put me in danger before. The Chinese corporate spies had murdered several women closest to him. Direct association with my ex-client and lover had become a very tangible threat to my life. I was used to dealing with criminals, I sat with them every day. I placed my hand over his. "I'm going back to Chicago today. I need to be in court this week."

"It will get your mind off this."

"It will."

"Greg Hauser will be there with you. He is a trusted friend."

"Like Travis King?"

"Not like Travis. That's not fair."

I stepped away from my lover. "When we came to Lake Forest, you gave me my own bedroom, my own apartment for that matter. You keep me at arm's length. Yet, you wanted me to sign your contract."

Too-professional, he said, "Our contract defines the extent of our relationship. That's important to me."

"Our contract defines our *sexual* relationship. That's all we have, Jonathon. A sexual relationship." I tied the black robe.

His stormy gaze held me as tightly as his arms would have. I would have been happier if he bound me to the bed at that moment. Instead,

I said, "For the sake of our relationship, for my own protection, I want out of the contract."

"No." As still as a statue, he didn't take a breath. Yet tension rippled through his shoulders and folded arms. "I cannot release you from the contract."

"There is no court of law that will find that contract binding."

A short, clipped laugh issued from his lips. "Leave it to you, the lawyer, to say something like that. And yet, Ms. Green, that is exactly why I've covered my bases. I've had my notary sign and stamp it. And you, as a lawyer, should know that the contract *is* binding. I will hold you to it. I want more from you that than the sex acts listed on that piece of paper. I want more than you can imagine."

"More? More than my submission? More than the power to dominate me? To whip and tie me up? According to you, I'm in danger. Is that not enough?"

"I won't let you out of the contract."

"Why is it so important to you?"

"Mina." Jonathon looked away from me.

"Help me to understand."

"There's so much that I want to share with you."

I brushed past him to the windows and threw open the heavy curtains. Trees blocked the view of Lake Michigan. "I'm going back to Chicago. I have clients who need me. I don't want to be part of this—situation."

"Do you think that by returning to Chicago Janko will keep from hunting you like prey? Do you think that by putting distance between us that I'll stop caring for you? Do you think that's all it will take?"

"What are you saying?"

"I'm saying . . . I'm in love with you." He took a step closer to me.

Love? I wanted him to love me. The word caried so much weight I wanted to lean into it.

No.

Not yet. Not with this hanging over our heads.

"I need to go back to Chicago." My emotions raged behind a delicate veil. Tears pushed to the surface as I said, "I can't stay here. I don't love you."

Jonathon settled on the edge of the bed.

I wiped my eyes and ducked past him to the bathroom. As I dressed for the day, I realized there was one thing I could do about this situation. I could fight Janko for Jonathon.

"I'll look into this for you, Jonathon."

"As my lawyer?"

"As a friend." I slid my feet into a pair of sandals and closed up my suitcase.

"I'll call," he said. "Every day, I'll call you Mina."

With my suitcase in tow, I walked out of the room.

-16-

Earlier than planned, I returned my friend to her brownstone near Northwestern University. I then drove home to my lux loft in Lincoln Park. Everything was just as I'd left it, a bit of a mess. Before going to stay at Jonathon's mansion, my condo had become a crime scene after Travis King's attack. Though the crime scene tape had been removed and the apartment swept for evidence, I still saw everything as it was when the police stormed in.

Travis had drugged me with fentanyl, and yet I woke from the haze and then fought him. He shot the Chinese associate he was working with and somehow I knocked the gun out of his hand and pinned him to the floor. I held the gun on him, threating him if he moved a muscle. Police arrived shortly afterward in response to the gunfire. I found out later that security had made the call.

A blood stain soaked into the hardwood floor reminded me how strong I had been. It reminded me to call a cleaning crew. It reminded me that I wanted to forget. That was all in the past, now.

I was a lucky survivor. A new rush of adrenaline flooded my veins. Here, I stood on the brink of a different cliff. One where I might launch into a new definition of myself.

Jonathon and his ropes came to mind. *I've fallen for you, Mina. In every way.*

Every relationship I'd ever had—which I could count on one hand—I'd ended. One was too needy. One guy couldn't hold down a job and kept asking for handouts. Another, the sex was meaningless and unsatisfying. Jonathon was none of those things. Was I doomed to repeat myself? Or. . .

Had I fallen for Jonathon?

After a restless night of sleep, I glugged iced coffee while getting ready for work at Milton, Wallace, & Edwards. Unsure if it would help, I planned to speak with Tig Wallace about Janko's extortion plans. It was the least I could do for Jonathon.

My ring tone—*Discipline* by Nine Inch Nails—turned a switch on inside me. The song announced a call from Jonathon, sending electricity zipping under my skin. I stood up from the kitchen stool and answered.

"Mina, has your security guard arrived?"

"Not this again."

"I need to be sure that you're safe."

"I *am* safe. I'm at my apartment. Jason, the head of security, assured me that safeguards in the building have been ramped up since—"

"A man is on the way," Jonathon said.

I tried to change his mind. "I told you my building has security."

"And who will be with you while you're walking the streets of Chicago? Who will watch your back when you go to meetings or the grocery store? I would if I could. But my life must go on as if nothing is wrong."

"So must mine."

"Text me the moment he arrives."

"Jonathon—" I looked at the blood-stained floor, "—alright," I said with the phone pressed to my ear.

"Mina, I care about you. You must know that."

Another call stole my attention. "I'll call as soon as he arrives."

I hung up. The call was from my building's security center. Jason said, "Greg Hauser is here to see you. He says he's your personal security detail."

"Ask him to wait in the lobby." Jason's primary duty was to the upscale residents of this elite apartment building. Almost six months earlier I had moved here because I needed the added security. Considering the types I worked with—sexual predators and rapists—it was worth every cent. The expense included guards and surveillance systems near each egress. Granted, those systems had failed the day Travis turned on me.

According to Jason, that wouldn't happen *ever* again.

I told myself I wasn't afraid.

Before leaving for work, I reapplied online for my concealed-carry license. The gun had belonged to my father, who'd been a Chicago cop before my mother died. When she passed away from ovarian cancer, we moved to Normal, Illinois, where he eventually became the chief of police. Now retired, he gave me his first gun, a Browning .9 mm. It was in excellent condition, and he taught me how to shoot and protect myself.

I submitted the online forms for my concealed-carry permit, but it would take a week or more for them to mail the license. Regardless, I holstered the gun under my leather jacket—hoping I wouldn't need to use it—and left for work.

I stepped out of the elevator in the lobby and walked toward the entrance. Out of the corner of my eye, I saw a slender, middle-aged man in a midnight blue suit stand up and approach me. Two men were with him. They followed him.

"Ms. Green?"

Glad for the weapon, I slid my hand under my unzipped jacket and turned on him. "Greg Hauser?"

"In the flesh." Hauser's blond hair was tousled. Though his suit was neat, and his collar ironed and stiff, his casual stance indicated an easy-going nature. He looked more like a former California surfer than a professional bodyguard.

He said, "Call me Greg. I'm here to help. This is Arron and Liam. They'll alternate the off hour shifts."

Arron was taller than the others, with a shaved head and a thick neck like a line-backer. Liam had trim brown hair and a stylish unshaven look that brought out his hazel eyes. He was leaner than Arron, but no less intimidating.

I removed my hand from the sidearm. I wasn't sure I wanted them following me around.

"I can tell you are dubious. I assure you Arron and Liam will remain invisible. You'll never see them."

I took a deep breath. It did little to calm my nerves.

Greg Hauser escorted me to work. Arron and Liam followed in a white Expedition. In Greg's Hyundai Santa Fe, he set the satellite radio to alternative rock, and we listened to Linkin Park's *What I've Done*.

Over the music I asked, "How is this going to work?"

"How do you want it to work?"

"I want it to work as if Janko never threatened Jonathon." *Or me.*

I wanted my old life back.

"Someday that will happen. But that day is not today," he said.

With the weighty feeling of the gun holstered near my ribs, I reserved judgement of Greg. He walked me to the elevators in my office building and then promised to wait in the lobby until my next venture outside.

On the way up, the elevator stopped at the second floor, and my investigator Gary Underwood stepped in. Wearing a dark gray t-shirt tucked into belted, faded jeans and a heavy leather biker's jacket, he took his hand out of his pocket and pressed number four.

"Hello, Gary."

"Ms. Green. You look —"

Gary was about to commit another social faux pax. I shook my head no.

"—how nice to see you again," he corrected himself then furtively backed into the panel and stopped the elevator's progress mid-floor. He faced me with a quick glance toward the ceiling. "Darn elevator's not working again," he said.

We'd met like this before. Without looking up at the security camera dome, I handed him my briefcase. Gary lifted it over our heads, blocking the hidden lens. Any work Gary did for me stayed strictly between us.

"I need to tell you what I learned about this Vorobiev character."

I smiled. "Your timing is impeccable, as usual."

"Good.

"Go on."

"Vorobiev Imports looks like a front. The business doesn't have any shipping records, but flight logs spiderweb across southern Europe and the Middle East."

"What are they doing there? What are they supposedly shipping?" I asked. I suspected drug trafficking based on the story Jonathon told.

"Though Vorobiev Export trucks and airplanes traveled from antique shops in Germany to Belgium and Turkey, I didn't find accounting ledgers. I'm afraid to tell you what I did find."

"I think I know." Was it enough proof to put Janko away?

Gary looked up at the briefcase and adjusted the height. He whispered, "Vorobiev has connections to government officials in Russia and Chechnya. He's also connected to terrorist cells in Saudi Arabia and Serbia. If you consider the rule *six degrees from Kevin Bacon,* then by association, Vorobiev is well connected to terrorists here in the US."

I nodded. "What *degree* is Jonathon?"

Gary swung the briefcase down to his side and gave it back to me. He flipped the stop-switch and as the elevator began moving again, he said, "I'll let you know."

A discordant arpeggio of nerves shimmied town my spine.

"Be careful, Wil," he said over his shoulder. Gary strode out on the fourth floor and rounded the corner out of my sight.

Terrorist cells in the US.

I hugged the sidearm under my suit jacket and hoped I'd never need to use it.

~17~

At work, I filed legal papers leftover from cases this summer and spoke quietly with my superior, Tig Wallace about Jonathon's predicament. Other than a lawsuit to draw his adversary out in public, we couldn't think of any way to deal with Janko.

I was studying a case file at my desk when Christina called. "There's a man here to see—You can't go in there!"

My office door opened and with the phone still at my ear, I stood.

"Hello, Mina." Looking smug as ever, Janko stepped into my office and closed the door behind him.

"Call security," I said to Christina and set the receiver back on the base. The hair on the back of my neck stood. "How did you get in here?"

"Greg Hauser, is that his name? Your *bodyguard?*" Janko said the word like it was a joke.

"What did you do to him?"

"I did nothing. He fell asleep in his chair, that's all."

Greg fell asleep?

Janko walked past me to the floor to ceiling window. He appeared to gaze out at the Chicago landscape. "I wanted to see you. To see why Jonathon is so taken by you." He turned to face me. Three feet from me, Janko's cologne smelled of clove and other spices. His gaze traveled slowly down my body as he seemed to assess every inch of my skin and took one long stride toward me. I tried to back away, and my calves bumped into my chair. "I see why he likes you." His hand was on my chin.

I swatted it away and shoved him backward. "Security is on the way. They'll make sure you'll never enter this building again."

"You're full of sass, too. I like that." Janko dropped back into the chair on the opposite side of my desk.

"What do you want?" I asked.

"He has not told you?"

"He'll never give you the money."

He smiled and his tongue flicked his lips like a snake would smell its food. "Are you so sure? I think he would give anything to keep you alive."

A chill rose up the backs of my arms.

Someone pounded on my office door, "Security! Is everything alright?"

Before I could answer, Arron and Liam barged into the room, weapons drawn. Three uniformed security officers peered from behind them as Greg pushed his way through and asked, "Are you okay?" He held a weapon pointed at Janko.

Janko stood and brushed off his slacks. "How was your nap, Mr. Hauser." He held up his hands.

Greg stared at him. "Who are you?"

"Nice to know you're well-protected, Mina." Janko turned to go. "You'll of course tell Jonathon that I stopped by. Let him know that I stand firm. I want the money by the end of the week."

Security escorted him to the elevators. They would make sure he exited the building.

Greg closed the door. "I'm so sorry."

"What happened to you?"

"I was drinking a Starbucks coffee and . . .I fell asleep. I don't know what happened." Dark circles bagged under his red eyes. Clearly, Janko drugged Greg without him knowing.

Janko's unannounced visit to my office shook me up. Knowing what Gary Underwood discovered worried me more. The Russian mafia were one of the most powerful organized crime groups in Chicago, and Janko had just proven what he was capable of.

While walking to the car, I asked Greg, "How do you know Jonathon?"

"When I worked for Pfizer, he asked me to demo the PPS software. I was amazed at what it could do. Jonathon, well, I call him Jon, offered me more than Pfizer paid to promote PPS to drug manufacturers. That's how we become friends."

"What did you do for Pfizer?"

"I kept all their secrets safe." Greg winked at me.

I cocked my head.

He explained, "Seriously, I design security software, and they use my products to encrypt their studies and test results. I kept the competition at arm's length. And when they needed brute force, well, look at me." His open palm flagged the length of his body from sternum to thigh. His eyes gleamed with conceit. "I'm a trained fighter. Well, actually, martial arts is my hobby. Pfizer doesn't pay me for that. But Jon and I have trained together for years."

"You're no bodyguard."

"Today, I am," he said confidently. "I'm a twelfth don black-belt in martial arts. I am a trained fighter and a weapons specialist. I can hit a beer can with a crossbow from fifty yards away."

"A crossbow will surely help us here in Chicago." I smirked.

"Today and for the foreseeable future, I am your bodyguard." He pulled back his jacket to reveal his concealed pistol, a Walther PPK .380 caliber.

"Carrying a gun doesn't make you a bodyguard." I showed him my dad's Browning.

"No. But now that we know what Janko's capable of, I'll keep my eyes open. I'll be watching for threats and attacks. I'll have your back." I was doubtful that he could stop Janko, but he seemed confident and friendly. I liked him more for that.

On the way home, Greg and I stopped at a local shooting range. I put on noise-cancelling headphones, and he stuffed ear plugs into his ears. I shot at the target until the hole in the center was as large as my fist, then reeled the paper in to look at it.

Greg took a turn next. He shot twice. Once to the center of the target's forehead, and the other to the exact center of the chest. We alternated for an hour. Greg helped me with my grip and aim until I could hit my target between the eyes. The exercise filed me with the confidence Janko had taken.

That evening we returned to my Lincoln Park apartment, Greg took a long black duffle bag out of the trunk of the car and slung it over his shoulder.

"Overnight bag?" I asked.

"The boss-man says I'm to sleep on your couch. Whether you like it or not, I'm going to stay near you until this thing blows over." Greg walked toward the elevator with a confident swagger.

~18~

Something was strange as we entered my condo. Confident that I'd turned all the lights off, it surprised me to see the blue seed-glass pendants over the kitchen counter turned on. Motion caught my attention out of the left corner of my eye and every nerve in my body sprang to attention. My free hand moved instinctively to the sidearm.

Greg saw my hesitation and pulled me back, his weapon already drawn. He recognized the intruder first. "Jon. We weren't expecting you," he said.

Jonathon stood near the couch with a bouquet of white roses in his hand.

After what happened at the office my heart raced as I lowered my briefcase to the floor. "You scared us."

Jonathon stepped nearer offering the roses to me. "I didn't mean to, Mina. I heard what happened today and needed to see you. To make sure you're alright."

Despite being startled at his unannounced visit, I was grateful he'd come. "I'm fine."

"Did he hurt you? Did Janko—"

"No. He was letting us know that—even at my office—he could get to me."

Jonathon turned to Greg, "Thanks for being there, Greg. Would you mind standing by? I need to talk with Mina."

"No prob, Bro. I'll be just outside the door." Greg left his duffle bag in my entryway and closed the door.

Jonathon handed me the roses. "White roses symbolize respect and new beginnings. I want us to start over, Mina."

I took the bouquet and smelled the flowers' soft, comforting fragrance. "How did you get in?" Clearly, the security people in my building lacked any skill or credibility.

"It's a long story." Jonathon wore a black suit with a midnight blue shirt and black tie.

I took the flowers to the kitchen and noticed an ice bucket with an opened wine bottle beside one of my crystal wine glasses. I laid the bouquet on the counter. Jonathon stepped toward me with his hand outstretched for me to shake. "Hello, Ms. Green. My name is Jonathon Heun."

"You didn't need to go to such lengths." Indeed, all I needed was his commanding voice and I would submit to him

"When I heard what Janko did today, it angered me." Jonathon had lines under his eyes that I'd never noticed before. "I don't know what I'd do without you."

Could his love be so strong when I still wasn't sure? I searched his eyes for a sign. He held my hand and caressed my fingers with his thumb.

He said, "Yesterday you mentioned our first meeting in Dubrovnik."

"Yes. Why didn't you remind me? Months ago, you could have opened with, 'Hi Mina, we met in Dubrovnik.' Or better yet, 'My friend and I bought you a bottle of champagne, remember?'" I tried to pull my hand away, but he gripped it tightly, pulling me toward him. The fragrance of his cologne wrapped me in a fantasy. Fresh sea spray and deep forest greenery collided with his masculine scent. My knees weakened.

He said, "I was embarrassed by that night. I guess I thought it was better left unspoken."

"And the longer it went on?"

"The longer it went on, the more convinced I became that I'd dodged a bullet." He took a long slow breath. "Please accept my apology."

I wanted to.

"My name's Jonathon. We met last year in Dubrovnik on the shore of the Pile Sea." He took my hand to his lips and kissed it while never removing his gaze from mine.

The podium of righteousness that I stood on crumbled, and my shoulders dropped away from my ears. I busied myself with putting the bouquet in a tall vase while Jonathon took the bottle of wine out of the cooler. I recognized the label at once—the South African Chardonnay that he'd ordered on our first date.

When Jonathon and I first got to know each other, I learned from a mutual friend that he was into BDSM. At the time, I'd never tried it, but I wanted to.

He poured a glass of Lewellen wine for me, and we moved to the couch. I said, "As long as we're starting over, I want you to tell me how you got into dominant/submissive sex. Why do you like it?"

He was near enough to me that I could smell his shampoo. He reached out as if to touch my thigh. I longed for the heat in his skin to warm me. I longed for his touch, whether caressing and pleasing or punishing and hurtful. It didn't matter.

"Please. Tell me everything," I said.

Jonathon's fingers hovered inches from my leg, then he rubbed his thighs as if he were nervous. "I didn't always know I was a dominant."

I encouraged him. "What happened that changed you?"

"I think I was a normal young man."

"So we're going way back to the beginning? First or second grade?"

I'd drawn a smile from him. "College. I had a sex drive that couldn't be sated. Girls in school—with their short skirts and skimpy blouses—turned me on. Girls in those tight athletic pants, girls in jeans and t-shirts. It didn't matter. Skinny and flat-chested, or curvaceous and full-breasted, I wanted them all. And I took any opportunity to be with them. I happened to be good looking—at least some girls said so—and it was easy to date any girl whom I wanted."

"It doesn't sound like much has changed."

"It wasn't satisfying. For me or for the girls I dated. Several years went by like this and I never stayed with anyone long enough to fall in love. In truth, they probably knew I wasn't capable of the type of love they wanted."

"Are you?"

"I believe I am."

"Handcuff me to the bed and show me."

"Touché." Jonathon set a hand on my thigh. "During my third year in college, I was already taking an advanced business class. You recall that I went to school at the University of Wisconsin, in Madison. The professor of a business strategy class had gone on personal leave and left this gorgeous TA in charge of the class. Her name was Elinor Fawkes. She was rounded in all the right places and wore snug-fitting clothes." He looked away as if lost in the memory of her.

A hint of green jealousy sprouted in my gut. Having never really been in a committed relationship before, I was unacquainted with the emotion in this context. I didn't like the nauseating feeling, so looked into my wine glass and waited for him to continue.

"Needless to say, Elinor caught my eye during that first session. Well, I should say, I caught hers. After class, I made a bold move. In those days, I knew the power of my looks. I had the ability to seduce a woman without ever touching her." He swung his head to look my way and added, "I know. None of this is insightful."

I nodded agreement with a slightly raised eyebrow.

"She agreed to go to dinner with me with the caveat that we could only discuss the class. Well, of course that rule didn't stick. I went home with her . . . to her off-campus apartment. That night we fucked like neither of us had ever been satisfied before. We were ravenous for each other. Starved for the feel of another body. The sex was violent in a way."

"Stop right there." I set my glass on the coffee table. "This has nothing to do with what I asked you."

"But it does."

"How?"

Jonathon stood and removed his jacket. He unbuttoned his cufflinks and dropped them into his pocket then rolled up his sleeves. "When it was over, I discovered that she'd clawed her fingernails into my back and left long red gashes. I'd never before experienced pain during sex, and Elinor awakened something in me. After that, we made a habit of discussing class at dinner, then going to her place for sex. She lusted for me, biting, and tearing at my flesh with her teeth. She clawed my back and spanked my ass. I couldn't get enough of it."

"Obviously, you didn't stay together."

He looked at the floor. "Although Elinor was a wildcat in the bedroom, she wanted more from me and our relationship. She suggested we slow down. So for the next few months, we took our time. The heat we first experienced in the bedroom began to cool off. It became habitual and uninspired. Our routine of eating out and then fucking twice a week bored me." Jonathon walked to the window. "And then one day she asked me to tie her up."

"She knew what she wanted. Like I knew," I said.

Jonathon turned away from the window and put his hands in his pants pockets. "I've always respected that about you, Mina. Not many women your age know what they want, let alone are willing to go after it."

I was beyond blushing about my kinky desires. Nevertheless, a warmth heated my core that had nothing to do with embarrassment.

"Elinor had played with ropes and whips before our relationship. I'd never explored any type of bondage. So, the first time she walked me through it. We used a couple of long scarves—the type she frequently wore around her neck or tied at the waist—and she instructed me to tie her hands to the headboard of her bed. She told me how to tie the knots so she couldn't remove them then had me slow down." Jonathon stuffed his hands deeper into his pants pockets and began to pace in front of my window.

I took another swallow of wine. The sun had set, and the city lights glowed in the distance.

I said, "She was in control of the experience. Like you say, the sub has all the power."

"I'm trying to convey that the dominant is nothing without a submissive." Jonathon came and sat on the couch beside me. "It's important you understand, because I—"

I love you. He didn't say it. Janko sensed it, and Jonathon admitted he'd fallen for me. We hadn't been together long enough for me to know if I was in love or not. I had zeroed in on Jonathon because of what he could *give* me. Not because of my feelings for him. Though I liked him, I needed more to take the leap of love. And I wasn't sure yet what that was.

I kicked off my shoes. "I imagine you've been with many women."

"I want you to understand who I am. It has everything to do with where we are now and everything to do with Janko Vorobiev."

"Janko?" I asked. When he'd told me Janko took him to the auction, many, many questions had arisen. "What do your past relationships have to do with Janko?"

"Everything."

My stomach growled.

He asked, "Have you eaten dinner?"

"No. You?"

I shook my head. "I've got some pasta in the pantry."

Jonathon knew I wasn't a great cook. He said, "Do you mind if I order something to be delivered? There's so much to tell you."

Indeed, I needed to comprehend Jonathon's position with Janko, and I felt safer with him here—whether I would admit that to him or not. We agreed on an Italian restaurant, and he dialed in an order. While we waited for the delivery, he paced and continued.

"With Elinor, I learned there was a level of euphoria that I'd never experienced before. I learned that I loved to be in control of the situation. I discovered that I *needed* to be in control of her experience, her pleasure, and her pain. I could become erect just watching her."

Jonathon's deep voice strummed my need. I imagined him tying her up, and I warmed.

"Elinor was willing. For the next month, we met almost every night to explore bondage. She and I even went to a sex shop to look at toys. That was when I bought my first whip. She thought it was overkill, but I think she liked it. I liked how it made me feel when I held it in my hand."

I perched on the edge of the couch with my legs drawn tightly together. "And how did it make you feel?"

Jonathon looked at me. The low light from my kitchen pendants added a cold blueish glow to his features. "Sadistic. Powerful. The whip had a good weight to it. The fat leather handle and dozens of long leather strips looked menacing—the way I wanted to be. And when the strips hit her back, I liked the sound it made. Like flesh on flesh."

I sipped my wine to cool the growing heat between my legs. Jonathon's story intrigued me. I *wanted* to be Elinor. "Did Elinor like the whip as much as you did?"

"She asked for it. But by then our games had begun to change. As did the balance of power. No one ever mentions how tricky it is to navigate power dynamics in a relationship. It's an unspoken truth. But in any relationship, when the control shifts, someone gets hurt."

"Aren't most good relationships based on equality?" I had asked Jonathon the question early in our relationship. At the time, he didn't answer. His glib reply had been, *"When was the last time you were in a relationship, Mina?"*

He said, "Not in my experience."

I poured another glass of wine. "Dominance and submission."

"All relationships are based on the elements of power. Depending on who's in control, the delicate balance of the relationship in their hands. They hold their partner's feelings and their needs. They hold everything."

I said, "There's always an enabler. One may think he's in the command seat, but the other partner allows it. It takes two to manage and navigate a relationship."

"Correct. I give so that you may give. You allow so that I am enabled. I permit so that you are empowered. And so on." He stood opposite the coffee table from me. "When the balance of power shifted with Elinor, things went awry. I was just learning, you see. And I didn't realize that I needed to give more choices to her."

"What happened?"

"The need to control her controlled me. The need to dominate her also dominated me. There were days when she hated me for it. As much as she craved the experience, I didn't allow her to make any choices.

Elinor wanted to dominate *me*. She asked me, hell, she begged me to let her be the top for a change. She wanted me to experience what she had."

"Did you let her?"

"No. I treated her badly. In my defense, I didn't know the difference between domination in the bedroom and control of an individual. She became sad and withdrawn. She refused to see me. It made me angry with her and with myself. I tried to temper my aggression by drinking and hated myself even more. I made it easy for Elinor to leave me."

~19~

Two caterers brought the four-course meal in white paper bags. They set my table with a white linen cloth. They arranged the plates on my table, and I set the bouquet of white roses in the center. Jonathon paid from a thick wad of bills. The pair thanked him and left.

Without a word, Jonathon pulled out a chair for me. I carried my glass to the table and sat, tucking my skirt around my thighs. I placed the black linen napkin in my lap and reached for a piece of garlic bread. He sat across from me, twisted open a new bottle of Perrier and poured it into a glass full of ice.

"I care about you, Mina. Not just about the contract. So I want you to understand who I am so you can make an informed choice. Out of respect, I owe you that much."

The solemnity of his voice, his seriousness, wiped every doubt from my mind that Jonathon loved me. He served me a hearty wedge of lasagna, careful not to drip any cheese on the tablecloth before serving himself.

"After Elinor Fawkes left, I felt lost. I longed for the sense of dominance again, but I had learned that with power comes a great deal of responsibility. It was around that time that I met Whitney Crewe."

Whitney and I had met that summer through Jonathon and become friends. She was the partner of Jake Barnes, the co-owner of PPS. Since she and Jonathon were both self-proclaimed dominants, I hungered for the intimate details of their sex life as I bit into the cheese-smothered pasta.

"Whitney and I met at a frat party on Langdon Street near Lake Mendota in Madison. My friends Jake Barnes and Darren Ward were there, too. We were drinking beer after returning from winter break. I remember it was the dead of winter and Whitney was sitting on the stairs of the frat house surrounded by a handful of male students who were clearly enraptured by the real-estate of her cleavage. Her fur-lined winter coat hung off her shoulders to her elbows and she held a frothy beer in both hands. Underneath her coat, she wore clothes that exposed her assets. Her skirt covered only a few inches of her espresso-with-cream thighs. Her knee-high black leather boots had spiked heels. And the rosebuds of her nipples protruded beneath the unbuttoned pink cardigan. I saw how the other guys looked at her and decided right then that I would have her."

Jonathon took a small bite then wiped the corners of his mouth with the napkin.

"I've longed to hear this story for quite some time," I said, picking up the water glass.

Jonathon turned to face the window. Dark clouds blanketed the city, underlit by Chicago. Maybe it was easier for him not to look at me. "Whitney noticed me, too, and as soon as she stopped holding court with the others, she made a bee-line to my side and introduced herself."

I set the water glass back on the table. "I heard that you two hit it off immediately."

"Of course we did. That night we returned to my place and fucked. But for me, something was missing. I wanted to control the experience. I wanted to control *her* experience.

"When I'd asked her to submit to me, she refused. I understood. Looking back on it, I don't know why I ever thought a strong, independent woman like her would ever submit to anyone. When I showed her my handcuffs, she wanted to put them on *me*. I wouldn't let her. Though she didn't know it, she inadvertently gave me a gift.

"She found a course in Japanese rope tying and asked me to take it with her. She wanted to tie me up. I was curious, but I never let her lay a hand on me. I paid for the class and attended the two-hour session. That was when I first became fascinated with Japanese culture."

"And ropes?" I added.

"Yes, ropes. And Japanese martial arts. And the gear used by dominants. I began to practice tying different knots and learned what types of rope were supple and soft enough for the skin. I learned how tight to wrap those bindings without cutting off circulation or bruising."

"But you and Whitney didn't remain together," I said. They'd both told me they were incompatible in bed. The art of domination eventually became Whitney's chosen profession when, a few years later, she became a high-paid dominatrix. Though I longed for more sexy stories from Jonathon, I had to ask. "I'm trying to understand, Jonathon. What connection does Whitney have with Janko?"

"I needed to tell you about these other women, Mina, so that you understand what follows. Elinor and Whitney were the important steppingstones to what happened next. In a way, they made me who I am. Without them, I never would have met Rory Bradford."

"Who is she?"

"She's the woman who introduced me to Janko."

"But wasn't that a few years ago? The story you're telling is from your college days."

"It seems like a long time ago, I know."

"Were you and Rory together for that many years?"

"No."

That burning jealousy fired up in my belly and I put my fork down.

"I'm trying to convey how Janko and Rory forced me into their web. How I became an ancillary target."

"All right," I said without admitting how curious I was to hear about Jonathon's other woman.

"Rory and I met at the rope-tying class." Jonathon bit into a piece of garlic bread. "She was studying Japanese culture as part of her major. And the way she spoke of it—her lust for everything Japanese—titillated me and drew me in as well. I began to take classes in a rare form of martial arts called Bujinkan. It's a Japanese offshoot of Chinese martial arts. Those who have made it their life study say it is the first Japanese martial art to diverge from the Chinese ways. Its purest form is Ninjitsu, where one uses the momentum of the attacker to ward off injury." He wiped his mouth with a napkin. "But I digress."

I nodded. "To put it mildly." I took another bite while listening. Jonathon had hardly eaten at all.

His gaze drew inward again. "At the beginning Rory was like you. She loved ropes. With her, I learned what it meant to be a dominant. I learned how to control her experience."

"How did you control her experience?"

He looked down into his water glass. "That's not important."

"I want the sexy details."

"Those details are irrelevant."

I set my fork down. I was through eating—it was impossible to focus on food. I could think of nothing but Jonathon in bed with these other women and I was envious. "Did you love her?"

"What?"

"Did you love her?"

Jonathon pushed away from the table. "Once. I think I did. But that feeling was replaced with loathing a long time ago."

"Tell me how you tied her up."

"I don't think I should continue."

"I don't care." I set my wine glass down a little too hard. "Tell me."

"*How* I tied her up has little to do with my point."

"Please." I had my reasons for asking for this. Two days ago I told my best friend that I wasn't in love. Had I been lying to myself this whole time? If Jonathon told me about Rory, perhaps it would loosen the grip of jealousy. If not, then I would know that I loved him.

He hesitated before sitting back down across from me. Jonathon set his elbows on the table and gazed past me. "I began with a fifty-foot length of rope. First, I unraveled it, found the midpoint, and with the rope folded in half, I strung the ends through the loop. I hung this over Rory's shoulders like a scarf. The extra length of rope pooled on the floor at her feet.

"Naked, she watched me tie the rope with a slight smile and her arms hanging loose at her side. With rope, I covered the flowery pink and red tattoo on the lower left side of her belly."

"Did you wrap her arms, too? Did you bind her ankles together?" As if asking a witness on the stand to divulge the backstory, I directed Jonathon's telling of his story. Maybe it was the wine, but I needed to know.

"No. Rory freely clasped her hands over her head so I could work. Careful not to cut off circulation or pinch her skin I wrapped the two loose ends around her chest. Inch by inch, I bound her breasts—leaving her nipples exposed—in a tight bustier made of the rope. The whole time, Rory gave me feedback. I made sure that she was never in pain. She assured me that she could breathe, even though she struggled with each inhalation."

I leaned forward, hanging on each word. Every detail—Rory's tattoo, the rope wrapped around her skin and her exposed nipples—was clear to me now. I loved what Jonathon and I did together. He clearly enjoyed performing these acts on women. He enjoyed taking their power and using his to elicit the most exquisite, the most elusive and sought after feeling that a human female can experience. The orgasm. "But she allowed you to continue," I said.

"She did."

"Keep going. Please." I couldn't disguise the longing in my voice. I wanted to experience the same things she had. I held the glass in my hands, grateful for its coolness. With parted lips, I eagerly waited for more. I wanted to *be* Rory. I wanted what she'd had with Jonathon.

Jonathon set his glass down on the table and stood. His bowed head and tucked chin evoked a moment of deep thought. He strolled to the window where wind now whipped against the glass and a spattering of raindrops ran down the surface.

He said, "At each moment, I made sure she wasn't hurting, and she assured me she was fine. That's when I took more liberties with her."

"How, Jonathon? How did you control her?" I was a hot mess and could hear it in my voice. I was sure Jonathon heard it too.

"Mina—" He shook his head as though he felt guilty about his actions.

He didn't understand. I simply needed more. "Tell me!"

"I laid her back on the bed and handcuffed her wrists to the head-board. I tied her ankles to each corner of the bed so that she was spread wide and exposed. Then I kneeled between her legs."

"Keep going."

"She couldn't take any more. She said she needed relief. Believe me, her relief was foremost on my mind. Watching her wait for it and building her climax while I took my time, slowly and deliberately teasing the orgasm out of her. I planned every touch, every tantalizing lick and pinch. I stroked her inner thighs and . . ."

I said, "You can't stop there."

"Rory begged me to let her come. I stroked her skin where the bindings had marked her flesh. Finally I sighed one hot breath on her, and she wailed with an orgasm that squeezed tears from her eyes."

I gasped. "You loved making her come like that."

He looked at the floor.

His story had only increased my desire for him. I longed for the restriction, the roughness and chafing confinement of Jonathon's ropes. I longed for him to touch me.

"No more tonight, Mina." He turned from the window and walked across the room with his hands loosely fisted at his sides.

"But I want more. Don't you understand? I want what you and Rory have. *Had*."

"That's why we're done tonight. *You* don't understand."

I jumped to my feet. "Then tell me! Explain it to me so I can stop desiring you."

Jonathon's hands went up like stop signs. "That's not what I want, and you know it. I've grown to care about you differently, Mina. Don't you see that?"

His stories confused me. Whether it was lust or love, I didn't know. I hated those women—Elinor, Rory, all of them. "Jonathon, I . . ." I inhaled raggedly. I wanted to understand what he was telling me. I wiped my brow with the back of one hand, then slipped my cool fingers beneath my long hair.

His gaze flitted around my condo like a bat seeking escape. When his anxious eyes met mine, he seemed to see what he was doing to me. Jonathon's head drooped like a wet flag between his strong shoulders. "You're getting the wrong impression."

I went to him and stroked his arm. "I want to know everything."

"And you will. But for tonight, we're done. The last thing I want to say is that I could never forgive myself if something happened to you, Mina."

"And yet you've put me in danger."

"I'm trying my best to rectify the situation."

"How? By sharing your past? By stoking the fire with these stories of other women? How does this rectify anything?"

"I thought by explaining who Rory was, you'd understand the nature of my predicament. Rory is the one orchestrating this whole thing with Janko."

"How?"

Jonathon's features hardened. "To understand Janko, you need to know Rory. She is at the root of all this. She is the conductor and the musician. She is the dungeon master, and she is a slave."

<h1 style="text-align:center">~20~</h1>

After Jonathon shared intimate details of his lovers, he seemed distraught. I sat with him on the couch after we cleaned up from dinner. But I could see that he needed emotional support. He spent the night on the couch. He stayed because he feared for my safety—because it gave him a sense of power over Janko—and he left before I rose in the morning. He had five days to deliver the money.

With Greg at my side, I returned to work and to the courthouse, where I observed a woman being escorted away in handcuffs. The sight of her brought to mind Jonathon. I relived the memory of my lover gripping my wrists. His refusal to allow me escape from his touch. I longed for him now and gazed at the cell phone in my hand. I was dying to hear his deep, soothing, yet powerful voice. His contact number with his photo—his smoky blue eyes staring right at me, daring me to break a rule—was a finger-tap away.

To get my mind off him, I immersed myself in the familiar—my work—and I dug into case files my client Bohdi Michaels might have been framed.

Madam Angelique Sartre had opened Red Lace Escort Service when the internet was young. In the state of Illinois, being an escort is a legal activity. It's not until the escort sells intimate favors for money or something of value—an expensive watch, drugs, a trip, anything—that it becomes illegal. Then, it's considered prostitution.

Angelique oversaw the umbrella business that appeared to be a legitimate escort service. As such, Red Lace had thrived for decades. Wealthy officials and businessmen sought Angelique's male and female escorts and paid the highest prices for their good looks and compliant behavior. Angelique paid for clothing and spa treatments such as manicures and depilatory procedures in return for seventy-five percent of the escorts' incomes.

Her percentage of that income remained consistent unless a sale of other goods occurred. Angelique's prosecuting attorney had already proved in court that she coerced her employees to sell more *services*, quote-unquote. Then her solicitation charges, class-A misdemeanors, were bargained away for information. I knew the DA who handled her case. He was as good as they come.

However, the US prosecutor, attorney Harvey Slater, wheeled-and-dealed like a true used-car salesman. Slater was Cook County's federal prosecutor, the man I'd be defending Bohdi against. The legal community of Cook knew Slater was corrupt, but no one was willing to forfeit their career to rat him out. He was one of the few powerful officials in line to be the next attorney general.

Several years ago a female defense attorney tried to bargain a deal with Slater for her client. The client was a high-profile businessman who got caught supposedly orchestrating an international Ponzi scheme. She argued that her client was framed, but Slater wouldn't budge. Some said he and his friends made millions on the scheme. Some said Slater targeted the poor schmuck so he himself didn't get caught. The Chicago Ponzi scheme crumbled with the arrest of that lawyer's client, and he went down for it. And in the aftermath, that female attorney never practiced law in Illinois again.

I pulled up her photo on my computer. In her brown eyes, I saw something of myself. Slater was connected and powerful. The man had influenced politicians and released prisoners on whisps of uncertain evidence. And he would oversee Bohdi Michaels' case. I had no desire to face-off with the US prosecutor or lose my career over one money laundering case. So I would need to tread lightly to get what I wanted. For me, and for my client.

Angelique had thrown Michaels under the proverbial bus. She told Slater Bohdi had deposited the illegal income on his own. That it was his idea to make small deposits over time and to layer transactions between multiple accounts owned by various pseudonyms—all linking back to

Angelique. He'd hid the money in overseas funds and purchased real estate properties, turning the meager deposits into gold.

Angelique was worth millions. And so—by default—was my client. I couldn't prove that he didn't do it. But without proof, I doubted I could meet with Harvey Slater and bargain down Bohdi's case.

I dug deeper and found that Bohdi Michaels was a Russian immigrant. I let out a quick breath at the coincidence. Both my client and Janko Vorobiev had connections to Russia. Michaels had come to the states from France eighteen years ago and integrated into American society.

Curious about his past, I looked for any related articles about Parisian banks from the year Bohdi Michaels left. His name didn't trigger any searches, but HC Paris bank did. An employee named Bohdanovyan Mykajlenko had been investigated by Europol. I finally understood the odd spelling of my client's name. Bohdi—not Bodhi—was the shortened form of a distinctly Russian name.

In the days surrounding this investigation, Europol had found an organized terrorist cell hiding in plain sight in Paris. They had been accepting illegal money from the Russian mafia to fund their next big event. The untraceable funds were deposited by Mykajlenko into private accounts. I found a photo of Mykajlenko and—no surprise—he was the striking younger version of my client, Bohdi Michaels. Charges were dismissed when he gave information linking his guilty associates to the crime. He was then told to leave the country.

The irony or the luck of the draw that both Janko Vorobiev and Bohdi Michaels were involved with the Russian mafia knocked the wind out of me. It was too much to fathom. The soft knock on my office door was a welcome break. "Come in."

Christina opened the door looking solemn and sad. With a shaky voice, she said, "Everyone is in an uproar, Ms. Green. Milton Sr. is calling a meeting for all the staff."

"What happened?"

"Gary Underwood has been murdered."

I hopped off my desk chair. She must have been mistaken. "Not Gary. I just spoke with him yesterday."

"The police have begun an investigation. They believe Gary was tracking some very bad people."

"We all work with *bad* people, Christina. Who?"

Christina mentioned organized crime. She said something about Russian gangs, but I stopped hearing her. Blood rushed in my ears—the full-volume white-noise sound of a waterfall. Suddenly I was in freefall, diving from Lake Havasu again. Thunder shook the ground and heat lightening rippled across the sky as chilly air blasted me in the face. The rippling water's surface, lit by another lightning flash, sped toward me.

Gary Underwood's death was my fault.

-21-

Milton Sr. held a somber meeting attended by everyone in our firm. Afterward, tears dried on my cheeks. I held a damp tissue in my hand and dabbed my nose with it. We all loved Gary, but knew he was secretive about his investigative work. I hated to think that he was killed working on my case, but that was the torturous truth.

A neighbor found Gary in his loft apartment, sitting in a wooden chair, his ankles and his wrists bound with duct tape. They had cut out his eyes and then shot him execution-style in the center of his forehead. The murderer left a clear message. He had seen something that was meant for no one to see.

Gary was probing Janko Vorobiev's past and the Russian mafia in Chicago.

I wanted to dive.

Jonathon met me at Milton, Wallace, & Edwards and gave me an affectionate embrace. Unspoken words hung in the air like a steamy breath in winter. Together we entered the conference room. With a stone cold expression and hands linked together at his belt, Erik waited in the hall beside Greg. Arron and Liam remained invisible, just like Greg told me they would.

Tig Wallace, the extortion expert at the firm, entered with a stack of papers in his arms. Jeff Lohmann, the chief detective of the Violent Crimes Division and an old family friend of mine was right behind him.

"Good to see you, Wil." He gave me a hearty, embrace and seemed to empathize at the sight of my reddened, puffy eyes.

I sniffed, hoping I wouldn't break down and cry during the meeting. Gary's death hit me like a dive gone wrong. As if I'd entered at an angle and broken my confidence.

Jonathon shook Jeff's hand, then Tig's.

After introductions, Jonathon and I sat on one side of the table across from Jeff and Tig. Jonathon told the story of his connection to Janko.

Jeff scribbled notes on a small notepad.

I asked, "Do you know what Gary found? What got him murdered?" My pen hovered above my legal pad.

"Not exactly. We only know that Vorobiev Exports or VE is only a small subset of a larger problem," Jeff said. "Europol is investigating VE because of connections to terrorists in the Middle East. EU investigators believe VE trafficked weapons to Saudi Arabia and to Pakistan, but there's no proof. There's loose evidence that VE supplies terrorists with guns and combat gear."

"Gary Underwood learned about it," I said.

Jeff set down his pen. "Underwood's apartment was tossed. His laptop was stolen. But . . ." He picked the pen up again and circled something on the paper in front of him. "We found a note pad behind his medicine cabinet where he kept track of all the cases he worked on. It listed all his jobs and most recently, the people connected to Vorobiev."

"Gary kept track of everything," Tig said.

Jeff nodded. "You might find some of those names interesting, Mr. Heun."

Jonathon raised his chin a fraction and asked, "Why would I?"

"Because your name is on the list."

I turned my head to look at Jonathon, who didn't meet my gaze.

"How are you and he connected, Mr. Heun?" Jeff asked.

Jonathon made a fist and placed his hand in his lap. "We are not *connected.* Janko is an associate, that is all. He's trying to extort money from me and has threatened Mina's life."

I said, "That's why I've asked Tig to join us. If there's anything we can do about the extortion threat. . ."

"Twenty years in jail, the price for an extortion sentence, isn't enough of a threat for this guy. A lawsuit won't keep the terrorists at bay." Jeff looked at his watch. "Because this investigation involves international terrorists, we're turning it over to the FBI and Homeland Security. The agent should arrive in a few minutes."

Almost on cue, there was a knock at the conference room door. "Come on in," Tig said.

The dark-haired woman who entered was dressed in professional attire, a black suit and yellow button-front shirt. She had a gun holstered at her hip. Confidence and her affirmative attitude glowed like an aura.

Jeff stood and shook her hand. "Thanks for coming."

"My pleasure, Detective Lohmann. My name's Agent Teresa Curbelo."

After Jeff introduced each of us at the table, she made eye contact with Jeff, Jonathon and Tig, then me. Her deep green eyes reminded me of the mossy foliage on the jungle floor of Australia. "I understand that your friend and colleague Gary Underwood was murdered and offer my condolences. The FBI will be investigating his case because it's become a matter of national security. I have some current information for you, but I also want to hear everything you know."

"I'll leave the meeting in your hands, Agent Curbelo. Do you need anything else from our task force?" Jeff gathered his notes and stood, offering the agent his seat.

"Stay, Detective Lohmann. I have some information that might interest you." Curbelo took the swiveling, black leather chair next to Jeff's. "The FBI has been following a set of individuals involved in a TOC group."

Jeff sank back down into his seat. "Transnational Organized Crime."

Curbelo nodded. "These TOC organizations have no regard for international borders or customs. They traffic weapons drugs, and human beings to more than fifty countries in the world. This organization infiltrates governments and banks. They're funded by the rich and powerful and nearly unaccountable."

Jonathon asked, "Is Janko Vorobiev involved with this TOC?"

"We believe so, but we have no proof of him trafficking anything. His little shipping company is only part of the bigger problem," she said.

I asked, "It's important for me to know what Gary Underwood uncovered. He was working an investigation for me and my client. Details are crucial to how we proceed."

Agent Curbelo opened a black zippered document bag and pulled out a thick file folder. From it, she took a photo and placed it in the center of the table. Two men appeared to be smoking cigarettes outside a corner convenience store. A stocky man with heavy jowls in an ankle-length black winter coat leaned toward a taller man in jeans and a red down-filled parka.

"This is Konstantin Tsezar." The agent pointed at the heavier man in black. "He is a known leader of Russian organized crime here in Chicago. An associate of his was arrested a few weeks ago for third-degree murder. Investigators connected the man, who shot the victim in a local nightclub, to Tsezar. They think he ordered the kill. But Tsezar's hands are clean. Too clean. We've surveilled his activity for over a year. And we know he's involved in weapons transportation and money laundering. He uses violence to get his way. He's not a man you want to cross paths with."

Tig added, "The Russian mafia has a large presence in Chicago."

"Precisely," Curbelo said. "Two days ago, we saw Gary Underwood watching Tsezar's apartment building from a parking lot nearby. Underwood may have run across Kostya Tsezar while researching Vorobiev. Records from his cloud files showed that he'd drawn lines connecting the two. He may have found evidence that connected Tsezar with one of the largest TOC groups in the world. This group is so well connected, they have people in governments and in law enforcement, even high-ranking officials on their side."

She reached for a pen from a corporate mug in the center of the table and examined it.

"How can I help?" I asked. As the agent spoke, adrenaline filled my veins. There was no reason for it, except that some part of me wanted to be part of this investigation. This was the reason I had endured all those horrible cases before meeting Jonathon. So I could be here today.

"Stay low, Ms. Green," Agent Curbelo said.

Jonathon said, "Janko Vorobiev threatened Mina's life. He wants fifty million dollars by the end of the week or he promises to kill her. How should I approach this?"

Agent Curbelo shook her head. "You can't take legal action against him."

"Why not?" Jonathon asked.

The agent drummed her pen on the paper. "We have a wide-scale sting operation going on in Chicago and other cities nationwide. I can't go into details, you understand. Any action you take could put our agents' lives at risk."

A red flush appeared beneath Jonathon's collar. "I'm supposed to sit here and take his threats to me and to Ms. Green?" Beneath the table, he clenched his fists. "We have four and a half days to meet his deadline."

As Agent Curbelo leaned forward, her folded arms slid on the table in front of her. "Of course not, Mr. Heun. Find solace in knowing the FBI is working on the case."

~22~

olace? It was the last word I would use to describe our situation. Gary Underwood had been tortured and shot. Who was next?

Gary had uncovered the Russian mafia connection between Janko Vorobiev and Konstantin Tsezar—a known leader of the Russian mafia—and been executed for it.

I hadn't known his name until today. In my research of Angelique Sartre, I found public records of Red Lace's office space leased by Tsezar. Twenty years ago, around the time Angelique moved to Chicago, he helped her get started.

In return for what? A lifetime of free fuckery?

It was a given that Tsezar was somehow involved with Bohdi as well. By default, Tsezar linked Janko and my client.

Jonathon had drilled the point home—to Agent Curbelo and everyone in the room—that I was in danger. Jeff promised more protection by ordering police cars to patrol my neighborhood.

After the meeting, I walked with Jonathon to the lobby. He instructed Erik to get the car—that he wanted to go to his condo in the Waldorf Astoria building. When Erik left, Jonathon turned to me.

"You don't go anyplace without your bodyguards. Do you understand?"

"Yes sir." Though his commanding voice pissed me off, I understood his fear. I wouldn't admit to him that Gary's murder frightened me. I would heed his advice to keep Greg Hauser nearby because of it.

Grave intent tightened his features. "I refuse to give Janko what he wants. And, Mina, I *refuse* to let him take you."

Because he loved me. I understood. "Jonathon, I . . ." I dropped my gaze.

The lobby security guard had turned our way. Jonathon softened to a mezzo piano. "I'm so sorry about Gary," he said.

"I'm afraid it's my fault." I stared down at my black stilettos.

"You couldn't have known." He placed a hand on my shoulder. "There's a Phillips Foundation cancer research fundraiser at the Navy Pier Ballroom tomorrow night."

"A fundraiser? What about Janko's deadline?"

"Janko is sure to be there because of his connections to the medical industry," he said. "I believe he expects me to be there. I plan to show my face, to show him that I'm not afraid of him or his threats."

I imagined unidentified mafia members—thugs—wearing tuxedos.

"I'd like you to come with me."

"Won't that put me in unnecessary danger?"

"Janko may expect you to hide. And he'll expect me to hide you. If you show up, we show Janko that we're not afraid."

"He's just killed my investigator."

His steady hand rested on the back of my arm. "I'll have six security men there. Greg and Erik will be there."

A thought punched me in the gut. "What am I? Bait?"

"No. Janko won't make his move in the middle of a public gathering. And I know for a fact that a number of Janko's associates are invited."

Janko had the means to follow through with his threat. His international connections could pull off any crime they wished. However, the plan appealed to me. The stakes were as high as any cliff I dove from. "I'd give everything to make Janko's arrest happen, and you know it."

"Then you'll go?" Jonathon's eyes opened wider, lit by something like hope.

"I've defended sexual predators for years. I regret every minute of it, but I was too young and foolish to take a stand against my employers. I won't be that person ever again. Now, I want to help capture and arrest any predaceous, loathsome man who crosses my path." And Janko *had* crossed my path.

For me, it was like standing on the precipice of the cliff in Acapulco. I could feel the gravel beneath my toes as I prepared to jump. This time, it was all wrapped up in an international crime syndicate. Fear of the unknown rushed through my veins.

The wrinkle in Jonathon's brow smoothed as he gazed at me. "Then let's go to the fundraiser and see if we can throw a net over Vorobiev."

It seemed a small risk in comparison to the Croatian cliffs where I'd almost lost my life. This fundraiser was a leap I could take.

Last night I had dreamed of diving from the cliffs at Mana Island near Croatia. The wall of jagged, white rock edging that island was sixty or more meters above the ocean's surface. In the dream, I had flown when I jumped and in midair, I flapped my arms and floated above the ocean. It had been years since I'd dreamed of flying. Those types of dreams told me I was on the right course.

Jonathan left me in the lobby after an emotional embrace, one which he returned with unmistakable affection. I watched him drive away with Erik and when I turned, Greg Hauser was standing at my side.

It was clear that Jonathon wanted our relationship to grow. Yet I didn't know how to manifest that when each hour Janko's deadline drew nearer.

~23~

Greg and Liam did a thorough sweep of the entire condo, closets, and bathroom before allowing me inside. Wanting privacy, I closed the door to my bedroom and fell onto my queen-sized bed where I struggled to see the point of Jonathan's story. How could this ex-girlfriend have so much sway over him?

She's the dungeon master and the slave.

What did that mean? How was she connected to Janko? And now that Gary Underwood had been murdered, what other dangers awaited? If I succumbed to the fear, like sinking under water with my breath held, I might never come up for air.

I gazed at the enlarged photo on my wall. The Mana Island cliffs in Croatia soared above blue-green water, inviting me to take a plunge because Gary's murder weighed on me. Exhausted, I stripped off my work clothes and fell asleep naked with cool sheets tempering my body heat.

The next morning, I sat up and threw pillows out of my way. I needed to research what Gary had uncovered before his murder. And learn how Jonathon was connected to Vorobiev. I put on jeans and a black tank top then went into the kitchen. First, I called Christina and told her I'd work from home today. She completely understood.

Greg made himself at home in the kitchen and perused the fridge. "What have you got in here?" He held up a moldy chunk of cheese. "This is a tragedy," he said.

I heated water in the kettle. "I haven't been at home. Do you want breakfast? There's a coffee shop down the block. We could have something delivered."

I poured boiling water over dark-roast grounds and opened my laptop at the kitchen counter.

Greg placed an online order at the nearest grocery store. Floating in a sea of unanswered questions—Gary's murder, Janko's extortion, the TOC and Russian terrorists—I drilled to the bottom of Bohdi Michael's case to find a loophole.

According to the search engine, Tsezar owned half a dozen small businesses in Chicago. His small liquor store chain had three locations—one in Skokie, one in the Russian Village, and one in the Lower West Side. His well-known nightclub in the theater district drew a late-night crowd from all over the city. Also, Tsezar owned a small hardware store and a tiny corner convenience store. I recognized it at once from the photo Agent Curbelo showed us.

As a well-diversified, ethnic business owner in Chicago, he had clout. He vocalized strong opinions about local politics on Twitter. He had influenced the directives of the Chicagoland Chamber of Commerce.

"There you are, Mina."

Jonathon's video call diverted my attention.

"Good morning. Did you sleep at all?" I asked.

"No." His rumpled hair framed bright eyes, and he showed no signs of a sleepless night. "You?"

"Some. Coffee helps."

He asked what I was working on.

"This morning I woke up thinking about Tsezar. I'm trying to figure out how he's connected to this whole scheme, so now I'm researching him. I left a message for agent Curbelo earlier. I want to see Gary's notes. I'm going to ask Jeff Lohmann if he can get them for me."

"Brilliant. I've been working on the same thing from my office," he said.

In unison, we both said, "Two minds . . ."

I laughed.

". . .that think as one." Jonathon completed the phrase. "Mina, with your legal skills and my connections, we could fight this thing with Janko. We could expose their corruption from the outside."

"Yes! Exactly what I was thinking. Kostya Tsezar seems to be at the crux of it all."

Jonathon nodded. "In his circle, he's quite a kingpin."

I reached for my coffee. "Tell me what you've found."

Jonathon leaned forward and pulled a notepad in front of him. "Tsezar was born in Balti, Romania, in the 1960s, but his family moved to Russia when he was very young. He attended college in Kyiv in the eighties and became an activist for Perestroika and the independence of Russian nations. He grew in popularity as an advocate for the Russian people, but his methods were as corrupt then as they are now. He used violence as a means to an end. Killed when it suited the movement and raised money for corrupt politicians."

"When did he move to the States?"

"Konstantin moved to Chicago in 2001. He thought he had an opportunity to influence immigrants here in the US. And he did. By then, many of his people knew his name. And here in the States, he thought he could sway American politics as well."

"With his connections to international crime organizations?"

"Yes. And using his influence, forcing people to see things his way." Jonathon shook his head.

"How are he and Janko associated?" I asked.

"I'm not sure. Janko has many friends. Many of them are not the type of people you would want to invite for cocktails—"

"Like Janko?" I reminded Jonathon. He had invited that gangster into his home.

"Right. But on the other hand, you want them on your side."

I sat back. For the first time in a long while, I felt like there was something pulling me toward this. I wanted to do something about the corruption in Chicago and thought maybe—just maybe—I had some influence. With Jonathon's money and popularity in the media, he had a unique brand and sway with important people. I wanted to take this dangerous dive with him and feel the freefall.

Jonathon said, "An acquaintance of mine is the senior editor of the *Chicago Tribune.* She has connections and no qualms telling the truth. I'll speak with her later today and let you know what I learn."

I sipped the last of my coffee before it went completely cold. "I have some ideas too," I said.

The frightened face of Bohdi Michaels eyed me cautiously. "You learned about Paris."

"Indeed." I worked from the privacy of the bedroom where my image and Bohdi's leered back at me from the computer screen. In order to discuss my findings with my client, I had sent him a secured Zoom link an hour ago.

He shook his head. "That was the past."

"Your past has caught up with you." I wiped my brow with a flat palm. "If you are innocent of the laundering charges, if you truly had nothing to do with it, you need to tell me who would blame you for this."

"It's a long story."

"If it helps me defend you, I need to know."

Michaels looked away, circling his chin to the ceiling. He bit his lower, quivering lip. When his gaze returned to me, tears filled his eyes. "I was born in the Soviet Union before it fractured into many countries. My city became part of Russia where you are forced to cooperate with the policy makers and leaders. It was not like here, where you have freedom. Do you understand? There, they kill your friends and blow up your car if you didn't do what they say. I moved to Paris to support my family, who had to stay in Russia. When a certain group of nationalists came to me asking me to raise money for the organization—they said it was for our country—I did what they asked. I had no choice."

"What happened?" I asked.

A tear rolled down his cheek. He wiped it away with the side of his hand. "Europol discovered them by tracing the stolen funds to me. Unless I wanted to spend years in jail, I had to tell the investigators exactly who asked me to invest the money. Then my sister's car exploded in the street outside her apartment building. She was not killed, thankfully. But the message was clear."

At his pause, I said, "I'm so sorry, Bohdi. Do you think they followed you here?"

"No, Ms. Green. This branch of the organization was *already* here."

I rubbed my chilled arms. "Is there anything I can use to help your case? Would you be willing to give names? Could you turn in state's evidence against one or two individuals?"

Bohdi thought for a moment, then said, "There is one thing."

After the call I stood up from the kitchen counter where I'd been working and paced to the window. Two hours ago, Greg left to pick up the grocery order. He assured me that Liam patrolled the building, but I didn't see him and my trust in bodyguards stood behind a thin line. I thought Greg would be back by now. Traffic below moved at a turtle's pace. A half dozen cars were parked along the curb of the one-way street. I wondered if any of them were police surveillance. Or Liam. Or Arron. Or Janko. One car remained at the corner for far too long. You meant "Or Liam."

Could the driver be Russian mafia?

Fear welled up from my toes. I darted to the door and made sure the deadbolts were locked.

~24~

When Greg returned, I locked and bolted the door after him. "What took you so long?" My voice sounded shaky.

"The grocery employees filled the order, but I still went inside to pick out produce and meats. If we're holed up here, we might as well make the best of it." He set three full, reusable shopping bags on the kitchen counter. After setting the bags down he looked my way. "Liam was in the lobby. You were safe."

"You said he was here, but I wasn't sure. This sounds so silly, but I saw a car outside. I thought someone was inside it, watching the building."

Greg went to the window. "Are you sure?"

I peered down at the street. "It's gone now."

"You have every right to worry. No judgement."

In an attempt to make everything normal again, I helped Greg put the groceries away. He told me what he planned to cook for the next three days, and I asked how long he planned to stay.

"As long as necessary," he said, his cheerless half-smile reminding me how serious the situation was.

As long as necessary.

Janko Vorobiev's threat was foremost on my mind. And Bohdi's involvement added a heaping serving of worry onto my plate. What I'd learned today scared me.

The Phillips Foundation Fundraiser raised money for ongoing research to fight Covid-19 aftereffects. The virus caused neurological damage and ongoing health issues for many long-haulers. I donated one thousand dollars from my personal savings.

When I spoke with Jonathon, I told him I wanted to go to a salon to get my hair and nails done for the event, he offered an alternative. Around three in the afternoon, a small team of beauticians arrived from the swanky Dennis Bartolomei Salon. They set me up on a stool in my kitchen where they highlighted, and styled my hair, painted my nails to a perfect luster, and gave my face and eyes a radiant glow.

A package arrived in the mail that day. After Greg inspected it, I opened the narrow Sack's Fifth Avenue box filled with tissue paper. A handwritten note said, "For the most beautiful woman at the ball. Remember to wear your collar."

It was signed JTH, but not by Jonathon. He had written notes to me before. I would always remember the first time he spelled out the word *love* in neat cursive. This card had been written by someone else, and I wondered to whom Jonathon assigned that task.

Folded inside the box lay a pale yellow dress that I could not believe was a full length gown—let alone big enough to fit me. I raised up the wisp of fabric and tried it on. The form fitting dress caressed my skin along my waist and hips. The open back exposed skin from my neck to tailbone. Its low-cut V dipped down between my breasts. Iridescent beads decorated thin spaghetti straps that didn't seem strong enough to hold it in place.

When I dressed, I was extremely aware of my uncovered nipples beneath the soft, silken gown, I could think of nothing but Rory, her breasts bound by Jonathon's hand.

Matching shoes included in the package completed the outfit. When I was ready, I joined Greg in the living room. He wore a black tuxedo and was adjusting the cuffs as I entered.

"Wow," he said. His eyes did that elevator thing.

Outside, the sky had darkened earlier than expected. A storm was coming. "Do you think I'll need an umbrella?"

"I have one in the car. And this is for your safety." He opened his jacket and showed the gun holstered near his side.

"Just in case." I lifted my dress at the ankle to show him the knife I had strapped to my calf.

Greg opened the door for me. Neither of us spoke as we rode the elevator down to the garage, and he opened the door to his Santa Fe for me. It was difficult to climb into the car in the tight-fitting gown. Taking a more lady-like approach, I gathered up the hem so it wouldn't get dirty on the side of the car, then stepped in. I sat with my legs drawn together. Cinderella headed to the ball.

Outside, black clouds blocked the setting sun. Paper and leaves scooted down the street as if seeking a place to hide.

~25~

Rain fell in a torrential downpour as Greg dropped me off at the Navy Pier Grand Ballroom. I gathered the gown and exited the car as quickly as I could. Large umbrellas held by event personnel protected me from getting soaked.

Inside the arched doors, Jonathon waited, wearing an elegant black tuxedo with black tie and red cummerbund. "Mina, how are you?" He took my arm and leaned in to kiss my cheek.

"I'm well, thank you," I replied. Jonathon had combed his dark wavy hair, but that did little to tame it. Though he might have been overdue for a haircut, I liked it longer.

The creases around his eyes revealed his angst. "Thank you for coming." He took my hand and lead me inside.

We ignored the camera-toting media and TV news people as best we could, stopping only for obligatory event photos. Inside the Grand Ballroom, white linen and crystal glasses covered round tables set for ten. Each chair was enclosed in a white seat cover. Tall centerpieces, vases filled with bold blue flowers and shooting silver stars accented the room.

A band played seventies rock on a stage at one end of the room and four big-screen televisions carried their images to each corner of the ballroom. Another screen near the stage flashed photos of people and organizations receiving benefits from tonight's fundraiser. Attendees were lavishly dressed in designer gowns and bespoke tuxedos. I recognized a few political figures and famous athletes walking about the room.

We were led to a table where two gentlemen and three women were already seated. The two men stood out of courtesy as the host pulled out our chairs. Introductions were made around the table.

"Jonathon Heun, good to see you again." A gray-haired man stepped around his female partner to shake Jonathon's hand.

"Good evening, William. How are you?"

"Never better. Meet my fiancé, Marissa." The young woman he introduced had to be thirty or forty years younger. She blatantly gazed at Jonathon's crotch.

He motioned to me. "William, Marissa, this is my guest, Wilhelmina Green."

After we sat, a waitress poured champagne into our glasses, and we toasted with the group. Inadvertently, I thought of the time Jonathon and Janko sent champagne to my table in Dubrovnik. The memory reminded me of why Jonathon and I were in this predicament.

At the time, I'd thought nothing of the coincidental meeting. I now watched the bubbles crawl up the inside of my glass and turned to Jonathon. "Dubrovnik," I said.

"Karma," he responded.

I pretended to smile and lifted my glass to him. Jonathon played along and lifted his in response. But his blue eyes saddened. "You didn't wear the necklace."

"What are you going to do about it?" I imagined him turning me over his knee.

"Nothing." He placed an elbow on the edge of the table and said, "You don't need diamonds to look beautiful. You're stunning, Mina."

"In the dress that you sent."

Jonathan angled his head in disbelief. "I didn't send the dress."

I rubbed the goosebumps playing an impromptu game of tag down my arms. "But you sent a note with it."

Now Jonathon pushed his chair back and faced me. "Mina, I didn't send the dress." His gaze stroked me from the hollow at the base of my neck down my décolleté to the beaded neckline of the dress. The way he looked at me smoothed the fine hairs on my arms. His hand moved to my crossed legs—I longed for him to touch my thigh, to caress me—and he pinched the silky, pale yellow fabric between his finger and thumb. "Who sent it?"

"I don't know. The note—I thought it was from you—asked me to wear the necklace. I thought for certain . . ." My chest heaved with a breath.

His hand floated gently to my shoulder. "I'll find out, Mina. I'll find out who sent it—who pretended to be me—and make them pay."

I trembled with disgust, but not at Jonathon's touch. His warm hand comforted me as the ardent desire to remove the dress tensed my leg muscles. I needed to bathe. I needed to strip off the feeling that someone—not Jonathon—could control me. I placed a hand on his and thought I felt the same angst within him.

Jonathon searched the room for a clue.

Greg and Erik strode to our table. Greg set his hands on the back of my chair. "Hello, Jon. Who the devil invited you to this party?"

Jonathon stood and vigorously shook his friend's hand. "I might ask you the same question!" He pulled Greg into a manly embrace. "Thank you for coming tonight, Greg."

Greg took the vacant seat next to mine and started up a conversation with the others at the table. Erik sat on the other side of Jonathon. Their arrival settled my nerves to a degree.

"Where are the others? You said you'd have a team of security here," I said to Jonathon.

My lover placed a warm hand on my bare shoulder. "There, beside the entrance. And there."

I followed his gaze and noticed two burly men in suits near the entrance. At the side of the room, a tough-looking woman and a thinner man stood at-ease with their hands folded at their waist. Clearly not attendants, the four wore earbuds and neckties—even the woman. The lumps under their armpits could be mistaken for nothing but sidearms.

"Arron is patrolling outside. We're connected through these earbuds." Greg leaned toward me. The ear-com was invisible, like a hearing aid. "If I need him, I'll call," he said, lifting his lapel to show me a tiny dot microphone.

I relaxed and sipped champagne.

As the champagne flowed and dinner was served, I kept an eye on the room, searching for Janko Vorobiev.

Jonathon ordered his usual Perrier with lime. He leaned close and said, "At the table to your right, that's Duane Hatfield. His family owns seventy percent of the oil in North America. See his son Norman next to him?"

I dabbed the corner of my mouth with a napkin. The young man shook hands with an Asian woman who appeared unimpressed. "Norman and I met in Vienna. The Asian woman next to him is married to Shao Shi Fen, the direct descendant of Chinese royalty. He's the man with the shaved head on her right."

She wore a race-car red satin dress and stunning diamond necklace. Shao Shi Fen wore a matching tuxedo jacket and black tie. They made a handsome couple.

Greg asked, "What are they doing in Chicago?"

"His presence here is political," Jonathon said.

"Isn't everyone's?" Greg asked.

At another table nearby, I noticed the unscrupulous federal prosecutor, Harvey Slater. Next to him sat a man with his back to me; he had trim black hair flecked with silver. Slater leaned back and guffawed at someone's joke, and as he did, his eye caught mine. I quickly looked away.

I noticed Jonathon's gaze had landed on the prosecutor's table too. "There he is. Janko's sitting there."

Janko was turned so we could see his profile, his strong Roman nose and angular jaw. He had hung his tux jacket on the back of his chair. His white shirt clung to broad shoulders.

"Excuse me." Jonathon set his napkin down, and he pushed away from the table.

He adjusted the sleeves of his jacket and slipped between the diners to the prosecutor's table. He placed a hand on the back of Janko's chair. The men and women seated there all greeted Jonathon as if they knew him. Hails and hellos were given with generous nods and wide smiles.

Janko craned his neck to look my way and a crooked, villainous grin stretched his mouth. I didn't return the smile.

While Jonathon made small talk with Janko, Slater pushed away from the table. I rose and intercepted his path to the bar on the other side of the room.

"Counselor Green. Lovely event isn't it?"

"For a worthy cause." I walked with him to the bar. "I just learned that you're prosecuting my newest client."

Slater's lip curled but not into a smile. "I hope that doesn't scare you, Counselor. I hear your career is skyrocketing these days."

"I'm not scared."

He stopped walking and put a thick, freckled hand on my arm. "You know . . . I really hate discussing work when I'm here to enjoy myself."

I didn't want to chat with him either, I simply wanted to make my intentions known. I said, "I understand. I just wanted to say hello and let you know to expect to hear from me in the near future."

"I'm looking forward to it." He had already turned away from me.

"Have a good evening," I said.

Soon after dinner, the speakers made their final pleas for donations. Plates were cleared, and a different band began playing jazz and R&B. The female singer in her sparkling dress caressed her microphone. Well-dressed people moved like stiff puppets on the dance floor. Guests grouped together near an open bar or huddled together in smaller clusters at tables and in the hallway. Jonathon and I walked the length of the room.

"Do you see Janko standing near the bar?"

I did. He was kibitzing with Konstantin Tsezar and two other men. One was Slater, who leaned in and patted Tsezar on the back. Like they were old friends. The way they guffawed and laughed at a joke that Janko told, made me think they'd known each other for years.

Jonathon turned his back to them. "I wonder how they know each other?"

"Slater is about as corrupt as anyone in the legal community. I wouldn't doubt that they help each other. Maybe when Tsezar gets in trouble, Slater wipes the board clean."

Marginally shorter than Janko, Tsezar carried his wide girth with the cocky assertiveness of one who has gained power through ruthlessness and merciless treachery. His formal bow tie was tight around his jowls. He held an amber drink in one hand and the other was buried deep in his jacket pocket.

I said, "Agent Curbelo thinks Tsezar is a mafia leader. Could Janko be acquiring the money for him?"

"I'm not sure. Tsezar is a dangerous man, and not only because the FBI have him in their sites. On the surface, he's generous to a fault. He gives to people and organizations that he deems worthy. In other words, he uses them to his advantage. He's known in Chicago for his draconian ways."

Janko caught sight of us and excused himself from Tsezar. He walked straight toward us with his eyes on me. I held Jonathon's arm.

"Mina!" Janko greeted me with his hands out.

I didn't take his hands at first.

He flicked his fingers and with a tilted head said, "We are friends, no?"

My chest filled with air, and I placed one hand in his. His clammy grip repulsed me. "Hello, Janko."

He lifted my arm wide, and his gaze slid down the length of the dress. "So lovely tonight. The dress is perfect on you."

I freed my fingers from Janko's, refusing to reveal any hint of the outrage and loathing that filled me at that moment. "Jonathon picked it out for me," I said.

"Did he?" Janko mocked me.

No!

The smile that lit Janko's eyes lifted one corner of his thin, fiendish mouth.

Jonathon moved with lightning speed. His flat hand pressed against Janko's chest, and he backed him up three paces.

"Don't mess with Mina, Janko," Jonathon growled. "Stay away from her."

Jonathon had drawn the attention of dozens surrounding us.

Janko looked at the crowd and chuckled. "I'm not messing with your woman, Jonathon. I'm simply showing you who's in control."

Jonathon lowered his hand, but his expression was full of rage. "You'll never get away with this. Stay away from her."

"You only have until Saturday, Jon. Then, she's mine."

"Never." Jonathon's lip curled.

"Janko, you must introduce me to your friends," Konstantin Tsezar trotted to Janko's side with his eyes on me. His thick accent gave away his country of origin.

As if he were my next depraved client, I showed him no fear. I stepped between them and held my hand out. "My name's Wilhelmina Green."

"You may call me Kostya." He raised my hand to his pale, dry lips.

I could see in his dark, smoke-colored eyes that he was a top predator used to getting what he wanted. I backed away and stood as near to Jonathon as I could.

Janko introduced Jonathon to Kostya, but the Russian's attention remained on me.

"Ms. Green, I heard what happened to your friend, the investigator. What was his name?"

The FBI believed he was directly involved with Gary Underwood's murder. "Gary was a good and decent man."

"Yes. What a shame." Kostya squinted, one eye closed, with his half smile. "When cold-blooded murder like that happens, I feel so badly. It gives our city a bad name, you know?"

"Gary's death was a tragedy," I said.

"Yes." Kostya nodded. "He was probably poking his nose into someone's private business. Where it didn't belong."

His unspoken message sent a shiver down my back.

Jonathon placed his warm, comforting hand on my arm and said, "Excuse me gentlemen. This is a party, and we're here to enjoy the music and festivities. I'm going to dance with the lady." Jonathon closed the conversation more pleasantly than I could have.

Though I wanted to leave—to tear the dress off and shower Janko's viper poison off my body—my gaze remained locked on Kostya who flashed his crooked teeth at me. I took Jonathon's hand. "Let's dance."

Janko said, "I'll say goodbye on my way out."

Jonathon said, "Don't bother, *my friend.*" We turned toward the dance floor. "Janko is testing my patience."

"And mine." I gazed toward them. Kostya still watched us while Janko whispered in his ear. "Can we prove his association with those criminals?" I asked. "Do the FBI investigators know?"

"There's not enough proof of Janko's involvement."

"How do you know?"

"I'm conducting my own investigation, trying to learn more about Janko's association with the terrorists."

"That sounds suicidal, Jonathon."

"It's certainly treacherous territory. I may uncover something that requires you to do as I ask."

I would do whatever it took. Whatever he asked. Regardless of his contract. "I'll do anything for you."

He smiled playfully. "Would you kneel in front of me right here on the dance floor?"

"Now?"

"I'm joking, Mina."

My heart skipped as Jonathon placed his hands on my hips and bare back. We swayed to the sultry tune. He held me close, pressing his hip against my waist. My feet followed Jonathon's lead like we'd danced together a hundred times. It felt so natural to move my thigh with his. His hand slid to my lower back, and he dipped me. I arched over his strong arm and my hair brushed the dance floor. Jonathon's warm breath against my cheek, and the woodsy fragrance of his cologne made me desire his closeness in other ways.

Blood rushed from my face as he pulled me back into his arms and I smiled, matching each and every step he took. Searching his blue eyes for the truth I found honesty and something unexpected. Jonathon was hurting. I assumed he was agitated by Janko's manipulative actions.

"You want to destroy him, don't you."

"As long as Janko is threatening me, I'll do everything in my power to protect you. Mina, I'm in love with you."

"Don't." I couldn't return those feelings. Not yet.

"It's how I feel," he said.

"It's the reason Janko is using me to threaten you. He knows it will hurt you if something happens to me." Jonathon reluctantly let go of my hand. He walked with me back to the table where Greg sat alone. Our plates had been cleared, all that remained were a few spoons and some half-full water glasses.

By the time Greg and Erik walked with us to the exit, Kostya and Janko had left . . . or crawled back into their snake holes.

"I'm glad you've been watching over Mina, Greg." Jonathon shook his hand.

"Whatever it takes," Greg said.

Jonathon said, "Good. I'm taking her back to Lake Forest tonight."

Puzzlement opened my mouth. "Wait—"

"Chicago's too dangerous, Mina. I've already arranged for your things to be sent," Jonathan said. "Greg, will you meet my security team at Mina's condo?"

Greg nodded. "Of course."

Jonathon said, "You'll join us in Lake Forest later tonight." He nudged me toward the door.

Greg said, "Whatever you need. I've got your back."

In a way, cooling relief washed over me. In Janko's dress, I felt like a pawn in their chess game. Easily moved and easily taken. I agreed to Jonathon's strategy because he had more security at his house. There, I'd be much safer than at home.

I glanced up at Jonathon who didn't return my gaze. Conflicting emotions ripped through me. My heart and body ached for Jonathon while the pragmatic lawyer in me said get out while you still can. There were only three and a half days until Janko's deadline.

~26~

The rain had slowed to a steady drizzle by the time we left Navy Pier. Water droplets dragged diagonal lines across the windows of the limousine. Jonathon raised the privacy window between us and the driver. He removed his tux jacket and laid it on the back seat between us. I longed to tear off Janko's dress in order to feel like myself again.

"I'm sorry I sprung this on you, Mina. I know you didn't expect to leave the city again tonight." Jonathon looked over his left shoulder out the window.

I turned to him. "It's fine." Despite the threat, I felt safer with Jonathon than anywhere else. Somehow I knew he'd do everything in his power to keep me safe. "Janko is insidious. How on earth did you meet him? How is your ex Rory Bradford involved?"

He took my left hand in his right and forced a little breath through his nose. "Rory Bradford. If I could turn back time and erase her from my life, I would." His gaze drifted far away.

I squeezed his hand. City traffic moved slowly up Michigan Avenue. Pedestrians hid from the weather under coats and umbrellas.

Two nights ago, Jonathon helped clean up the caterer's meal. He said he had more to discuss but wanted to give me time to think about it. I think he was trying to find a way to tell me the rest because something about it vexed him. I kissed his hand.

"Rory became obsessed with submission. And her obsession carried me like a tidal wave into the very darkness that these men—Janko and Kostya—are involved with. If it wasn't for her, I never would have befriended Janko."

"What happened?"

He let go of my hand. "She was focused on Japanese culture as part of her foreign studies major at UW Madison. She began to collect books on the Japanese history of women in particular. She studied the geisha and oiran with a passion bordering on madness. In the US, the geisha have the reputation for being sex workers, but they were not. And they are not the submissive slaves that people commonly stereotype them as. The geisha were—and are—entertainers. They are musicians and dancers trained to be works of art."

"I didn't know," I admitted. The whir of the tires on pavement lulled me into a pleasant state. I waited for him to continue.

"It's easy to understand why people confuse geisha and oiran, their dress and makeup are similar. Both required years of training from childhood." Jonathon paused. "Oiran, however, were the real sex workers. Their training took years. To become oiran, one needed to be good looking and very smart. Women had to learn how to carry themselves. They were taught to paint and play an instrument as well as how to please a man. Rory became obsessed with this training. She wanted to experience what those women might have gone through. She begged me to train her."

During our last foray into bondage and discipline, Jonathon had not been the cruel dominant I imagined him to be. He'd delivered punishing strikes with the Japanese reed but showed unexpected kindness and compassion afterward. The message confused me. On one hand, he said he didn't want a relationship outside of the contract. On the other, he resisted performing the acts outlined in his document. He had more to tell me. Of that I was sure.

"While she was studying these things, I got involved with the Japanese martial arts community and began obsessive studies of my own. I learned about weapons and learned how to fight. I learned about staffs and swords, ropes, and smaller devices. And I became curious about implements for causing pain."

"The Japanese reed?" I recalled the burn it left on my thighs and the bottoms of my feet.

"Among other things, yes. I began to collect these devices. Rory asked for my help with the research—to tie her to the bed—while we explored the feel of different whips and paddles, thin switches, twigs, and batons. I . . . I discovered that I loved wielding the weapons. I refined my flicking technique to cause the most pain. Specifically, I reveled in the power of controlling Rory's pain and pleasure. Together, we learned to balance both. We learned how the loss of control and the sting of a reed followed by sensuous stimulation would bring the ultimate orgasm."

Jealousy surfaced again. I had begun to imagine a life with Jonathon. I asked, "Why is all this important to your connection to Janko?"

Jonathon looked away from me. "Looking back on it, I think Rory's obsession turned her from a submissive into a dominant."

"Is that possible?"

"Why wouldn't it be?" He shrugged.

I couldn't imagine wanting to hold the whip. I wanted to be on the receiving end. I turned toward him as much as I could with the seatbelt confining me. "I'm curious about the details, Jonathon. She did something that threw you off your game. Please tell me more about you and her . . . together."

Jonathon gazed my way. "I don't want you to get the wrong idea again."

"I won't. I'm just . . . I'm worried about you."

He nodded. The driver's attention was on the wet roads. He couldn't hear through the partition.

Jonathon tucked his chin to his chest and spoke quietly. "On a typical night, Rory would begin by kneeling at my feet with her knees spread wide, wearing only her lingerie. And she would stretch out her arms and place her forehead touching the floor between them."

I knew the pose as Extended Child's Pose from my yoga classes.

"This was how she begged for me. I would reprimand her if she didn't keep her big toes touching. But she always tested the boundary. I would catch her shifting her position and clear my throat. It was a game. She was asking for the paddle because she knew what came after it."

I thought I knew but asked anyway. "What?"

"We learned that pain and ecstasy are sisters. For her, the sublime strike of a paddle or whip was foreplay. Normally, I would lay four or five devices on the bed in front of her. She always smiled at me before choosing, and I noticed a trend as our relationship grew, so did her addiction to pain."

"Jonathon," I interrupted. "Before we were together, I was seeking pain but I never thought of punishment as sexual."

"I know. That's another reason I want us to slow down."

I placed my hand on his. "Go on."

"One evening, Rory came to me wearing a new shade of scarlet lipstick. She asked me to spank her, told me she'd been very bad. Indeed, she had pocketed the lipstick at a superstore and walked out without paying for it. It stunned me to think she'd go to such lengths to receive punishment. She chose the studded paddle."

I said, "I've seen one like it in your basement."

"Yes. It's about three inches wide and eight inches long. Fastened to the face, dozens of half-inch metal buttons lay in diagonal rows."

"How does it feel?" I asked.

"Would you like to try it sometime? Would it turn you on?"

I paused a moment, but the answer was there. *Yes.* I thought of the heat that radiated, the afterburn from the reed. "Yes, it would."

"The paddling made Rory hot, too. But this time, after her punishment I refused to touch her. By this time in our relationship, I was fed up with her acting out so she could have sex. I stopped pleasing her because none of it brought me pleasure anymore."

As soon as we were outside the city, a shadow fell across Jonathon's face. Only occasional streetlamps allowed me a chance to witness his tenebrous expression as he spoke.

I asked, "Did she know? Did she demand more from you?"

"Yes, of course. But she was never satiated. There was nothing I could do to please her anymore."

We had arrived in Lake Forest, and Jonathon's house was mere minutes away. But I wanted to hear the end of the story. I needed to know how she hurt Jonathon.

"Since those days, Rory has become a very powerful person."

"Is she the reason you give the contract such relevance and significance?"

"Yes. She's the very reason I presented it to you in the first place. But truthfully, the contract is only a device. It's the umbrella under which we play the game."

Erik slowed the car and pulled into the driveway.

Back in the bedroom that I'd left less than a week earlier, I wondered what future Jonathon and I could have together. Since Greg hadn't arrived with my things yet, Jonathon laid out a few garments for me and went to get coffee from the kitchen. I threw the evening gown in the waste basket, then chose his long-sleeved gray, pajama shirt, which loosely covered my bottom.

Jonathon entered the room with two cups of coffee then sat in the chair next to me. He had changed out of his tuxedo into a pair of silky dark gray pajama pants—the match to the shirt I wore—and a black T-shirt. He was barefoot, like me.

I carried the hot cup to my lips and sipped. The liquid scalded my mouth. I held it, letting it cool slightly before swallowing. It allowed me a moment to verbalize my next question.

"I've told you I'm willing to participate in these *games*, as you put it. I'm interested in exploring those feelings you've detailed in your stories. Pain and pleasure are entwined for me in ways you can't fathom. I'm drawn to that darkness—the domination and submission, the punishment—because it helps me to escape the guilt and the emotional pain of my life. So tell me. What did Rory do to you to make you want a contract?"

He faced the unlit gas fireplace and said, "I need our relationship to be as clear as the horizon from the edge of the Pacific Ocean in Mexico. What we do needs to be as clear as the stars on a cloudless night at Lake Havasu in Nevada. Or in the forest at the top of the waterfall in Wollongong. I don't ever want to hurt you *because* I care about you."

His mention of my last three tombstoning sites placed images firmly in my mind. I understood.

I set the cup down and moved to his side. I placed my hands on his shoulders and massaged the tight muscles beneath his black T-shirt.

Jonathon melted at my touch. "Rory kept pushing. She began to exhibit strange behavior that, even to me, seemed over the top. We had graduated from the university at this point, and I was working hard with Jake and Darren on creating our software and our partnership. It was an exciting time for us, and I was gone a lot, meeting with them until late every night. I didn't have as much time to devote to Rory.

"I would come home after working fourteen straight hours with the guys and Rory would be stark naked and kneeling on the kitchen floor. She'd tell me she waited for me all day. I'd tell her to get up. Usually I was in no mood to deal with her. She'd become extremely needy and very demanding. She refused to take no for an answer. Then, I'd become angry and lash out at her. Anger grew between us, and the relationship became and emotionally and psychologically abusive. But believe it or not, Rory was the one who held all the cards. Although she kneeled at my feet, she'd become the dominant in our relationship."

He placed a hand on top of mine—still on his shoulder—then turned in my arms.

"Rory left me because we never set any boundaries in our relationship. We didn't have any rules. *Our* contract—the one between you and me—defines our relationship. It gives us guidelines."

I gazed into his turbulent eyes. A warmth flooded my heart and a desire to give him all of myself.

Love?

"I don't *need* the contract. I'm not going to leave you, Jonathon."

"Mina." Jonathon gripped my waist and pulled me to him. His burning lips met mine as he seized the back of my head with a firm hand.

I returned his passionate kisses with a fervent intensity, opening my mouth to his and allowing his tongue to explore my teeth and tongue. It had been so long since we'd touched. Since we'd kissed. His lusty heat warmed my core and sent tendrils of anticipation to my pelvic floor. I lusted for his embrace. His touch.

He held me at arm's length. "I care for you, Mina. Deeply. Until you understand what I'm telling you, we can't be intimate."

I whispered, "I want you, Jonathon. But I also want more than the guidelines in our contract. If we're going to be in a relationship, it has to be without a list of rules."

"I don't know how." He took my hand and gazed it for a long moment. Jonathon was willing to put aside any sexual intimacy until we reached an understanding. *Was I?*

"Maybe you just need time," I said. Rory had cut him deeply.

He nodded. "Maybe so." This man—the man I was growing to love—was so full of angst I didn't know how to help him heal. If I could, I wanted to be there for him when he was ready.

"Good night, Mina."

As he walked away, I said, "You never explained how Rory and Janko are connected."

He looked tired and drawn in the low evening light. Stress lines appeared on his forehead, and he didn't look at me as he said, "I've never told anyone. It was punishing, what they did to me."

His use of *that* word hit the core of my being. How could anyone *punish* Jonathon? He was the Master. He was the dominant.

I said, "I'm here when you're ready."

~27~

Around three in the morning Greg arrived at Jonathon's Lake Forest mansion with my personal items. I tossed and turned for a few more hours then got up, found my suitcase inside the bedroom door and my laptop case beside it. I showered and dressed, then took my laptop to the kitchen.

Greg awaited outside my bedroom door to shadow me wherever I went. A team of security professionals, some with sidearms holstered beneath their jackets, others carrying Uzis, patrolled the grounds around. Men and women flanked the entrance and prowled around the pool house. They congregated near the back porch, gazing ahead with eyes hidden behind dark glasses.

The sun hid behind dark clouds today. The light I flicked on in the kitchen cast a yellow glow over the room. Neither Grant nor Jonathon were around, but the invigorating aroma of simmering fresh coffee filled the room. The house was unusually quiet considering the number of people wandering the grounds. I poured myself a cup, added cream, and spread out my work on the table in the dark, windowless dining room.

Kostya Tsezar could be the key to many things. At the fundraiser last night, he had admitted to knowing what happened to Gary Underwood. He had no idea whom he was messing with. More than anything, I wanted to learn his relationship with Janko and my client, Bohdi Michaels. We had three days to meet Janko's deadline.

I called my old family friend, homicide detective, Jeff Lohmann.

"Good morning, Jeff, it's Wil."

"I was just thinking about you. Is everything okay?" The noise from the precinct hummed behind him. I heard a door close.

"I'm fine. Jonathon and I are fine. I'm wondering what you can tell me about the Gary's murder investigation."

"Nothing. The FBI took the case, you know that." Jeff would never go against protocols. It was a long shot asking him.

"But it was your jurisdiction at first. I need to know what Gary found. Those thugs killed Gary because he was working for me, Jeff. We saw Tsezar and Janko Vorobiev at a swanky fundraiser last night. Tsezar knew about Gary's death."

"What did he say?"

"Nothing incriminating. He was intentionally vague, but he nearly admitted to killing Gary."

"You shouldn't get anywhere near a man like that, Wil."

"Like the men I work with every day? Like Senator Peterson? I'm in the fighting ring, Jeff."

"Are you safe?"

"Yes. I'm at Jonathon's home under the watchful eyes of a dozen security guards."

Jeff sniffed. I could picture him with a snarl on his face. He hated criminals like Tsezar. It was why he worked so hard to arrest men like him.

I said, "You told us Gary hid the notes of his investigation behind his bathroom mirror. I need to know what Gary learned. I need to know what was written in his notes."

Jeff was silent for a moment. Years ago, he and my father were colleagues. Jeff even dated my mother before introducing her to my dad. When we moved to Normal, Illinois, Jeff and my dad remained close. We spent summers together. My brothers and I grew up loving his kids like they were our cousins, and we still celebrated the holidays together when we could.

He said, "After meeting Agent Curbelo two days ago, I assigned six patrol cars to watch your building, Wil. Yesterday, the afternoon shift spotted three different guys parked outside of your place. When they ran the plates, they all belonged to a shell corporation called Luka Shapiro Investments. Have you heard of it?"

"No." It validated the dread I felt looking at cars on the street below my apartment. "What did Gary discover?"

An hour later, I received an encrypted email from Jeff. If his superiors knew he was sharing evidence of an ongoing investigation, he would be fired. He took the risk because we were family and he thought I could do something about it. I would be forever grateful.

The information he shared blew me away. As I suspected, Harvey Salter and other local government officials were directly involved with Tsezar and other figures in the local Russian mafia.

With a shaking hand, I called the prosecutor.

"Good afternoon, Councilor Green. Did you enjoy the Phillips' fundraiser last night?" His congenial and chummy how-dee-do fit everything I knew about the prosecutor, mainly because his deceitful reputation preceded him.

I had no desire to chit-chat with him, and I got straight to the point. "As I mentioned last night, you'll be prosecuting my new client, who was charged with money laundering. I want to work out a plea bargain on his behalf."

"Does your client have prior convictions?"

"In Paris, France, the charges were removed from his record because he turned in evidence against the men he was forced to work for." If that didn't scare Slater, nothing would. "Otherwise, he wouldn't have been able to move to the US. So, no, not in the States. But he did generate substantial income over time. The thing is my client didn't know the deposits came from illegally earned income. He's an investment broker at Houghton Chambers Bank."

"I know who Bohdi Michaels is."

"Do you?"

Slater didn't hesitate. "I've already read through the case points."

Bohdi's initial hearings weren't scheduled for another month. Slater was either way ahead with his paperwork, or—considering what Gary Underwood discovered—he was working the case from another angle.

"But refresh my memory about the case," he said.

"His long-time employment as an investment broker speaks volumes for his trusted practices. I think he's someone's fall guy. He doesn't deserve twenty years in prison, and I'd like to—"

"First of all, Ms. Green, I know your reputation, and I like you. However, you still have me at a disadvantage. I wasn't aware he hired you, and I don't have his paperwork in front of me."

"Yes, sir." The last thing I wanted or needed was for Slater to turn against me. "I was hoping I could walk you through the details."

Slater softened a little. "I'd like to hear more about your client's case. Perhaps over lunch."

"Thank you, sir."

"I'm free . . . let me see. Oh, I'm free today. Meet me at the Tortoise Supper Club at noon. We'll talk about it then."

Greg drove across the river on Dearborn and turned right at the next street to go around the block. He parked near the restaurant where patrons dined on the covered sidewalk outside the restaurant and where a host's podium had been set up.

"Table for two?" the male host asked Greg.

"No, thank you. The lady is meeting someone. I'll wait at the bar."

"Ah. Who is expecting you, miss?"

"Harvey Slater." I'd heard this supper club was a regular haunt of his.

The host set his pen on the podium and lifted a dark green leather-bound menu off a stack. "Right this way."

Greg and I followed. Inside the restaurant, my eyes adjusted to the candle-lit atmosphere as grilled steak and savory herb aromas wafted my way. The host pointed Greg toward the bar and lead the way to a secluded dining area.

The prosecutor sat in a booth along the far wall. He was sipping an amber-colored drink when he spotted us.

The host left a menu on the table and asked if Mr. Slater needed anything.

"Another Macallan." He wagged his glass above the linen tablecloth. "And bring one for Miss Green."

The host bowed and left as I slid into the booth opposite my adversary. "Thank you for seeing me, Mr. Slater."

"Not a problem. I looked back at the notes from your client's arraignment. You didn't represent him at the hearing. Why not?"

I adjusted my skirt and settled onto the booth's bench cushion. "He didn't reach out to me until later. I represent him now, though. He's in a real predicament."

Tight-lipped, Slater nodded as if he knew the layout of the mouse hole in which Bohdi had been cornered. "He pleaded innocent on the grounds that he didn't know Red Lace Escort operated an illegal business."

Without disturbing the place setting in front of me, I rested one forearm along the edge of the table and the other on top of it. "That's correct. Angelique Sartre accused him of laundering because she was faced with a 25-year sentence for solicitation and trafficking. She was looking for a scapegoat."

Slater slurped an ice cube from the remains of his scotch as two more glasses arrived. It was much too early in the day for me to drink alcohol.

"Angelique Sartre isn't the accused in question," he said, crunching on the ice cube.

The waiter held the tray in one hand while he set cardboard drink coasters on the table and placed the drink glasses on top of them.

I said, "Bohdi Michaels has worked for the Houghton Chambers Bank in Chicago for eighteen years. He's never been charged with a criminal offense in the United States."

Slater waited until the waiter left. "Do you take me for an idiot, Miss Green? Michaels was charged with a similar offense in Paris. Isn't it true that's why he immigrated to the US? To Chicago? He was expelled from France and from working in European banks because he was caught laundering money for a terrorist group."

"He wasn't exiled, he left for his own protection."

"You can't put a bow on it, counselor. The man worked with criminals."

"He's reformed."

"He's not!" A lock of his thick, slicked-back gray-brown hair had come loose at his little outburst. He smoothed it with one hand. "Bohdi Michaels has been working with the Russian mafia since Paris. He's amassed more than thirteen million in illegal investments. Most of that he kept hidden within fictitious entities and offshore shell corporations. He has used the money to purchase oceanfront real estate in fictitious names. I have multiple sources who have confirmed this." Slater's unedited reveal exposed he knew as much as I did—and maybe more—about Bohdi Michaels.

"He's willing to turn in state's evidence," I said.

"Against whom? Against some faceless Russian gangsters? Nothing he says will help him in federal court."

Faceless? His word choice could seem as if Slater had no idea who the Russian gangsters were. I knew differently and tread cautiously. I'd seen Slater patting Kostya Tsezar's back at the fundraiser, and Gary's notes proved the two were in cahoots. One hand washed the other, as they say.

How deeply is Slater involved?

I sat back and examined Slater's sagging features and the fleshy hammocks under his eyes. I folded my arms across my chest as I watched him swallow more scotch.

Tactfully, I said, "So, excuse me for asking, but I still believe the Category IV criminal offense charge is too high for my client. It's his first offense in the US. He doesn't even have a parking ticket. Can we at least bring the charges down to Category II with a shorter prison sentence?"

"Michaels has committed a federal crime, Miss Green. This is not his first offense. I consider his action to be a Category IV criminal offense and we will proceed as such."

"You're not going to bargain his charges with me at all then."

"By your reaction, I see you haven't done your homework. I hope Michaels's expectations of your ability to acquit were worth the price he paid. Go home, counselor. You're in over your head."

I moved to the edge of the booth and gathered my things but verbally stood my ground. "I don't think so."

"Your colleague Charlie Reid turned this case down. And for good reason."

What?

I pursed my lips, unable to imagine why she'd do that. "Well, I didn't. Like every client I've represented, I'll fight for this one, too."

"May you live to regret that decision."

Was he threatening me? The US prosecutor had ruined careers. I stared at him. "What are you saying?"

Slater peered down his nose into his scotch. "Exquisite alcohol takes meticulous nurturing and years of refinement. Like anything worth something in this world, the greatest, the ones who reach the top, need the right atmosphere and careful encouragement to become the very best. You're on your way there, anyone can see that. But this case could set an aspiring female defense lawyer back in more ways than she could imagine."

Before I could stop the words from running out of my mouth, I asked, "Is that a threat?"

Slater narrowed his eyes at me. "Now, Ms. Green. I would never do that." His lips curled in an icy smile that never reached his eyes.

<h1 style="text-align:center">~ 28 ~</h1>

Greg drove us out of the city. My hand shook as I dug my phone out of my purse and called Charlie Reid. I had to know why she didn't take Michaels's case. The call went straight to voicemail.

"This is Charlotte Reid. If you got this voicemail, I'm in court. Leave a message so I can decide whether to call you back." *Beep.*

"Charlie, it's Wil. I need to talk to you. Call when you get a chance."

As soon as I hung up, my phone rang again. It was Charlie returning the call. "Thanks for the call back."

"I'm having lunch down at The Office. Join me," she said.

The Office was a hangout for many other lawyers from around town. Charlie liked to show her face there, just to remind them of her presence and intimidate them.

"Not today. I have a question for you."

"You sound a little off. What's on your mind?"

I gazed out the window at the gray city. Dirty concrete darkened in the shadows of the amber afternoon sun. "Why did you turn down Bohdi Michaels's case?"

"Don't tell me *you're* representing him."

My lungs had inflated with air, but her tone flattened me.

"Oh, Wil."

On the phone, I heard the clinking of glassware and low music in the background. Charlie wasn't one to let the silence simmer. Yet now . . . I interrupted the lull. "Why did you turn it down?"

"Are you in trouble?" Charlie sounded genuinely concerned.

"I just met with Harvey Slater to bargain Michaels's sentence down. I think . . . he threatened my career." There was a definite quaver in my voice.

"You couldn't have known."

"What? What couldn't I have known?"

"I'm sure Bohdi Michaels is seeking the very best representation he can find. He can afford you, that I know. But you'll never win this case."

"Bohdi thinks I can."

"And what do you think?" Her open-ended question inserted doubt in my mind.

Greg turned onto northbound I-90 and accelerated.

I said, "Bohdi Michaels is a scapegoat. He's taking the fall so someone else won't. There are bigger fish in that fishbowl. I'm aware of the Russian mafia's presence in Chicago, and I think Slater is somehow involved too. I'm just not sure to what degree." And Janko Vorobiev's threats brought their unscrupulous, depraved methods full circle.

Charlie said, "After I turned the case down, three other top financial crimes lawyers did the same. No one would touch this until you. You're so naïve, Wil."

"Why didn't Jim Milton vet this one?"

"Come on. Why would he? Look what he put you through over the last three years."

True. Milton's choices in clients were the worst of the worst. I'd been schooled by taking those cases. Clearly, I had more to learn. "What am I missing?" I sank into the leather car seat. Greg's gaze was straight ahead, but I knew he was listening.

"Hold on. I'm going to the bathroom where it's quieter." A minute passed before she continued. "Whether he knew it or not, Bohdi Michaels worked for one of the biggest criminal organizations in the world. His arrest and conviction will keep the feds happy for a few years. You're right. He is a scapegoat. But you won't win the case. Chalk it up to experience and stick a feather in your cap. Don't fight it, Wil. It won't be worth it."

"But I have to. Michaels is expecting—"

"Michaels knows he can't win. He's desperate, and you're his last shot. But they won't let him go free. Slater won't give you an inch."

"How is Slater involved?"

"He's getting a cut. Almost every case that involves members of this organization—every *Chicago* case—goes through Slater. He's . . . he's the gatekeeper."

I'd never heard fear in Charlie's voice before, but it shaded her tone now. The revelation that she would back down from something frightened me, too.

"That's why you declined Michaels's request for representation," I said.

"I'm getting old, Wil. I'll retire someday. I'll stop fighting. My millions will buy me a nice condo on the shore of some tropical island. There, I'll lay in the sun and turn brown with salt in my hair and sand between my toes."

It sounded like she'd exited the bathroom. Glasses clinked and laughter came alive in the background again. Someone called her name.

Charlie said, "Take care, Wil. Best of luck with this one. You're going to need it."

My hand with the phone fell into my lap.

"Is everything okay?" Greg asked.

I barely shook my head, *no*.

~29~

The presence of the security team at Jonathon's mansion reminded me of Travis King, the bodyguard who had attacked me, and how even they might be swayed to turn against us by the promise of power . . . or a deeper purse than Jonathon's. They made me leery.

For the rest of the day I worked in solitude on my laptop from the bedroom. Jonathon—busy with work and his own investigation—checked on me several times. Jonathon had a private team of analysts looking for ways to avoid giving Janko the money. We discussed the limited options which included shipping me off to someplace remote and having the FBI make an arrest during the handoff. He seemed preoccupied but never too distracted to forget to kiss me or rub my shoulders. Every moment brought us closer together.

I began to long for more time with him. His woodsy fragrance. His caress. It had been too long since we'd been intimate.

With Bohdi Michaels' trial weeks away, I looked deeper into terrorist groups and specifically the Russian mafia. I tried to glean the scope of their reach. While it seemed improbable, I'd uncover blacker crimes committed by them—selling weapons to terrorists, funding corrupt politicians, and promoting war in the Middle East—it turned out it was not impossible. I trolled the U.S. Justice Department files for more information. The darker subject came out of a single article I found about Tsezar from nearly thirty years ago. Proof that Konstantin Tsezar had been involved in human trafficking.

He had a criminal record.

When Tsezar first came to the United States, he was arrested and charged with solicitation for his peripheral involvement with a ring of human traffickers. A gang of men and women had trafficked the young adults from Turkey, Hungary, and Croatia with the lure of traveling to the US for sightseeing. The college-age kids were promised the price of round-trip airfare and a chance to see the great cities of North America. The *tour group* traveled from New York to Chicago and Los Angeles before supposedly going home with an experience to pad their resumes.

The too-good-to-be-true travel adventure had a catch. Once these young people came to the US, they no longer had access to their money or their passports. In return for the all-expense paid trip, the victims had to work for money that they would never see. While on this trip-of-a-lifetime, their captors sold them every day to perform sex acts with anyone they desired. They became sex slaves with no hope of returning to a normal life.

Tsezar wasn't directly responsible for bringing the young women and men into the United States, but he had aided the gang of traffickers once they arrived in Chicago. He provided them with passports and paperwork and also helped to find work for their victims.

At the time of his arrest, he possessed dozens of Turkish, Croatian, and Hungarian passports. Of course, he claimed no responsibility. In his statement, he said the passports were planted in his apartment.

Tsezar walked away from a trial because the evidence was mismanaged from the start. The prosecution's case fell apart because the passports were lost. Criminal evidence *never* gets lost. It was an indication of foul play. Even the victims disappeared from town. Recorded comments from one social worker stated that she hoped the victims were sent home. The young prosecutor who oversaw Tsezar's case was none other than Harvey Slater.

Acid gurgled in my stomach. I pushed the cold cup of coffee away.

It was years before Harvey Slater was appointed as a federal US prosecutor. A young raptor at the onset of his career, Slater easily embraced his role. He was a hunter. A predator. He quickly moved up in the ranks to become one of Cook County's best and most formidable attorneys. With many government officials on his side, he became the youngest federal prosecutor in US history.

Just as cliff diving had become instinctual with muscle memory to support my sport—a split-second decision made by each cell in my body—I knew with every fiber of my being that Harvey Slater was still directly involved with Konstantin Tsezar.

It had taken Gary's notes and hours at the computer to learn this.

Jonathon needed to know. I dashed out of the room and ran down the hall toward Jonathon's study on the other side of the house. I passed through the kitchen where Grant and a small staff cooked for the army of security guards. My shirttails whipped behind me as I rounded the corner of the dining room and turned into the back hallway. His office door was closed.

I lifted my hand to knock, then heard Jonathon's voice carry through the heavy wooden door. "How can you use that against me?" His furious tone stopped me in my tracks.

"Show me the proof!" he argued.

Someone tapped my shoulder and every nerve in my body jumped to attention.

"I almost lost you." Greg's kind smile didn't diffuse the tension in my chest.

I flashed him a fake grin and pressed my ear against the door. Jonathon's deep voice rumbled, "Meet me in one hour." The sounds followed of shuffling papers and drawers slamming.

Who had Jonathon been talking to? Janko?

Jonathon said, "Erik, pull the car up front. We're going out." As I heard his footsteps crossing the office I backed away from the door right into Greg. A nervous gasp escaped my lips when Jonathon opened the door.

"Mina." Jonathon seemed surprised to see me.

I made an excuse for standing outside his door. "I needed a break from my computer, and I can't seem to shake this guy."

Greg backed up a few feet.

"Who were you talking to? I heard you through the door."

"I can't talk right now. I've got to run. But I'll be back by dinner time."

"I need to talk to you."

His hand slid to the small of my back as he gave me a moment of his full attention. "Not right now," he said. "Tonight, though. I'll see you tonight."

I made an excuse and tried for more. "Could I come along? A couple of these guys could take me to the Water Tower. I need to do some shopping."

"Sorry, not today."

I matched Jonathon's quick gait. "Was there a problem at work?"

He kissed me on the cheek and spun on his heel. Over his shoulder, he said, "Something like that. Have Greg take you shopping. As I said, I'll be back around dinnertime."

In the entryway, Erik met Jonathon and opened the door for him. The Alfa Romeo purred in the circular brick driveway. Jonathon rushed out the door to the car without a backward glance.

What's he hiding? And who had angered him on the phone?

Before the front door closed, I said to Greg, "We're following them. Get the car while I grab my things. And hurry!"

"Wait, Mina. We can't—"

"We can and we will." I sped past him back to my room where I snatched up my gun, the holster, and my knife with the ankle strap.

~30~

Greg drove fast and caught up with the Alfa Romeo as it exited the Lake Forest neighborhood onto North McKinley Road. He kept two cars between us, a Lexus, and a restored, decades-old Mustang convertible. Erik turned onto the I-94 southbound, and we followed.

"Don't lose them," I said. "I need to know where he's going."

"I don't like this, Mina. Jonathon's business is his business."

"When it involves threats on my life, it's my business too."

Greg quieted down and while he drove, I maneuvered the shoulder holster around my body and slid the Browning into place over my striped, sleeveless summer dress. Sweat made it difficult to stuff my sticky arms into a black blazer that hid the weapon. I hiked my dress up to my hip and strapped the knife belt onto my thigh.

Once I clicked the seatbelt in place, I gazed ahead at Jonathon's car. The three-act play was coming together—Tsezar and Slater, Janko and Rory, and Bohdi Michaels and Angelique Sartre—but I still couldn't determine Jonathon's role.

Was he the hero or the villain? Mentor or trickster?

I'd been daydreaming of a cliff in Vermont that I hadn't dived from in years. Imagining the dangerous dive, standing on the towering cliff's edge, and launching my body into the crisp, freezing air seduced me. I craved the rushing wind and punishing blow on entering the water.

Erik exited on West Davidson Street near Pulaski Park in Chicago. When he turned right on West Augusta, I knew he was headed toward the East Village, where many members of the Russian community lived. Confirming my assumption, Erik drove Jonathon to West Iowa Street where he parked in front of what appeared to be an abandoned warehouse or old industrial site. We were blocks away from St. George

Orthodox Cathedral, a known Russian congregation. This was the heart of the Russian community in Chicago.

Greg slowed as he passed the street where Erik parked, then he did a U-turn and stopped in front of some brick apartments. We watched Jonathon and Erik exit the Alfa. Jonathon straightened his black double-breasted suit jacket and looked up at the three-story brick building. Despite the extreme heat of the day and the anxiety I'd perceived in him about rushing to this meeting, Jonathon appeared cool and put together.

Arched, black metal window frames checkered the side of the historic building. Filthy glass panes didn't allow clear sight into the inner domain. I read the name *Koval* mounted above a small wooden door and looked it up on my phone.

The manufacturer had gone out of business decades ago though their sign still hung on the side of the building. Google listed the edifice as vacant. The title transferred through a sale about ten years ago, but the new owner's name was not available.

I clutched my phone to my chest. "Who is Jonathon meeting?" I asked, though I didn't expect Greg to know the answer.

Greg had shut off the engine and tilted his seat back. He shook his head. "I don't know Jonathon that well. He's a very private man."

Yes, he was.

Greg said, "I've never been to this part of town before."

I said, "I only know the East Village because years ago, I had a client from this area. The people here don't like strangers. They're wary of outsiders." I leaned forward to watch Jonathon through the windshield of Greg's Santa Fe. Behind Jonathon, Erik in dark glasses, scanned the surrounding area, furtive as a fox. I held my breath as he looked our way for a moment then moved on.

"What are we doing here, Ms. Green? I should take you home."

"No. I need to know what Jonathon is up to." I sank lower into the car. "Are you sure they won't see us?" I whispered as if they could hear.

Jonathon knocked on a green door, the single entrance on this side of the building. I was only able to see the arm of the man who let them in. I wanted to peer through the darkened windows. To comprehend what was happening for Jonathon's sake—he was my friend and lover after all—and my own personal safety.

A heat advisory was in effect till the end of the week. August sun baked the asphalt and Greg's black car warmed quickly. The air inside thickened. Greg turned the key, and the A/C came back on, but I needed out.

I swiftly exited the car and closed the door on Greg's protests. Hoping to remain hidden, I stayed close to the wall nearest me and slunk to the apartment's corner. Thick humidity glued my dress to my thighs.

To the beep-beep of the car-lock, Greg dashed to my side. "I'll have to advise against this, Ms. Green."

"I'll let Jonathon know."

He grunted a laugh.

For several minutes we stayed close to the apartment wall in case someone inside the warehouse looked our way. A passing man shot me a wary side-eye and walked by. He was followed by an older woman conversing with a young man. Their conversation came to a stop as they observed us hugging the wall.

I took Greg's arm and laughed. "What are you doing? Come on."

We passed them, and the young man turned around to watch us cross the street in front of the abandoned warehouse. A small oak tree growing from a cutout in the sidewalk gave us little cover from the upper windows. Opportunistic weeds filled in the cracks. I took note of three cars parked on the street. One red Lexus, one spanking-new silver Hummer, and a Porsche.

We hustled to the end of the block where a garbage-strewn alley separated the old warehouse from the next building. Small shrubs and tall weeds lined the periphery. A rusted storage pod filled the dead-end alley. A heavy padlock hung on a bolt on the green side-door.

Greg sauntered up to a door and tried turning the knob. He pulled his Walther PPK .380 and he manually locked the slide. The same gun had been admitted as evidence in a trial last year and I remembered that this modification to the Walther silences the sound of the gunshot.

He shot the padlock off the bolt with only the rattle of the smoking metal echoing off the brick walls. I turned my gaze to the entrance of the alley and watched for bystanders as he removed the busted lock.

"It's open, now," he said.

"You're a handy guy to have around, Greg." Across the street, movement from a second-story window caught my eye. A woman watched us with great interest then lifted an old-style phone to her ear. I said, "We're being watched."

He pushed the creaky door open and looked inside. "This appears to be a back room. No one's inside."

I followed Greg and left the door ajar for an easier escape. Just in case.

Inside, the smells of old cardboard and machinery oil hung in the still air. Years of footsteps had trod a light-colored path on the grimy-colorless laminate floor from the entrance to another door. This room was in the back part of the building where perhaps workers would congregate for a break. Cigarette butts, food wrappers and wads of paper trash had taken up residence in the corners. Ahead of me, Greg crouched behind a second door.

Men's deep bass voices hummed and the muffled phrases, " . . . proof of your involvement . . ." and " . . . settling scores . . ." rose above the rest. One voice, thick with a Russian accent like Janko's, sounded vaguely familiar.

Greg whispered, "Do you want to go in?"

"No!" I whispered. My brow knit together. "I have no idea who Jonathon's speaking with."

"But you want to find out, right?"

Tentatively, I nodded, wary that Greg might expose us. Sweat trickled down the side of his neck where the spiraling chord from the earbud hung outside of his shirt. He had disconnected his com-link to Jonathon's security team.

He quietly opened the door one inch and allowed me to look first. Dirty glass windows in the expansive room allowed little natural light and they hadn't bothered to turn overhead lights on. A man sitting at a desk had his back to me. Jonathon's silhouette faced the right side of the desk.

"I can't let you do that," Jonathon said. He slammed his hands down on the desk.

The man at the desk stood. "You can and you will. We made a deal."

"I want to see the photos. I want proof," Jonathon said.

Another man who I recognized him from the fundraiser faced us on the opposite side of the room. He wore a prominent gun on his hip.

I backed away and asked Greg, "Who is the third man with the gun?"

Greg leaned in to look. "It's Fayed Almahn. He's involved with the Russian mafia, but I'm not sure exactly how. I can find out if you want."

"How?"

"Some of the security guys have experience with that crowd." He backed away from the door.

I hunched forward to peek through the opening again. This man was stockier than Jonathon's frenemy, Janko. He replied to Jonathon in a threatening whisper at the same moment an airplane noise shook the building from overhead. The jet engines drowned out their voices, but the Russian threatened Jonathon with his poised fist.

I scanned the room for Erik but couldn't find him. Perhaps they'd required him to wait outside the room.

Jonathon began to pace. When the airplane noise faded he said, "You can't always get what you want. Not this time. Not from me."

"If you don't give us the money, we will hurt you in ways you can't imagine. Those photos will go viral. We will prove you are involved in international drug trade, in distribution of deadly fentanyl."

"You can't prove anything."

"We will. And if you still won't cooperate, your beloved Ms. Green will disappear," the Russian said. This time, I placed the voice with my memory of the fundraiser. It was Kostya Tsezar. The photos he spoke of must have been taken at the auction Jonathon told me about.

I couldn't pry my gaze from the room. A welcome draft cooled the sweat on my neck, but it blew the door open another inch. I stood very still and held my breath against the pounding in my chest.

Someone's cell phone rang with a creepy ringtone. Fayed Almahn dug into his pants pocket and answered.

"What is it?" Kostya asked.

Almahn hung up and took two long strides to the Russian's side then whispered something in his ear. Then, he turned his head and directly looked my way.

Through the one-inch crack in the door, we made eye contact. Jonathon also looked toward me. Behind the bulky door I felt exposed. I gasped and backed away.

"Stop!" a deep baritone shouted.

"Let's go," I said to Greg as I shut the door and hurried to the outer door. With an explosion of speed, we exited and raced down the alley. Greg grabbed my arm to stop me from running out into the street. I gazed up at the window where the woman still watched, the phone no longer to her ear.

Greg led the way, keeping me covered with his Walther at his side. We ran toward a cluster of pedestrians then melted into the group. Behind us, the deep voice yelled, "Stop them!"

A Russian thug—waving his pistol in his hand—came rushing toward us. The crowd parted, all eyes landed on Greg and me.

Greg pushed me forward as we rounded the next block. We ran. Six, seven, eight doors down, we ducked into a restaurant. The Russian thug followed. I side-stepped a waitress—tray in her hand. Greg couldn't avoid her. The tray, plates and full glasses smashed on the floor. We ran through a smelly, steamy kitchen leaving a wake of broken plates and splattered food. The waitress and cooks screamed but I didn't understand their words as I bolted out the back door.

Another alley. I jigged to my left and into the hot sunlight. Greg was at my side, tugging me forward. Bigger crowds mobbed the sidewalks here. We slowed our pace and merged with them, ducking low.

When the Russian gangster emerged from the alley, we were well out of his sight.

"That was close," Greg said.

I breathed in the sizzling summer air. Relief was a long way away.

-31-

Greg and I hopped in a cab and drove in circles for an hour before asking the driver to let us off near his car. By then, Arron and Liam joined us. When the four of us exited the elevator on the floor of my condo, I took the Browning out of the holster and put a finger to my lips in the sign for *quiet*. If someone were waiting—Janko knew where I lived—I needed to protect myself. We had no idea what Jonathon was involved in or what those gangsters were capable of.

The image of Gary bound to a chair with his eyes gouged out haunted me.

Arron and Liam flanked the door like unmatched bookends. They nodded at each other and at Greg, who placed a ready hand on his weapon. His grave look confirmed my sense of imminent danger. None of us wanted to confront a dangerous intruder.

As I slid my key into the slot, Greg stopped me. He raised a finger to his lips. He motioned me to wait and unholstered his Walther, holding it tight to his chest. His index finger laying across the barrel.

When he nodded, I rolled the doorknob in my hand and the latch clicked, echoing in the quiet hallway. I stepped back.

Greg pushed the door open with his left arm, looking left and right into my living room. The spacious loft had twenty-foot ceilings that absorbed all the tiny tics and moans of the plumbing.

Arron stalked through the doorway after Greg. Liam followed. My heart razzed against my chest as I took shallow breaths, my hands gripping my dad's Browning. Pointing the weapon into my kitchen, I hoped not to use it. And yet, if any of those men came into my home, I'd make them pay.

Greg slinked inside, keeping his back to the wall and his gun out front. He swept his weapon left, then right.

My pulse pounded in my ears as I followed him in and closed the door. From the doorway, I couldn't see behind the kitchen counter. I nodded in that direction, and three strides carried Greg to the edge of the counter. The area was clear.

Floorboards creaked under Greg's feet. In the entry, I removed my noisy, glossy beige stilettos. Liam looked behind draperies as I moved down the hall. I rounded the corner and flicked the bathroom light-switch. The clear shower door spotlighted an empty stall. Arron brushed past me and moved to my bedroom. My unmade bed, with pillows mounded under the sheets, looked like someone still lay there. I threw the sheets off, and Arron moved to the walk-in closet.

I didn't relax when they announced the all-clear.

"Halt!" Arron ordered. He was in the living room.

The hairs on the back of my neck stood at attention. *Who had followed us?*

"Don't take another step forward," Liam commanded.

I followed Greg down the short hallway with two hands on the grip of my Browning and the weapon pointed at the floor. I almost bumped into Greg's backside as he came to an abrupt halt.

Greg said, "What are you doing here?"

A wave of prickly chills scattered down my back.

I strained to see past him. "Jonathon!" His name escaped my lips with a breath.

Greg backed me up as I rounded the corner and stepped cautiously into the room. Liam and Arron both pointed their weapons at my lover.

"I had to see you."

"How do we know we can trust you?" Greg asked.

Jonathon made sure the door was locked. "Kostya demanded to meet me. I had no choice. I left the warehouse as soon as the meeting broke up. I saw you there, Mina. I tried calling your cell."

I hadn't received any messages that I was aware of. "It didn't ring."

My three musketeers still hadn't holstered their firearms.

Jonathon held his hands out, his gaze darting from each man and to me. "I'm on your side. You must believe me."

Greg holstered his weapon first and he gave a signal to the others. Mine was still pointed at Jonathon.

Jonathon said, "You shouldn't have followed me to the East Village."

"Did I have a choice?" I didn't know the anger buried inside was rage directed at Jonathon.

"Put the gun away, Mina," Jonathon said. "Please."

"Who else is here?" I asked.

"I'm alone. Erik is waiting downstairs." Jonathon turned his gaze to Greg, beside me. "Greg, can you and your team wait in the lobby? I'll call when we're ready to go."

"Not unless Mina wants me to."

"Greg," Jonathon said.

"It's okay, Greg," I said. "You can wait outside."

Greg looked from Jonathon to me.

I nodded. "It's okay."

Greg crossed the room while shaking his head. He passed Jonathon without looking at him and Arron and Liam followed. When they shut the door, Jonathon locked and bolted it.

I holstered my Browning. "What in the hell were you doing with Kostya Tsezar?"

"It wasn't my choice to meet with him. Until recently, I didn't realize Janko has worked with Konstantin for many years." Jonathon had dark circles under his eyes that I hadn't noticed before.

I yanked my jacket off and threw it on the back of the couch. "You make me so angry!"

Jonathon loosened his tie. "I'm so sorry. I had to know for sure. Tsezar is working with Janko. They've threatened to take you away forever and I *cannot* let you become a victim."

"Victim! Ha!" It was the last word anyone had ever used to describe me. Yet Jonathon's contract came to mind. *"I won't release you from the contract. You gave me control."*

I lifted the hem of my dress and dug at the leather knife-strap around my thigh. The buckle came away with my prying and I unbelted the blade. Holding it up in front of him, I asked, "Do *you* see me as a victim?"

Jonathon stepped out from behind the couch. "No, Mina. I see you as a powerful, fierce equal. I see you as my peer and my match." He crossed the room as I set the knife down on the counter. "You are my colleague and my counselor. You are a leader and a champion who rivals the most powerful women in the world."

He stood in front of me.

A pressure valve opened. I shoved unwanted emotions downward, refusing to let them control me.

"I didn't know you felt that way—"

He put a finger on my lips then pulled me closer. "Shh," he said. His steely eyes met mine and passion welled in my core.

Jonathon's hands were on my shoulders. In my hair. His mouth was on mine, occupying the same space. His possessive kiss took my breath. It was no use resisting. I leaned into his lips, and he gathered me to him, claiming me. I wanted him, and I wanted to be his.

He slid his hands down to my sides, stopping at the holster. I unbuckled the leather strap of my gun holster. We separated long enough for me to set the gear on the table. Then we reconnected, our passion ignited.

Jonathon whirled me around. He cupped my breasts as I unbuckled his pants. We danced. His pants pooled on the floor, and I removed my dress.

Walking backward while I unbuttoned his purple shirt, I drew him forward to my bedroom. He peeled the garment off and dropped it in the doorway.

Jonathon pushed me back onto the bed and then crouched over me, like a mountain lion pinning his prey. I lay back and wrapped my arms around him.

With one hand supporting his weight on the bed beside me, Jonathon eased a lock of hair away from my mouth and caressed my cheek. "Mina, you are everything to me. You must know that."

His soft touch weakened me. My fingers found their way beneath my panties. I moaned his name as my fingers slid past my hardening clit to the moist ravine between my folds. I needed very little stimulation. Jonathon's hand covered mine and soon, his fingers surpassed mine. He strummed the moist folds between my legs. He took control.

With pleasure, I closed my eyes and allowed the sensation to overcome me. I lifted my hips and pressed against his.

"Each day, I long to be with you. Each day, I long to possess you." He cupped my pussy and squeezed with a commanding grip.

I arched into his fist—pressing my breasts into his chest—and I looked into his eyes. "And each day, I long to submit to you. I long for you to take me."

Heat between our bodies made our skin slick. I pinched my nipples and offered them to him. Jonathon took one between his teeth and bit down. The sharp pain brought my senses to life. I groaned. "Bite it again."

His free hand took a fistful of my hair and pulled. The sharp pain reminded me I was alive. It reminded me that I was strong. I demanded more. "Again."

He pulled my hair and alternately chewed one nipple at a time until both were aching and hard. My head tilted back, my mouth opened, and I let out a gasp.

Jonathon lifted me toward him and plunged his erection deep into me. I closed my eyes and thrust my hips into his. I let him take me. I let him slam his cock into me as I met him with equal force.

He kneeled between my legs and lifted my ass up to his thighs. With a sudden smack of skin on skin, he slapped my ass with his flat hand. The sting opened my eyes. I hummed, "More, Jonathon. I want more."

He slapped me again.

"More!"

The sharp sting of his hand on my flesh warmed my skin and fanned the flames of desire. I thrust my hips toward his erection. Deepening our connection. Jonathon gripped my thighs and repeatedly pumped me with his engorged cock.

I needed this. I needed Jonathon. I needed Jonathon's brutal fucking.

He was the only one who could own me like this. He alone knew how much pain to deliver. How much punishment I could take. His thrusts pushed me to the peak of orgasm. I cried out with the release, the overwhelming sensation of orgasm.

Jonathon grew inside me until I thought we both would burst. With a war cry, he called my name "Mina!" His ferocious thrusts and explosive release gave rise to another climactic wave. Together, we moaned in rhythmic song. Together, we collapsed on the bed.

~32~

Sticky sweat glued our bodies together. Satiated and basking in the incandescence, we moved slowly, unwilling to let go. I wanted to lie in his arms until Janko's threat and all that surrounded it disappeared. I *could* love Jonathon.

When finally the source of summer heat sank beneath the horizon, I opened a window and let in a cooling breeze. Our stomachs growled. Jonathon and I sat up from my bed. His hand on my back. My fingers on his cheek. His lips on my shoulder.

I donned panties and a t-shirt—still too hot to wear anything else. Jonathon slid into his slacks and hung his shirt to smooth the wrinkles. He took a call in the bathroom. When he exited wearing only his slacks, Jonathon said he checked in with Greg and Erik. The second shift bodyguards had arrived so they could get dinner. They would stand watch in the building lobby and the underground garage.

"Let me cook for you," he said.

"I didn't know you had the talent."

"There is much you still don't know about me."

Truer words hadn't been spoken. I looked into my lover's eyes and found a man I wanted to know better. A man I wanted to be with.

I said, "Let me help you. We'll make my favorite, grilled cheese." It was one of the few things I knew how to cook.

Jonathon said, "Grant taught me a gourmet version, if you want to spice it up."

"I always want extra spice." I slipped my arm around his trim waist.

Jonathon gazed down into my eyes. I had longed for that smoldering, steel blue gaze, the hunger in his eyes. "I know exactly what you mean, Mina."

I raised up on my tiptoes and kissed him.

Jonathon found the chilled bottle of Chilean Sauvignon Blanc in the fridge. He opened it then set a glass in front of me.

"Tell me more about Rory. How did she and Janko meet? How is she involved?" I asked.

"Rory and I split up around the time PPS stocks had gone public. I was about to move to Chicago."

"Was she heartbroken?" But what I really wanted to know . . . "Were you?"

"The breakup was mutual. We'd fallen out of love." He gathered an onion and a few jalapeños Greg had shopped for earlier that week and set them on the counter beside a cutting board. "Our disfunction had become so normal by then. For a few years, we'd been moving our separate ways. She traveled for work and so did I. When we saw each other, once a month or less, she seemed bitter. Resentful." A wave of emotion rippled across Jonathon's brow, disappearing so quickly I thought I imagined it.

I found a brick of Gouda cheese—which Greg must have purchased—a stick of butter and loaf of nutty, 21-grain bread.

"But you didn't answer my question. How did the breakup make you feel?" I pushed. I longed for Jonathon to open up. Deep inside, I believed we could be closer. That we could be more than sex partners.

Playful, slightly resentful, eyes looked up at me. "You don't miss a thing, do you?"

"Well?"

He paused and seemed to direct his gaze inward. As if the emotions were hard to access. As if they were locked behind a forgotten door. He washed the peppers in the sink and answered with his back to me. "I was sad. Rory was my first love."

Jonathon seemed to hold those emotions in the locked fortress of his heart. I suspected that much like me, he maintained fragile domination over them.

He placed the vegetables on a cutting board and reached for a knife. "Sex had become violent with her. I thought she enjoyed pain and punishment too much."

I enjoyed it, too—at least I thought I did.

"Not only did she enjoy receiving it, but she also longed to deliver it." His knife hovered over the pepper. "When we went our separate ways, I heard she got a job in New York with her multilingual skills. She became a translator for a medical manufacturing firm. She traveled overseas to sell the products to hospitals and medical suppliers."

"She works in the same industry you do." I set plates on the counter and took four slices of bread out of the bag.

"Years passed before I saw her again. When we did meet, it was in Vienna at the Austrian International Business Bureau's gala event I told you about."

"Wasn't that where you met Janko?" I swirled the wine glass, eager and listening.

"Yes."

Slices of jalapeño and onion slivers lay piled on the cutting board as Jonathon heated oil in a small skillet.

"How did you feel when you saw her again?"

"Though I was glad to see her doing well, Rory had changed since we first met. Years before, she was curious about life and people. In Austria, she had hardened and there was something malicious about her." Jonathon grew introspective as he focused on the task of preparing dinner. "She wore a shimmering black gown that hugged every curve of her body. Her heels were at least six inches high and when she stood next to me, we were eye to eye. Yet we weren't. The way she spoke to me—and everyone around her, for that matter—was punitive. As if she blamed the world for something. After all we'd been through, I didn't know her anymore."

"People change, Jonathon."

"I understand. But she was no longer the submissive woman that I met at a college frat party. I sensed she enjoyed inflicting pain and punishment more than anyone should."

"Don't you?"

Jonathon looked up at me. His wounded, anguished gaze informed me all I needed to know. I'd opened a lesion. "Mina." He set the knife down and washed his hands. After drying them, he placed his palms on the counter and leaned toward me. "I enjoy drawing out your orgasm. I find pleasure in sparking sensation and teasing your excitement and drive. And I'll do whatever it takes to help you obtain the highest rush, the sexual climax or peak of uncontrollable euphoria. Because for me, your pleasure is also mine."

"And all the painful devices in your *torture* chamber? The whips and racks? You can't tell me you don't intend to use them to hurt a submissive or me."

"The devices are merely tools that fascinate me. They represent an idea. For me, and for someone like you, they illicit a little bit of fear and excitement. In the right hands, they can be used to stimulate and arouse."

"And in the wrong hands?"

"What do you think? I'm quite sure that in Rory's hands, those devices could be deadly."

It seemed Jonathon's fascination with the toys and how to use them had become a crutch when he was with Rory. A way to hide from his feelings. "I misunderstood."

He whispered, "Please don't compare me to Rory again. We are not the same."

"I'm sorry." Ashamed for hurting him, I lowered my chin.

"It isn't your fault. You couldn't have known."

"How can you be so sure she'd become . . . malicious?"

"There were many clues, trust me. The young man cowing at her elbow appeared to be at her beck and call, for one. His gaze never left her. I knew the type. From watching him, I was certain that Rory had become a Domme and he was her sub."

Jonathon picked up the knife again and finished chopping. He dropped the onion slivers and sliced jalapeño into hot oil. The fragrances of onion and pepper bloomed with the sizzle.

"That night at the gala, she held court with some of the most powerful businessmen in Austria." Jonathon said, "Janko wasn't one of them, but he was clearly friendly with leaders and high-profile businesspeople.

He lifted his glass with the wealthy directors and presidents of international corporations. And he rubbed elbows with government officials."

"Janko and Rory met through the Dubrovnik hospital clinics?" While the veggies cooked, I arranged the cheese slices on buttered bread.

"She said they were colleagues." Jonathon seemed to access the memory by looking up at the ceiling. "I shook Janko's hand and Rory told him about PPS. That we'd been friends for years. He seemed vaguely interested. She launched into a description of the purpose of the software while Janko acted indifferent, looking around the room. His attention wasn't directly on me or Rory until she said, *'He's one of us.'* As if it were a code word. Because from that moment on, Janko focused in on me. From that day forward, he refused to let it go."

"Let what go?"

"He kept referring to that phrase—*you're one of us*—each time he reached out."

"*You're one of us?* What does that mean?" I asked.

"There were many ways to take the comment. Out of context, it has no weight at all. At first I thought it meant that like them, I was involved in the medical community. You know, she sold medical equipment to hospitals, so, essentially, did I. But like a stalker, Janko called my direct line to ask for demonstrations of the software. He wanted access to workshops and tutorials when he didn't yet possess the software."

Jonathon pulled the skillet off the stove and scraped the caramelized veggies onto the sliced cheese sandwiches. Next he wiped out the pan and flicked a slice of butter back into it. When it began to sizzle he lowered the two sandwiches into the hot pan and covered it. The sweet and savory smells drew a growl from my belly.

"By that night in Dubrovnik, Janko and I had known each other for two years. We finally reached a deal. I had agreed to send my liaison to the Dubrovnik clinic the following week."

I flipped the sandwiches.

"We finished eating, and Janko drank another scotch. His tongue became loose. He flirted with the waitress and discussed his love of women. When you arrived, he watched you—his eyes on you like a tiger selecting a gazelle from the herd. He began talking about you, wondering who you were. American? Local? What were you like in bed? He wanted to do things to you. I glanced over my shoulder at you and, yes, I was taken with you, too. But Janko seemed obsessed. He began to tell me about the women he liked. His preferred stock were soft. Pliant. Docile and demure. They did his bidding. His type was *submissive*."

Jonathon's head hung. The implications—what he and I understood—were clear. Now I understood why Jonathon needed the contract between us. It was an agreement that protected him. With the contract in place, he couldn't be implicated in anything abusive or felonious. He had covered his bases.

I pushed my wine glass away.

Jonathon stared at the sandwiches. "Janko sent the bottle of champagne to your table. He told me he would have you by the end of the night. And then he launched into all the ways he would get you to beg for him. I listened without judgement because at the time, I also enjoyed having someone submit to me. When you and I shook hands, you said you were from Chicago. Later, I researched your name. I learned everything I could about you and yes, I followed your activities and travels. I became worried Janko would somehow follow through with the menacing taunts, his unrealized overtures to you."

As the memory of that meeting reanimated in my mind, many things became clear. I thought I'd been imagining things like Jonathon stalking me. He had known things about me, like my tombstoning trips, that I'd never shared with my closest friends. I had been leery of him, yes, then let my feelings get the better of me.

Tendrils of smoke rose from the pan. Jonathon quickly pulled it off the heat and set it aside. He slid the grilled cheese sandwiches onto plates, cut them into triangles, then set one plate in front of me and another beside it. With his glass of Perrier in hand, he sat on the stool next to me.

"Smoked gouda grilled cheese sandwiches with caramelized onions and hot peppers. Grant taught me how to make them. I hope you enjoy it." A humble smile graced Jonathon's mouth.

"I'm ravenous. You could have made a bowl of cereal, and I'd have been happy." I sank my teeth into the crispy, aromatic bread and let the savory flavors mingle on my tongue.

His head hung and he still hadn't taken a bite. "I'm sorry for any angst I've caused you, Mina. The truth is, since that day, I've always tried to look out for you. Janko is a predator. And now I've done the unthinkable. I've lead you right to him."

"Oh, Jonathon." I put a hand on his thigh. Armed with these insights—to Jonathan's behavior and his past.

"I love you, Mina. I can't bear it if something were to happen to you," he said. His hand traveled to my back, his blue eyes locked on my gaze.

Clearly Jonathon loved me. Through his actions, through his words, I warmed to the truth. And still I hesitated. What would it mean if I were to dive from this cliff with him? Growing up, I'd had no role models for love. My mother died of ovarian cancer when I was four. My father pined for her as did my brothers and I. But I didn't know what it would mean to have love in my life. I was afraid, and cautious. "I—"

A loud knock on the door stopped me mid-sentence.

He put up a cautionary hand and looked through the viewing lens.

I swallowed. "Who is it?"

"One of my security team." Jonathan didn't open the door. Instead he dug into his back pants-pocket for his cell phone as apprehension rippled the muscles in his shoulders and back.

The person rapped harder on the door again, the tempo urgent. A man's voice—whom I didn't recognize—called, "Mr. Heun? Are you in there?"

"What's going on?" I hopped off the stool and joined him at the door.

Before answering, Jonathon swiped through screens on his phone. He glanced at messages and scrolled quickly through an email list.

"What are you looking for?" I asked.

"I missed a message from Erik about a half hour ago." He opened the door.

I recognized the man in my entryway at once from the warehouse. Fayed Almahn.

"Who is this?" I asked. I gripped Jonathon's arm.

Almahn was built like a line-backer, his wide shoulders and thick trunk rose from narrow hips and muscular legs. Black hair cut short matched his late-day beard growth. His pinched lips held something at bay.

"There was a shift change. Fayed works for me, too. He's spying on Janko and reporting back to me." Jonathon asked Fayed, "What is it?"

"You need to come with me now. Erik went on break and he's been shot."

~33~

onathon was paying Almahn to spy on Janko. Until that moment, I hadn't known how deeply Jonathon was investigating his frenemy. It was a light bulb moment. One that illuminated the kind of power money could buy.

Erik sat on a bed in his white undershirt and slacks. The glass privacy door was closed, and the white curtains shut out the emergency room nurses and staff working at their computers and bustling around. His shoulder and upper arm were bandaged, and he was in good spirits for having just taken a bullet through his upper bicep. His suit jacket, with a shredded, blood-soaked sleeve, hung on a hook on the wall.

"Missed the bone." Erik smiled.

"You're lucky," Jonathon said.

"All in a day's work," Erik said. "I know who shot me,"

"I do too. Janko called and took credit shortly after we heard the news." Jonathon sat in a swiveling chair with his hands on his knees. I stood beside him, one hand on his back.

"His car is in worse shape. I ran him off the road at the intersection of north Lincoln and Sedgewick. The driver hit a hydrant and their airbags deployed. I'm sorry to say the Alfa will need some repairs. They shot out two windows. They might have hit the coolant reserve, too."

Jonathon shook his head. "I'm not concerned with the damn car."

I asked, "Have you spoken with the police?"

Erik's white button-up shirt lay wadded on the bed beside him. Splattered blood stains had ruined it. "I came straight to the emergency room. Officer James came by the room and filed my report. I told him I worked for you and that you'd been threatened by Vorobiev, and a member of the local mafia. I didn't draw my weapon when they shot at me. I just tried to get the hell outta there."

"Was there anything else?"

Erik said, "Officer James confirmed the reports of gunfire and an accident at the corner of Lincoln and Sedgewick. Their car had ridden up onto the hydrant. When officers arrived at the scene, there was water everywhere, but no one was in the car. It had no license plate or tags. The VIN number was scraped off too, so there's no way to find the owner."

Jonathon said what I was thinking, "The mafia."

"Will the police track them down?" Erik asked.

"No. They have too many connections within law enforcement and government," Jonathon said. He stood. "Take the next few days off, Erik."

"Are you kidding? They came after me. Those foreigners sent you a clear message that I plan to ignore. I'll be at work in the morning, boss."

"You need to rest," I said. A navy blue and white sling held Erik's left arm.

"No way." He looked up at Jonathon with a smirk on his face. "I'm not leaving your side till this thing is over."

The beeps of hospital monitors and equipment played a soundtrack, reminding me how close Erik had come to dying and what Janko and his men were capable of.

As we left, Erik reiterated that he'd be back at the mansion first thing in the morning. Erik and Jonathon agreed to disagree.

The day had taken its toll on me. I yawned as we walked to the Mercedes, parked in the pick-up zone at the emergency room entrance. I glanced around at other cars, wondering which might hide another shooter. Janko threatened all our lives. Would Jonathon be next? Would I?

Almahn opened the car door, and I slid inside first. "What now?" I asked.

"I'll tell you what's next. We're going to sink their ship, Mina. Because you and I have the power to do so."

Almahn started the car as Jonathon sat beside me in the back seat of his black Mercedes. I tapped Jonathon's knee and pointed to the driver.

I whispered, "He's working for you. But today at the warehouse, he took the call. . ."

"Forget what you saw. Almahn is with me. He's helping me be one step ahead of Janko."

Jonathon refused to let Janko scare him into giving him the money. He had the money and power to do so.

Janko's deadline was in two days.

~34~

Harvey Slater had it in for my client, but why? Bohdi Michaels was a scapegoat and a snitch who may have laundered money for the Russian mafia. I wouldn't let Slater dictate Bohdi's fate, but much work needed to be done. Since I couldn't remain locked up and guarded at the Lake Forest house, Greg drove me to visit Angelique Sartre. She had turned my client over to authorities. I needed to find out what knowledge or evidence she had about Bohdi's involvement with the Russian mafia.

I caught up with her at Red Lace Escort Services. Her business offices were located in a high rise on Randolph Drive near the theater district. I pulled on a long chrome handle on a heavy glass door and Greg followed me into the lobby.

A perfectly groomed young woman with long white-blonde hair and deep burgundy lipstick stood at the polished chrome desk with a phone to her ear.

"Let me check," she said in a low-register, sultry voice. "Yes. Celine Divine is available on the twenty-third. I'll drop you into the schedule and let Celine know. One of us will reach out for details of the arrangement about a week before your event. Thank you so much, Doctor." She hung up and typed notes on the computer that I couldn't see behind the elevated desk.

Without glancing my way, she asked, "How may I help you?"

"I'd like to speak with Angelique Sartre. Is she available?" My briefcase hung heavily from my left hand.

The young woman looked over at Greg. "I'll need to check. What's your name, dear?"

"Wilhelmina Green."

Her attention moved from Greg, who sat awkwardly on an ornate, fuchsia loveseat that looked about as comfortable as a wooden bench. The whites of her eyes shown behind the lash extensions. She picked up the phone and pushed a button. "Ms. Sartre, a woman and her, um—"

"He'll wait here."

"Her name's Wilhelmina Green. Um hm. Are you sure? Okay." She hung up without a smile. "She says you can go on in."

I headed to a door beyond the desk. It opened before I reached for the handle.

The woman who stood before me wore a short pink dress that flared at her hips to show off her well-toned thighs. The lacy straps of her black garter belt peeked out beneath the hem of the dress, and they clipped to black stockings. She towered above me on white vinyl platform high heels that gave her unnecessary added height.

"Ms. Green?" She looked down her nose at me then over my shoulder toward Greg. "I'm Angelique Sartre. How may I help you?"

"I'd like to talk with you about Bohdi Michaels. I'm his defense attorney, and I believe you can help his case."

She looked me up and down, appraising my black skirt suit and white button-front blouse. Her gaze stopped on my thousand-dollar Valentino Garavani, rock-studded, caged black pumps. With a welcoming hand to indicate the way, she said, "I have nothing to hide. Right this way."

"Thank you."

I sat in a bright yellow-green chair covered in busy, Middle Eastern fabric. I set my briefcase on the floor and admired a painting of naked bodies twisted together on a red blanket. Yellow accents on the walls added variance to the cool upholstery colors. Huge windows offered a view of the glass skyscraper across the street.

"I love the color of your chairs." The style wasn't to my liking. I simply tried to make friendly conversation. I wanted her to feel comfortable enough to let down her guard.

"I just had it redecorated this spring. Bought all new, contemporary furniture and this antique desk. Chartreuse is all the rage these days. I love how it pops and catches your eye." Her fingers grazed the surface of the desk. She pushed aside a few papers that appeared at a glance to be contracts.

"My office needs upgrades. I just haven't had the time." I smiled and smoothed the arm of the chair with my hand. "So tell me. How long have you known Bohdanovyan Mykajlenko?"

"Bohdi and I have known each other for a long time." I noted she didn't skip a beat at the mention of his Russian name. A name he hadn't used in eighteen years.

"Would you consider him a friend?"

"Absolutely." She sat up tall, acting like she thought she held all the cards.

"If he's your friend, I'm trying to understand why you turned him in to the police. What did he do to deserve your punishment?" There was no better word for it.

"Punishment? No. Bohdi never made me angry." I began to notice a slight Eastern European accent the more she spoke. She hid it well.

I moved to the edge of my seat. "Then why did you tell the police he was guilty? Why did you tell them he was the person who invested your illegal income?"

She tipped her chin and tossed a wink my way. "A girl has to do what she must, no?"

I mirrored her pose and tossed a sly smile her way. As if we were friends, too. "Are you saying you told investigators what they wanted so your solicitation charges would be dropped?"

"I won't admit to that. My lawyer has advised me. Listen, Bohdi is part of the system, too. He's been involved for longer than I. He knew what he was doing when I invested with him at HC bank. He knew where the money came from. All that money he invests comes from the organization. Then it all goes into the big account overseas. I get my cut and he gets his." Her accent began to slip, a word here, a phrase there. "Only this time the feds came too close. They—the ones in the organization who make those decisions—wanted someone to take the fall this time. I heard about this, you know? And I decided that *someone* was not going to be me."

I dropped my gaze to my briefcase. She had just inadvertently admitted to working for organized crime. I didn't want to scare her off by writing notes, so I lifted my chin and watched her closely. "Who is your contact?"

Her thin smile stretched across surgically tightened skin. "Who is asking?"

I rubbed my palms together. "I'm trying to decide whether or not to put you on the stand at Bohdi's trial."

"I have nothing to say that will help my friend. Mr. Slater said Bohdi will go away for a long time." Her fingers pushed a loose black curl back into place.

I crossed my legs, dangling my studded pumps. "Harvey Slater can't promise that, and you know it."

She shrugged. "I have to believe what I'm told." Her half-closed eyelids showed off the blue jewel-tone on her heavily made-up eyelids.

"Did you know that Mr. Michaels is facing a possible jail sentence of twenty years? Is that what you want for your friend?"

"Does it matter what I want?"

I leaned forward. "It does, Angelique. Are you being threatened?"

Her complexion momentarily blanched. She lifted a hand to gaze at her deep red nails. "When Mr. Slater comes here, he gets what he wants. My boss says so."

"And who is your boss?"

Now she looked up at me. "Bohdi's going to jail, there's no way around it. I can't help you, Ms. Green. I can't help Bohdi."

"You can't or you won't?" I asked, then stood to go with my briefcase in my hand. "Angelique, who owns Red Lace Escort Service?" I knew from my research that Tsezar owned the lease. It was a logical conclusion that he also owned the business. At the very least, he had controlling or vested interest and had a say in the way things were run.

She didn't reply, and instead turned away. The back of her head faced me so I could count every hairpin that held the updo in her over-dyed and processed hair.

"I'll find out. Those are public records," I said.

I got the feeling she sought escape from an organization that held her in chains. With her gaze out the window, she softly said, "Konstantin Tsezar."

Hairs on the back of my neck stood at attention. "Thank you, Angelique. My paralegal, Christina, will be in touch. I'm going to use you as a witness."

"You are putting my life in danger."

"Am I? I think you'd give anything to get out of this business."

Her gaze dropped to her nails. To her lap. To the floor. "I can't. They own me."

The Russian mafia controlled Angelique's business. They dictated her life. Now was my chance to help someone who was clearly subjected by the system. "What would it take? Police surveillance? Witness protection?"

Angelique shook her head. "Don't make me take the stand. I can't help Bohdi."

"I can help you get out of this."

"No, Ms. Green. You cannot."

As I turned for the door, she said, "Nice shoes, by the way." As if she hoped the last-minute compliment would change my mind about her.

On the way down in the elevator, I called Christina and asked her for a subpoena to see a list of all Red Lace clients from the past five years.

~35~

ohdi Michaels's psychiatrist, Dr. Richard Beaman, worked and lived in a three- bedroom flat on the thirteenth floor of a high-rise close to Chicago's University of Illinois campus. He invited me into his bookish study.

"Welcome. Please sit down." He pointed to a brown leather divan along the side of his office.

I tucked my skirt under my thighs and seated myself. While pulling my laptop out of my briefcase, my gaze was drawn to the lamp on his desk. It might have been an antique and featured a short, black metal sculpture of a blackbird with some leafy foliage. Empty bird cages and four small paintings of birds graced the walls. Behind and in front of me, bookshelves were stuffed full of research material. I noticed many psychology textbooks strategically planted at eye level as if the certificates on his wall didn't give enough credence to his PhD.

"What can I do for you, Ms. Green?" In jeans and casual shoes, a blue pinstriped shirt and gray blazer, he sat across from me much like—I imagined—he would sit and listen to his patients.

"You must know why I'm here."

"You're Bohdi Michael's lawyer. But I'm not sure how I can help."

"I'm looking for character witnesses for the upcoming trial."

Beaman pushed a lock of light brown hair away from his glasses. "Character witness? Don't you mean expert witness?"

"No. Due to the nature of the charges, I'm sure you don't know much about financial planning and investment brokering. But I imagine, after five years of listening to Bohdi Michaels spill his personal problems in your lap, you have a good idea of his true nature."

"HIPAA."

He referred to the Health Insurance Portability and Accountability

Act that protected patient's privacy. "In a court of law, HIPAA won't protect his privacy. If the defense subpoenas those records, they'll be used, regardless. For now, I'm not asking you for a diagnosis or details into his private life."

"What are you asking me for, then?"

"Bohdi Michaels is scared. I'm here to protect him and help him in any way I can. I'm hoping for an acquittal, but with the evidence stacked against him . . ." *and,* I thought, *the prosecutor's unwillingness to work with me,* "I think the best we can get is a lowered sentence."

"I'm sorry to hear that." Beaman crossed his legs tightly—Eagle Pose in yoga—and placed an elbow on his thigh.

I said, "I'm trying to give Michaels some hope. But I'm telling you it's not looking good for him. He seems to have become someone's fall guy. That's why I need your testimony."

Hunched toward me, Beaman said, "Well . . . " and considered my request with three fingers massaging his chin. "I'll help you if I can."

"I need to understand the scope of your knowledge as it pertains to criminal behavior. Have many of your patients been criminals, Dr. Beaman?"

"I'm not at liberty to say. And please, call me Richard. However, the psychopathology of criminal behavior usually leads a person toward violent—not white collar—crimes. You must also know that persons with mental illness are much more likely to become victims of crime than perpetrators."

"I'm not sure where you're heading, Richard."

"Sometimes criminal behavior is a cry for help. In those cases, criminal intent can be simply part of their psychological profile. In other words, the patient has trouble discerning right from wrong."

"Has my client given any indication that he doesn't know right from wrong? Has he been diagnosed with mental illness? I'm asking because the prosecuting attorney will cross-examine you if I put you on the stand. He will ask you questions about your background and your degrees. He will grill you and try to disqualify all your credentials." I pointed to the certificates on the wall. "So for me to be Bohdi's advocate,

I need to know what's coming before the jurors do. I need to hear what you will tell them. So that I can present you *and* our client in the best possible light."

Beaman unwound his legs. "No." He took his time with the answer. "Bohdi has not been diagnosed with mental illness, per se. He's a victim of abuse. For the most part, that's what we discuss. I can't give you details, but Mr. Michaels has endured severe psychological trauma."

"Like PTSD?"

"Like that, yes. He's had several codependent relationships where he gives everything for very little or nothing in return. And I wonder if it's why he's fallen into this situation."

"Can you give me specific examples?"

"I cannot."

"When you're on the stand, you will be under oath. You may be forced to answer that question." I held my fingers poised to type his answer on my laptop.

Richard said, "He has lately felt threatened. He's paranoid and skeptical—no, not skeptical, distrustful. He's uncertain who's telling him the truth."

"Do you know why?"

"Why don't you ask him?"

As soon as we finished, I would. I changed the line of questioning. "In your opinion, would Michaels perform criminal acts if his life were in danger?"

"Wouldn't you?"

"No, I wouldn't." The backs of my legs stuck to the leather divan. I shifted my weight. "Tell me why you think Bohdi Michaels didn't go to the police when he had the chance."

Dr. Beaman looked at the floor and bounced his knee up and down three times. His palms flattened against his thighs, and he massaged his jeans, or maybe he was wiping the sweat from his palms.

He looked at me and said, "Someone killed his family. It was years ago, but . . . he believes the threat is still real. And I believe him. Look,

I'm not comfortable talking about this anymore. Subpoena the records, and I'll let you read them over."

"Will you take the stand?"

"Yes."

I closed my laptop and gathered my things. "Is there anything else I should know, Richard?"

"Take care, counselor. From what I've learned, he has every right to be afraid. He believes that there's no reckoning with the people he's involved with. To tell you the truth, the mere association with him scares me. Some of the stories he's told . . ." Richard shook his head. "The only reason I've kept Bohdi as a client is because I thought he deserved an ear. I've never felt I could help him escape from his past."

~36~

I removed my suit jacket before climbing into the air-conditioned Mercedes. Disheartened, I sank into the leather seat and looked at my phone. I called Bohdi Michaels, and he picked up on the second ring.

"Ms. Green?"

"I have a question for you."

Greg slid into the driver's seat and started to put the car in gear. I held up my hand, asking him to wait till I finished.

"Go ahead," Michaels said.

"I've just visited your psychiatrist—"

"Oh, Jesus!"

"—I need him as a character witness. So I asked him a few questions." Bohdi's reaction made me think he'd really opened up to his doctor. I suddenly worried what might be exposed if I put him on the stand.

"Why him?"

"Because Dr. Beaman is a respected professional who knows you well. Trust me, it's a good call."

"Okay," he softened. "I trust you."

"Slater would need a court order to have your records released. And I can see no reason your medical information would be necessary for this court hearing. But that doesn't mean Slater won't call for it. Bohdi, your personal life, your immigration status, and some of your discussions with your psychiatrist are going to get revealed during this trial. Slater is not going to be kind. We need to be prepared for it. *You* need to prepare for it."

Michaels coughed like I'd gutted him. "You said you had a question."

I pressed the phone to my ear and watched pedestrians cross the street. Gently, I said, "Dr. Beaman said your family was murdered. Why didn't you tell me that before?"

"It was a long time ago."

"Who is using violence and threats to coerce you?" I asked.

Bohdi paused for a long time. I heard his deep, irregular breathing on the other end of the call.

"Is it Konstantin Tsezar?"

"You know of him?"

"I do. Tell me the truth, Bohdi," I whispered into the receiver.

"Tsezar . . . He makes the calls. Some tough-guy does the dirty work. That's why they call it an organization. There are many, many . . . Oh, God." He wheezed, and I thought he was laughing.

"What did they do?"

"They . . . killed my sister. Before that, they killed my parents. I have few loved ones left, and I have told them to hide." He snorted and coughed. "But there is nowhere to go. . . Oh, God!" Bohdi coughed and then inhaled again. "What have I done? They're going to kill me, Ms. Green. They're going to kill my brother, his beautiful wife, and their three small children. I'll never be free from this!" He sniffed and coughed again, but then I realized it wasn't sardonic laughter. Bohdi Michaels was crying.

I tried to calm him down, but my heart raced. Tsezar had ordered this man's family to be killed. If that were true . . . We knew Janko was working with him.

Cold fear crawled up my spine. I looked at Greg. *My bodyguard.* And I hoped he could live up to the task. To build Bohdi's confidence and my own, I said, "They won't kill your brother, Bohdi. I'm not going to let that happen. I promise."

It's a promise I can't keep.

By the time I hung up with Michaels, he had sniffed away his tears. But the man was scared. His fear had rubbed off on me and my breathing grew shallow.

"Where to?" Greg asked.

"Not to my apartment."

"We'll return to the mansion. I'll have you safely home in no time."

Safely? If Tsezar could kill Bohdi's family in Europe, then how could I be safe? Chicago was Konstantin's playground.

Greg began to drive toward Lake Forest when my phone rang again. The sudden vibration sent a shrill of neurons firing up my spine. I relaxed as I checked caller ID. "Hi, Traci." A call from my friend might lighten my mood.

"How are you, girl? I miss you!"

"I miss you too." A quick smile curled my lips.

"Are you in Chicago? Do you have time to meet me at the Flea Market? I'm looking for a new necklace to go with a dress I bought."

Shopping with my friend sounded like just the lift I needed. "I'd love to, but isn't it only open on Sundays?"

"How long has it been since you've gone? This summer they're open Sunday and Thursday."

I was game for shopping therapy with Traci, and I offered to pick her up. "Do you need a ride?"

-37-

Jason had taken the last night shift and had the day off. Greg called Liam for backup. He'd been following us around town in another car—staying invisible—and I hadn't even known. He agreed to meet us at the market.

Traci and Greg chatted in the car on the way to the market while I changed clothes in the back seat. Just in case I ended up at home or at Jonathon's—I never knew these days—I'd brought a bright green spaghetti strap top and a blue jean skirt. I slipped out of my business clothes and removed my pricy pumps, switching to a pair of flat sandals. Instead of folding my white blouse, I put it on over the tank top and tied it at my waist.

Traci had pulled her hair up into a loose knot, which seemed a terrific way to get my long hair off my neck. I took a band out of my purse and emulated her up-do.

"When I told him who I worked for, he looked at me and said, 'Yes Mr. Hauser, I'll take care of it right away,'" Greg said, finishing his story. He and Traci both laughed.

Her melodic voice filled the car with joy, and it made my lips curl up.

Looking into the rearview mirror, Greg said, "It's nice to see you smile, Ms. Green."

The pair helped me forget my troubles. Even so, I said, "I'm not sure I'm going to be good company today."

"I had a feeling you needed me," she said, reaching into the back seat and placing a hand on my knee.

Greg parked in a ramp near the market. Liam got caught in traffic and called to let Greg know he was delayed. Greg insisted on parking and walking the mile-long strip with us, and I appreciated his presence.

The large flea market near Des Plaines supported vendors selling goods that ranged from produce and cut flowers, to hand-crafted items made by local artisans. An army brass band played jazz as we entered the row, and by this time of day, the market was shoulder to shoulder with people filling the street.

Paced by the slow-moving crowd, we made our way, sampling cheeses and fresh berries. Sweet bakery smells enticed Traci to buy a breakfast danish for tomorrow morning. I bought a loaf of warm cheese bread to take to Lake Forest for the weekend. She stopped at every jewelry vendor looking for just the right necklace to match her dress.

A stocky man wearing shorts that exposed tattoos covering both his calves pushed a double stroller in front of us. His blonde significant other held the hand of a girl, maybe six or eight, who ate a donut as they navigated the crowd.

Immersed in the spectacle of savory delights, artwork, and music, we nibbled and chatted about nothing and everything. We bought iced coffees and sipped them. Greg remained right behind us, watchful of everything around us.

"Have you told your dad about Jonathan?" Traci asked.

"No. I don't want to get his hopes up." Our relationship wasn't smooth-as-glass due to my career requiring me to help acquit criminals. Quite the opposite of his objective as a cop, and he made his strong opinions known. If I looked deeper, his voice was the one I heard when shame wrapped me in its death shroud.

"Did something happen between you and Jonathon?"

"No." I deliberately withheld details of Janko's threats from Traci. I didn't want her worrying. "Nothing happened. He says . . . he's in love."

I almost said the L-word, didn't I?

"And . . ."

"And what?"

"Are you?"

"Well, Jonathon offered refuge after Travis and Kanji Zhao attacked me, and I accepted. We're taking it slowly—" *Were we?* I couldn't mention that we were involved in this TOC situation with Janko "—because I'm not sure I have the same feelings."

"You're so analytical. He's a sweetheart! He's a freakin millionaire and he gives you the treatment in bed. What's not to love?"

"Okay." She'd drawn another smile from me. Jonathon was actually a billionaire, but what difference did that make?

"What are you doubting?"

"I want the happily ever after."

"After all this time, you found the man who fits your criteria. All those lists you made in college, you read them to me! I know you, Wil! Jonathon is perfect for you. I can't see you being satisfied with anyone else. And if what you said about him in bed is true . . ." Traci focused on a nearby hot pepper stand and didn't see the tattooed man in front of us stop to talk to his toddlers. She walked right into his back side, spilling her coffee all over the front of her pale-yellow silk top.

"Sorry!" he said.

His partner said, "Bummer." She stared at Traci's wet shirt until the toddlers grabbed her attention again.

"I'm so sorry," the man apologized.

Greg moved to our side. "Everything okay?" I was glad for his immediate response.

"I wasn't paying attention," Traci said. Then under her breath, she cursed. Dark coffee soaked her shirt.

I looked through my purse for a tissue or napkin as we stepped to the side of the slow-moving crowd.

A woman at the nearby pepper stand pointed us in the direction of running water. "There's a restroom inside the bank building," she said.

Traci said, "Thanks. Darn it, this shirt is brand new."

"We'll rinse it off, Traci." I led the way and Greg waited outside the building.

Inside the restroom I offered her the white button-front blouse I'd tied over a pastel green tank-top. Traci took off her coffee-stained top and doused it under cold running water, then wrung it out and put it in a plastic bag previously filled with cherry tomatoes.

As she tied the white blouse in a knot at her waist, Traci said, "It was an expensive shirt too, believe it or not."

"That was strong iced coffee."

"I like it that way. Strong and powerful." Traci winked at me in the bathroom mirror and pulled my white blouse over her shoulders. "I know you like that too. Jonathon's a great match for you."

"Is he?"

"I just want you to be happy. And I haven't seen you as happy as you are with him in a long time. Besides, now that I've found David we need someone to double date with."

"You're still with David?"

"Chalk off another week. Must be some kind of record, right?" she joked. Traci looked into the mirror while adjusting her loose up-do. We could have been sisters.

Back outside, I searched the nearby area for Greg, who wasn't beside the bank where we'd left him.

"Where's your watchdog?" Traci asked.

"Maybe he's using the bathroom."

I tried his cellphone, and it went to voicemail, which unnerved me. I called Liam next, and he was just arriving at the parking ramp. We waited for five minutes, and Greg didn't return. I looked up and down the street for him. Music from two live bands mingled and the heat gave me a headache. I was tired because for the past few days, I hadn't slept well.

Baskets of colorful peppers temped Traci, whose palette was stronger than mine. We strolled to the pepper vendor to sample sauces and dressings. Red peppers bundled with string hung from the tent awning. The woman who had helped us said, "Looks like you got your shirt all cleaned up."

"Oh, no," I said. I couldn't believe she had mistaken me for my friend.

"We switched. I don't know if that shirt will ever be the same," Traci answered.

"Ah, well. Can I get you anything?"

While keeping an eye out for Greg I dipped into salsa samples with pretzels and cucumber slices.

Traci pointed at a bowl of smallish light green, wrinkled peppers.

"You've discovered the hottest peppers in the world. They have a Scoville rating of nearly one million points. Try one." She pointed to a green bottle that looked deceptively cool.

Traci tasted it then fanned her mouth. "That will sure spice up my chili. Try some, Wil."

"No thanks." My tastebuds couldn't handle *the hottest pepper in the world.*

"I'll take a bottle." Traci smiled. "David will love it."

As the vendor took Traci's money and thanked her, Greg returned my call. He'd had no cell-phone service in the restroom. He insisted that I wait by the bank, but I told him to find us on the next block.

At the busy intersection, crowds pushed into us while we waited at the corner to cross. Over a dozen heads, I saw a traffic cop waving her arms. When she blew a whistle allowing our group to cross, people jostled me from all sides, separating me from my friend.

Across the four-lane street, I waited for Traci to catch up, watching a Black woman wearing a fancy red gown dancing to Cajun music as if mesmerized by the guitar's rhythm. Shiny red high heels clicked on the pavement. While I struggled to understand the words of the song, someone took my elbow. I expected Traci to be at my side. "There you are."

It was Greg.

"Where's Traci?" The anxiety pulsing through Greg's jaw panicked me.

I looked behind me for my friend. No Traci. I searched the faces nearby and looked for my white shirt. My friend wasn't nearby. She wasn't standing near the pepper stand across the street either. I thought perhaps she'd walked on, and I stood on my tiptoes to get a better vantage of the crowd.

Greg kept a grip on my arm as he looked left and right. "Did she cross the street with you?"

"I thought she did." I expected to see her brown up-do through the mob. Politely nudging my way between people, I dragged Greg to the next vendor's stand where a Chicago artist displayed his photography.

Still no sign of her. Exasperated, I dug my cell out of my purse and called. As it rang, we waited for the traffic cop to let pedestrians cross so we could go back the way we'd come. Traci's voicemail answered.

Once able to cross the street, we hurried back the way we'd come. Perhaps she didn't hear her phone. I called her again. Her voice mail picked up a second time.

Where are you?

A sea of shoppers moved past us, Liam among them. Sweat dripped down his temples as he rushed to meet us.

"I'm sorry I'm late."

"We're looking for Traci Lambert," Greg said. "You didn't happen to see her, did you? She looks a lot like Mina."

"No."

I dialed her number a third time. As I listened to her ring tone through my phone, and heard it echo in the distance. Greg and Liam were at my heels, and we walked upstream, against the flow of people, against the traffic and closer to the sound of her phone.

A guy wearing an orange t-shirt stooped over, disrupting the flow of pedestrians. He picked up a ringing cell phone.

The world shifted abruptly as I heard her voice mail pick up and moved toward the man holding Traci's phone.

"Is it yours?" I asked.

But I knew the answer.

~38~

I paced back and forth on either side of the intersection. Greg mirrored me on the opposite side of the street. Every white shirt caught my attention and every brunette. None of them were Traci.

The thought that she was wearing my shirt shook me to my core. Janko's threat—a day and a half until the deadline—Bohdi's murdered family. . . In my experience with Jonathon, missing women rarely returned home. Timing was crucial. We had to act quickly or risk losing my friend forever.

A half hour passed. If she'd been taken by Janko or abducted by the Russian mafia, they'd be far from here by now. We located a pair of police officers standing near a lamp post. I tried to remain calm as I told the story to a short female officer and her partner, an older Latino. I showed them Traci's scratched and stepped-on cell phone and brought up a photo of her on mine.

Officer Beth Roland took notes. She said, "Technically, we can't file the report until she's been missing for 24 hours, Miss Green. She could have accidentally dropped this without realizing it. You don't know that she didn't duck into a restaurant or catch a ride home. Maybe she'll borrow a phone and call you in a while."

Time was ticking. "I'm telling you something is wrong!"

The Hispanic officer looked away.

Inconvenient tears rolled down my cheeks. Panic kicked my butt.

Greg explained, "She's not overreacting. We need to take Traci Lambert's disappearance very seriously. The Russian mafia threatened Ms. Green. That's why she has me . . . I am her bodyguard." He appeared to be just as rattled by Traci's disappearance as I was.

I wiped the tears of frustration away as the unsympathetic officers radioed mounted police and nearby patrol cars to look for a brunette fitting Traci's description. None had witnessed suspicious activity.

Greg and I sat at a picnic table under a shady tree while we waited for responses. Liam paced in the distance. More than a hundred people passed us in fifteen minutes. Brown-haired women in shorts. Brown haired women in flowery dresses. Not one was Traci.

Officer Roland suggested the possibility Traci would call, fertilizing the expectation that flowered in my mind. It grew like a climbing vine and wrapped comforting tendrils around my darkest thoughts. I gazed down the street at a nearby restaurant. Could she have gone inside without me?

I gripped Traci's phone in one hand, mine in the other. When Jonathon's caller ID lit up my phone, I let it go to voicemail. Moments later he texted.

We need to talk.

I texted back.

Something happened. I'll call when I can.

Greg drummed his fingers on the table. He adjusted his slacks. Removed his earbud and reinserted it.

An additional half-hour passed before Officer Roland received a radio alert. All patrols reported back. Nothing unusual. She wrote up the report. Traci was here. Then, like a magic trick with mirrors, she was gone. I was terrified of what might become of my best friend.

Officer Roland said, "I'll follow up tomorrow morning. I've got your number."

The officers strolled away—all in a day's work—and Greg wanted to take me home.

But what if Traci returned? What if she emerged out of a restaurant or jewelry shop like Officer Roland said.

I refused to leave right away. For the next hour, Greg reluctantly waited with me, pacing between a large oak and the picnic table. Numerous times, he suggested we go.

"Go where?" I wandered back down the street and called her name until my throat felt as dry as the pavement. Strangers asked if I'd lost a child.

At the end of the day, I followed Greg back to the car. Jonathon texted me again.

Where are you?

I dialed his number.

"Mina, I'm so glad you're safe," Jonathon said.

"Traci is *gone*, Jonathon. She disappeared."

"What!?"

Greg opened the car door for me.

I explained what happened. "I'm worried sick about her." Iced coffee had burnt my insides leaving my stomach acid-singed.

"I'm so sorry, Mina." Jonathon's voice soothed my open wound. "We'll find Traci. I promise. I'll help you find her."

His compassion touched me, triggering tears.

"Come to Lake Forest. I might know where she is."

What did Jonathon know?

~39~

Fury scorched me inside. If Jonathon knew something about Traci's disappearance, he'd have hell to pay. Once we arrived at Lake Forest, I flew around the house looking for him. He wasn't in the kitchen, nor was Grant. The empty black leather desk chair in his office faced the window as if watching for someone to return.

Two at a time, I leapt up the stairs and opened the Kendo room door—hushed quiet. I exited quickly. Down the hall to my left, Jonathon's stark bedroom. I swung the door wide and let it crash into the wall behind it. *Benjamin Kyle* stared back at me.

"Jonathon?" I called.

No answer. Frustrated and angry, I backed out of the room and right into Jonathan's arms.

"Mina. I—"

"What the hell, Jonathon?" I backed away from him and faced him head on. "This is your fault!" I was furious. I was frightened. I was losing control.

"I'm so sorry." Jonathon didn't say a word in his defense. He looked me in the eye. "I'm calling FBI Agent Curbelo now. We need to inform *her*." Jonathon already had his fingers poised over his cell phone.

As he took control of the situation and spoke with the agent, I heard fear in his tone of voice. These people, Janko, Tsezar, and Rory frightened him. There was nothing that his money or prestige could do to hold their threats at bay.

He put the call with Agent Curbelo on speaker, and she recorded my statement. She and a team of investigators were on their way to Lake Forest. They would take Traci's disappearance very seriously.

Thick, end-of-summer humidity bathed us in its heavy atmosphere as the sun sank below the trees, dipping us in dark shade. Jonathon and

I stood on the patio outside the living room. He pulled out a chair for me, and though I was beyond exhausted, I didn't sit.

"I think I know who has Traci," he said.

"Who? Janko Vorobiev? Kostya Tsezar? You run with a sinister crowd, Jonathon." I stood with my arms crossed. Every muscle in my back and arms wrapped like rope around my furious bones.

"That's not fair. Neither Tsezar nor Janko is my friend," Jonathon said. Fire had finally lit behind those blue eyes.

I wanted to see more of it. More emotion. I craved his touch and his meanness and his anger. That rage was better than the passive, quiet man he had become. My arms remained crossed protectively around my chest. "You claimed that Rory, your old girlfriend introduced you to Janko—who, by the way, deals fentanyl to terrorists. Did she abduct Traci? It happened in broad daylight, Jonathon. In the middle of a crowded street for God's sake."

I said the words that had been eating at me all day. "Janko missed his mark."

"I think so. I've been putting off the transaction—wiring the money to Janko—hoping that time would help the FBI's investigation. Hoping their investigation would lead to an arrest."

"At what cost? They tried to kill Erik."

"A man has been arrested for it," Jonathon said.

"Not Janko."

"No." Jonathon faced me.

I sank into a chair. If hope was available to me earlier, it now crumbled like a child's wood-block tower. "Does Agent Curbelo know you were photographed with drug traffickers at an auction?"

"I've shared the details with her. They're using what little information I have to investigate Tsezar and his overseas associates."

My heart pounded in my chest. "You said you knew where Traci is."

"I have an idea. They could have taken her to the warehouse in the Russian Village."

"Why do you think that?"

"Janko called just before you arrived," Jonathon said.

"He did? What does he want? Is Traci okay? Is she—?" The word *alive* clung to the back of my throat, choking me.

Jonathon said, "He's not with Traci. His men realized they made a mistake and handed her off to someone else. He won't tell me who. Janko said I can't *'protect you forever.'* If they don't get the money by the end of the day tomorrow, they will kill her and come for you, Mina." Jonathon's hardened features showed willingness to battle his adversary.

"Let's go to the warehouse." I stood, anxious to rescue my friend. "We need to save her."

"No, Mina. We need to wait for Agent Curbelo."

"But if you're sure she's there—"

"I don't know for sure." Jonathon explained that when Janko called, there was a familiar echo to the room. He said, "We can't go there, Mina. Janko said he'll call to arrange a meeting and we need to let the FBI handle this."

I tried not to imagine all the things they might do to her. Evil deeds performed by many of my clients came to mind, and I was unable to suppress them.

Jonathon wrapped his arms around me. Maybe it was the look on my face. Maybe it was out of compassion. He held me as I burrowed my head in his chest, succumbing to fear and exhaustion, and I cried. He held me until the tears rolled down my cheeks onto his pressed burgundy shirt. When he'd wrung the emotions out of me, like squeezing the dishwater out of a sponge, he peeled me off him and we got to work.

~40~

Jonathon put Erik and his team on high alert. They called in more security. My friend Jeff in the Chicago PD called the Lake Forest PD and asked them to station cars throughout Jonathon's neighborhood. They were happy to provide police protection right away.

The investigation had begun. Traci had been missing for only eight hours, but time was ticking. If we couldn't find her in forty-eight hours, we likely never would. Janko's deadline for fifty million dollars was 24 hours away.

Grant fed me, I don't remember what, and Jonathon went back to his office to make calls. To arrange the transfer of money and sales of investment capital. Now, he didn't have a choice.

Though I was infinitely exhausted, I lay awake in bed for hours trying to make sense of what happened. I recalled the last conversation with my dad. He said, "You're the toughest woman I know."

But I felt weak.

Before dawn the next morning, the FBI arrived. I paced with a second—or was it third?—cup of coffee in my hand. Agent Teresa Curbelo steered everyone to their workstations. She guided and organized the entire setup. Since Janko said he would call again to arrange a time to meet, they placed phone taps and sensors all over Jonathon's house.

With the agents and the rest of the team, we waited for the call and devised a plan. While the others were occupied, Jonathon came to my side in the kitchen.

"Is there anything you need, Mina?" His eyes searched mine with a softness that melted my hard, outer shell.

Weary and drained of strength, I leaned a hip on a kitchen stool. "No. I just want things to return to normal."

Jonathan pulled up a stool and perched on it. "What would that be for you?"

I looked at the floor. "I don't know. Representing sexual predators in the Cook County courthouse. Escaping daily life to travel and tombstone. Going barhopping with my girlfriends." A million memories of Traci floated into my mind.

My brow felt heavy above my lashes. I ran a hand through my unwashed hair. "I should call our friends and let them know what happened. I just don't know what to say."

"Wait until we find her. We *will* find her. We *will* get her back." Jonathon placed a hand on my shoulder and his thumb circled around a tense, sore muscle.

I leaned into the massage. "You're right. I'll wait."

Agent Curbelo, her white shirt-collar ironed to a stiff point and her deep brown ponytail swishing down her back, found us in the kitchen. She said, "Though we don't want Jonathon to give any money to this TOC group, we need to ensure Ms. Lambert's safety and the safety of all involved. To find her, I'll be asking for more than your help. I'll need everything you can give." Her intense gaze narrowed in on Jonathon.

He didn't shrink in her headlights. Jonathon said, "I'll tell you everything."

"First, let me tell you what we discovered," Curbelo said. "A week ago, an officer saw a van parked near the Lake Forest subdivision and asked the driver to move on. He wrote up a report after speaking to the driver, Malec Krolo, a Croatian immigrant. This morning, patrol officers found the abandoned van in a gas station parking lot near the Russian Village."

Jonathon asked, "Did they find the owner of the van?"

"No. They scrubbed the van for DNA. Forensics are testing hair samples, syringes, and empty vials."

I said, "It might be a long shot, but then again. . . can you find out if the owner is connected to the Russian mafia or to Janko Vorobiev?"

"We can and we will," Curbelo said.

I said, "I'm worried that Traci will be trafficked by those men. You have no idea what Janko's capable of."

"We're aware of Vorobiev's past, Ms. Green. He's worked with Konstantin Tsezar for almost five years. Interpol is building a case against him even as we speak. When Vorobiev calls, we'll be ready," Curbelo said. Her gaze pinned me and Jonathon. "Keep your phones with you at all times."

I inadvertently glanced at my phone on the counter. I had no new messages or calls but unlocked it and scrolled through my recent phone calls while the agent and Jonathon talked.

Curbelo nodded. "It's clear that Vorobiev and Tsezar aren't above trafficking."

Jonathon said, "Janko *thought* I'd be interested in what he sold."

"Why did he think that Mr. Heun? What might you have said to lead him to that conclusion?" Curbelo asked.

Jonathon stood up taller.

"I'm not sure. Rory Bradford, an ex-girlfriend introduced us. She works with health care systems in Europe as a translator. Somehow, she's involved with this too. They're making fentanyl and distributing massive quantities to US cities. I refused to be part of it, but I'll tell you everything I know."

"You run with a sinister crowd, Mr. Heun." Her words echoed my own.

"I believe Janko will murder Traci to prove his power over me."

His statement chilled me.

"We can't let that happen," Curbelo said. She placed a hand on my arm. "We're doing everything we can to bring your friend home alive, Ms. Green." The agent began pacing with her hands on her hips. "The situation is potentially deadly—especially for Lambert—and we're being cautious. I'm working with the Foreign Corrupt Practices investigative team and the DOJ. The FBI's International Corruption Unit head the investigation. You and Prevail Pharmaceutical Software are protected under the FCSA."

I argued, "But my friend Traci is not. No act or law enforcement agency can help her if you can't find her."

She turned to Jonathon. "Mr. Huen, you said you thought Janko called from the old Koval warehouse, so we're sending in a SWAT team. If he is there, if your intuition is right, they will find Traci and take Vorobiev into custody."

This news settled my nerves a little bit. "I hope they find them," I said. I would gladly trade places with Traci. There was nothing Janko could do to hurt me that he hadn't already done.

~41~

The sun rose over Lake Michigan, and early morning mist evaporated. I looked at the clock on my phone. Thirteen hours and seventeen minutes had passed since my best friend vanished. Optimism was difficult to conjure.

When Jonathon's cell phone rang from inside his office, he leapt to his feet. Tracing software had been installed in both our phones to identify the cell towers that relayed the next call. I followed him, anxious that this was the call we awaited.

Agent Curbelo and Agent Morris Holt were standing by. They moved out of Jonathon's way when he entered his office. Agent Holt worried a toothpick between thin lips and slicked back his thinning hair with stubby fingers. Every eye in the room watched as Jonathon lifted the phone to his ear. Curbelo stood right next to him as he placed the call on speaker and answered, "Janko."

"My old friend."

"I am *not* your friend. Where is Traci Lambert?"

"Do you think I'll tell you anything? You broke the rules of engagement, Jon."

Jonathon's black eyebrows merged. "How?"

Janko's voice grew louder. "You sent a fucking swat team."

Jonathon looked at Curbelo who steadied her gaze on the phone. He said, "You kidnapped Traci Lambert. What did you think, Janko? That I'd sit here and do nothing?"

Curbelo looked at Jonathon and patted down air with both hands.

Tone it down. We're in negotiation.

Curbelo nodded and wrote something on a piece of paper for Jonathon. He read it and said, "Put Traci on the phone."

Janko laughed wickedly. "I can't do that. She hasn't woken from her beauty rest."

I strode forward, placed my hands on the desk, and blurted out, "What have you done to her?"

Janko asked, "Is that Ms. Green? Tell her, Traci is beautiful. If only she were younger . . . But she will fetch a fair price." Janko's calm, musical voice angered me.

I held back. Held my breath and cringed.

Janko said, "I want that money, Jon. I want one million in cash in the form of unmarked bills, and I want it by noon. Wire the rest, forty-nine million, to the account number I will send through an encrypted email."

"The deadline is tomorrow morning. I won't send the money until I know she's alive."

"You don't have room to negotiate. The woman will die."

Jonathon's face purpled with rage. "Tell me where to meet you with the cash."

Janko hissed like the slithering snake he was. "You bring the money to my associate by noon."

Jonathon glanced at a painting hung on the wall. Curbelo's hawklike eyes followed his. "I can wire it to you on the phone right now. I just need to know that Traci is alive."

"Not so fast. You will hand the money to my associate. As soon as she acknowledges receipt, then she will tell you where to find Ms. Lambert."

"You've fucked with me from the start, Janko. How do I know you'll keep your word?" Jonathon growled.

"Because I still have photos of you at the auction. I can prove that you placed bids on four hundred pounds of fentanyl."

"I did not!"

"You want this evidence destroyed, I imagine."

Jonathon's lip curled. "That's no promise."

"Meet her at 201 West Madison Street."

I knew this address.

"Come alone, Jon. Just you and your Mina. If I hear one word about police or swat teams in the building, Traci will die. If I see one cop car on Madison Street, Traci will die. If you two are not alone, Traci will die. My associate is waiting on the twenty-seventh floor."

"Will Traci be there?"

"Trust me, my friend." A click indicated the call had ended.

Agent Holt rushed out of the room and Curbelo called out, "Agent Matz! Did we trace the call?"

I blurted out, "She's at Red Lace Escort Service. Konstantin Tsezar owns the lease for their office space. His contact must be Angelique Sartre."

"Are you certain?" Curbelo asked.

"Yes. I was just there . . . yesterday." So much had happened in the past twenty-four hours that it was hard to fathom. I'd met with Angelique only yesterday.

Jonathon reached for an abstract painting on the wall and removed it to reveal a steel-gray wall safe.

"Matz?" Curbelo called one more time.

"We got it!" Agent Matz collided with Curbelo in the doorway. "The call came from a car driving southbound on I-90 just outside of Chicago. We're still following the car with cell tower tracking software."

"Notify all law enforcement in the area. See if we can stop him," Curbelo said.

"On it." Matz said.

I said, "Janko was at the Koval building. He must have been."

"He knew the team was there." Curbelo made a call and stepped out of the room. Moments later, she returned and confirmed that the swat team had indeed arrived in the Russian Village.

"People in that village watch out for one another. Someone tipped off Janko and he fled," I said.

After removing stacks of one hundred dollar bills from the safe, Jonathon closed and locked it again. He filled a black leather duffle bag with the bills.

Curbelo said, "Come with me. We'll outfit you with vests and a micro-transmitter. Ms. Green, Vorobiev asked for you to be there. Since we don't know his motives for asking for you, I can't let you go."

"Agent?" Jonathon asked.

I said, "It was clear to me that Janko wanted me there."

Darkly, she said, "I can't allow it."

I matched her grave tone, "He'll kill Traci if I don't go. I want to be there when we find her."

"And I'm not going *anywhere* without Mina," Jonathon said.

—42—

A heavy-set man in a black suit opened the tall glass doors of Red Lace Escort Service for us. I recognized him as the man who—weeks earlier—handed me the titanium business card with Bohdi's number. He pulled back his jacket and showed us his pistol. I followed Jonathon into the brightly lit office, where two other thugs were waiting. One stood near the office door with his automatic rifle in hand. One had been reclining on the fuchsia loveseat and when we walked in he sat up at attention, pointing his Uzi our way.

I had left my Browning with Greg. Curbelo had outfitted us both with bullet-proof vests. The heavy armor made my breathing shallow. I wore the micro-transmitter—a necklace that looked like a tear-drop pendant—because Curbelo was afraid Jonathon would be frisked.

"Ms. Green," the heavy man said. "'Dis way." He pointed to the hall that lead to Angelique's office but didn't follow us. I understood now that the organization wanted me to represent Bohdi because they didn't think I'd win. They had another thing coming.

The door to Angelique's office was open. She sat at her desk with her gaze out the window. Her sleek updo without a single stray hair glistened in the daylight pouring through the window.

"You're working *for* Tsezar," I said.

"A side gig." Angelique spun in her chair. "I told you, you can't do anything for me." Her gaze went immediately to Jonathon and slid down and up his body, stopping at his crotch. "This must be Jonathon Thomas Huen. I'm surprised we've never met. Your taste in women must be unusual."

"I have no use for what you're peddling," he said.

She shot a look at me and stood, kicking the desk chair out of the way. A tight black bustier pressed her round breasts upward. The black pants she wore had a dull sheen like leather. Her arms straightened and in her clasped hands, a handgun I couldn't identify aimed at me.

Soviet issue?

"The money?" she asked.

Jonathon set the duffle bag near her feet. "Here it is. Tell us where Traci is."

"When I'm sure this is what Vorobiev wants, I'll tell you where to find Ms. Lambert." She stooped and tentatively unzipped the bag, keeping her gaze on us and the pistol aimed at my head.

"What made you turn, Angelique? Was it money? Did Kostya offer you escape from his chains?"

The cold hard glint in her eye told me not to fuck with her. "Shut up," she said. "Down on the floor! Both of you. On your bellies." The weapon didn't quaver in her hand.

I looked at Jonathon, and his hurricane gaze fired at her. "Do what she says, Mina." He lowered to one knee. As a skilled fighter, Jonathon had agility and speed at his immediate disposal. I trusted him.

I dropped to my hands and knees and turned to face Jonathon. The tension built in his body as he held back for good reason. We still didn't know where Traci was.

Jonathon's well-manicured fingers met the ground beside me. "Tell us where she is," he growled. Tension poured off him like vapor from dry ice.

Once Jonathan was flat on the ground, Angelique sat at her desk. From the floor, I could only see her glossy red stilettos as she typed a fascinating rhythm on the computer keyboard.

"As soon as I verify the rest of the money has been wired to Janko's accounts, I'll give you your friend's location," she said. She typed a flurry of words. "Why does it say the deposit is pending?"

Jonathon looked up. "The bank can't transfer that amount in a few hours. They have to gather the funds from investments and holdings."

"How long will it take?"

"Up to ten business days. That's why Janko wanted the cash. It was for security."

She unplugged the computer, shot out from behind the desk, and fired her gun at the computer, reducing it to pieces of twisted metal. With two hands, she grabbed the heavy duffle bag.

Jonathon touched my arm. He squeezed. A signal to hold back. We needed to wait. Patience would give us Traci's location.

Angelique dragged the bag toward the door. Her hand was on the knob as she said, "The FBI will arrest Vorobiev as soon as they catch him. Tsezar will not be implicated. Only Vorobiev."

"How can you know this?" Jonathon asked.

"I have my sources."

I wondered who.

She opened the door. "There's a note in the top drawer of my desk telling you where to find your friend. She has been drugged."

"With fentanyl?" I asked.

"Possibly." She nodded. "Probably."

My heart wept for Traci, but I held my emotions back.

"Don't try to follow me." She turned her back on us and closed the door.

Jonathon leapt to his feet and followed her out. As I rushed to the desk and opened it, I heard the men shouting from the lobby. I pushed aside papers and pens to finally find a folded piece of paper with an address, which I read out loud, hoping the agents listening would hear me.

More shouts from the lobby followed Angelique's shrill cries. "Stop him!"

The sound of gunfire exploded. Glass shattered and something heavy hit the floor. I cowered behind the desk for several minutes until the noise ceased. "Jonathon?" I called.

Since there was no response, tiptoed out of the office. One man lay wounded on the floor, his gun and everyone else were gone.

Where is Jonathon?

I ran out through the double glass door toward the elevator. The second gunman was collapsed face-down on the floor in the elevator bay. Blood pooled beneath him. Jonathon, Angelique, and the foreigner I'd recognized were not standing by, but the numbers above two elevators ticked downward. One ahead of the other. I had to assume Angelique and her bodyguard were in one, Jonathon in the other.

"Curbelo?" I spoke out loud, hoping she would hear me through the transmitter. "They've gone down the elevator. Can you meet them on the ground floor? I think Jonathon is following them. Angelique has the cash."

I had no idea if she heard me or not, the transmitter was a one-way device.

By the time I made it down twenty-seven flights, the agents had handcuffed Angelique and her thug outside the building. Jonathon standing by, rushed to my side.

"You're not hurt?" I asked.

"I'm fine. Did you get the location?"

"I did."

Agent Holt approached. "We have the location on GPS. Come with me."

~43~

The FBI had initiated a car chase. Agents had locked on Janko's vehicle as he fled the city. The last we heard, five vehicles were in pursuit near I-290 and the I-350 interchange.

On the way to the address where Traci was held, Agent Holt told us that the location was a known underground brothel. Exigent circumstances and the threat against Traci's life, gave us permission to enter the building without a warrant. The smell of wet cardboard and rodents hit me as we burst through the weathered door of the old brownstone. The building appeared to be vacant.

Agent Holt entered ahead of me, his weapon out like a divining rod. Jonathon and Greg flanked me. Curbelo and two others had our backs. Our hollow footsteps echoed through the old floorboards. Agent Holt lead us to a stairway where a rat slinked away.

Holt and I took the stairs two at a time. We reached the top floor, where a hallway lead to five bedroom doors.

He methodically called out, "This is the police, we're looking for Traci Lambert." When no one answered, he opened the first door with his pistol raised. A cot lay on the floor where a thin young woman peered up at us, her watery gaze full of awe. She was not Traci.

One by one, we opened the rooms, finding five young women and two young men. All appeared to be abused and under the influence of drugs. Outside, sirens grew louder as the police and paramedics we had alerted began to converge on the building. The final door was bolted.

"Stand back," Holt commanded as he shot the deadbolt off the latch. Wood splinters flew across the hall and fell to the ground. He entered first, with his elbows locked and his weapon out front.

My eyes took a few seconds to adjust to the darkness and my heart pounded out an entire etude in the lengthened moment. I couldn't tell if the growing siren sounds were inside or outside my head. In those terrible moments, I doubted that Janko and Angelique told us the truth. I doubted we'd find Traci alive.

My gaze stabbed through the dusty air.

Where is Traci?

There in the corner. A blanket.

Holt rushed toward her first. I skidded to Traci's side and dropped to my knees.

"Traci! Are you okay?"

No response.

Her body was limp and unresponsive, but warm. The agent checked her pulse. My heart thudded in my clogged throat. Tears dripped off my chin.

Jonathon was at my side. His hand around my waist.

Paramedics backed us away. They checked her vitals, started a saline drip, then took her away on a stretcher.

<h1 style="text-align:center">~44~</h1>

A quarter-mile procession of vehicles and police squad cars followed Gary Underwood's black hearse into Crown Point, Indiana. Old oaks and fruit trees stood sentinel over perfectly rounded shrubs and headstones. Calumet Cemetery Park, with its green lawns and water features, was a gentle resting place for the kind and beloved man.

Jonathon and I arrived in the middle of the procession of cars. Erik parked the Mercedes on the lawn behind Tig Wallace's orange Corvette. Behind us, a seemingly unending train of cars followed suit, parking where they could. Ahead of us, dozens of funeral attendees—policemen in uniform, women in dark, flowing dresses, family, and friends—had exited their cars and were walking toward the mausoleum where Gary, in a simple cremation urn, would be laid to rest. Gary, a former Chicago cop, had touched many lives.

Jonathon held my hand as we walked beside Tig and his years-younger second wife. Erik and Greg followed a short distance behind, then they stopped beside the thick trunk of an old maple tree. We continued ahead to the rows of folding chairs that extended out to a fountain. The centering sound of flowing water calmed my nerves and reminded me of many waterfalls and cliff-diving sites, my solitary escape.

We walked up the grassy lawn to a marble vault where Gary's brother, father, sister, and her family greeted guests. Near an opened vault, a shiny black urn rested beside bouquets of white lilies and colorful cut flowers. I shook Gary's father's sun-spotted hand.

"Mr. Underwood," I said. "I'm so sorry for your loss. Gary and I worked together for seven years. I considered him a good friend."

Gary's father glanced from me to Jonathon, holding my hand between his long cool fingers. "What's your name, dear?"

"I'm Wilhelmina Green. Gary had been working on my case when he was murdered. I promise you I'm doing everything I can to bring those criminals to justice." Heat rose in my throat, and I swallowed back tears.

The elderly man's kind eyes wrapped me in warmth. "I'm so sorry, Wilhelmina. But please don't feel guilty. You know Gary loved his work."

"If I had only known . . ."

If I had understood how dangerous those men were. If I had investigated them myself. If I hadn't asked Gary to look into it. If I had trusted Jonathon more . . .

The ifs kept coming.

Gary's father said, "I'm certain there was nothing you could have done. Gary would have put himself on the line for any of you."

Jonathon stepped forward and spoke his condolences. Mr. Underwood let go of my hand and shook Jonathon's. He looked up at Tig, who stood behind me, and embraced him. "Tig Wallace, thank you for coming."

"Gary was a trusted friend, Mr. Underwood. I'll sincerely miss him," Tig said.

Jonathon took my arm, and we made our way to a seat near the back of the assembly. He said in a low tenor voice, "I'm here for you. Let me know if there's anything I can do, Mina."

"Thank you, Jonathon. I'm sorry to be so emotional. Gary's murder is my fault." I swiped tears from my cheeks.

"Don't apologize." Jonathon reached into his lapel pocket and handed me a travel pack of tissues. As I took the packet from him, he captured my gaze with kind, forgiving eyes.

Jonathon's strong arms had held me when I told him the news of Gary's murder. Now, his silent presence beside me at Gary's funeral soothed me. I knew Jonathon loved me. More than ever, I longed for the sting of his whip to take me away from the sense of responsibility and blame that I placed on myself.

Agent Holt had promised to call when Janko was captured. Instead, he informed me that when the FBI had apprehended the vehicle, Janko wasn't inside. He'd moved the tracer to an innocent woman's car. Janko was still missing and the pending deposit of forty-nine million to Janko's account was canceled.

I visited Traci before and after she was released from the hospital. The sight of her, roughed up and still shaken, saddened, and angered me. My best friend's face showed signs of her struggle. No doubt she'd fought her captors and tried to get away. A swollen black eye and fresh red bruise bloomed on her high cheekbone. Her captors had injected her with fentanyl-laced heroine, an extremely high dose, and raped her.

I gazed off at a distant fountain and my eyelids filled with tears. Anger for what they'd done to my friend. And sadness for the loss of a trusted friend. Tears dripped onto my dress, and I found myself thinking of tombstoning. I wanted to curl my toes over the rocky cliff near Stiniva beach. I craved those seconds in midair with the water's surface rushing toward me.

Quiet mourners arrived by the dozens. Police officers from Gary's days in the Chicago PD shook hands with Gary's father. Gary's ex-wife and their two sons sat in the front row. My entire firm had come to grieve. Christina and Troy hugged me. I didn't know if they could sense that I shrouded myself in guilt.

"Mina," Jonathon whispered. His gaze was on a woman sitting a half-dozen rows in front of us. Her brown hair was scooped into a loose bun on the top of her head. "That's my friend Elaine Goodman. She's the senior editor at the Chicago Tribune. We've emailed back and forth, and she knows I'm here with you. We'll talk with her when this is over."

After Gary's family finished speaking loving words, mourners proceeded to lay single white roses in front of his urn. Jonathon searched for Elaine as I spoke my condolences to Gary's brother and sister. Groups of friends clustered on the lawn or made their way back to their cars.

I caught up with Jonathon and Elaine who had moved away from the service. Jonathon introduced me.

Her green-gray eyes assessed me. She was older than I thought. Probably in her forties. She wore a form-fitting sheath dress and high heeled shoes that sank—like mine did—into the turf.

She said, "I'm so sorry about your friend Gary. His murder must have been a shock."

"Thank you. It was." I shook her hand in greeting.

"I've heard so much about you," Elaine said. "One of the journalists on my team covered the Peterson trial earlier this summer. He has great admiration for your skill in the courtroom."

We moved toward a sidewalk where we could both stand comfortably.

"How do you and Jonathon know each other?" I asked.

Elaine smiled. "I've reached out to Jon many times for interviews and private meetings."

"You made yourself known to me. There's no denying that," Jonathon said with a glimmer in his eye.

"I'm a journalist at heart, Ms. Green. And also a single woman." She touched his arm.

"And I've always said no," he said. Their playful, friendly banter showed their respect and admiration for each other.

She said, "I didn't feel completely defeated until you entered his life."

They both looked at me. Jonathon dropped his chin with lips tightened in agreement, and he gave a subtle nod.

All the clues were there—Jonathon loved me and even Elaine knew it. He had professed his love.

Am I capable of giving him more?

He'd made many sacrifices for me and Traci. After Angelique's arrest, Jonathon donated the million in cash to the Lake Shore Women's Shelter. He wanted to donate it in my name, but instead, I talked him into donating the goodly sum in Traci's name.

We had reached the paved walkway and headed toward the cars parked along the cemetery drive. Elaine said, "Jon tells me you have a story you want published."

"We do. Gary was killed looking into a case for me. However, the risk in exposing the killers is very great. We're treading on dangerous territory. Some of these people wield great power, and I'm just beginning to see the fringes of their reach. It frightens me, Elaine. It will take some savvy investigation and journalism, but I think we need to do it."

"It sounds juicy. I've never been one to shy away from dangerous men," she said, peeking around me at Jonathon.

I smirked. "Jonathon's not dangerous." I could say that now that I knew how kind and generous he was.

"No?" Her gaze seemed to undress him from top to bottom, and I had the sudden urge to step between them and claim Jonathon for myself.

Unfazed, Jonathon continued, "This story needs to reach the public so they can judge for themselves. Do you have time, today, to listen to Mina's story? Can we go someplace private to discuss it?" He inadvertently looked over his shoulder.

Flanking us, Erik with his arm in a sling and Greg standing tall tailed our movement from several paces away. Their dark glasses hid eyes that I knew were scanning the crowd.

Elaine said, "Let's walk." And she led the way.

We strolled along a paved path that curved around the pond. Erik and Greg remained about ten paces behind us. She said, "One of my team members covered Gary's murder investigation. She knew it was an execution-style shooting, something the police didn't want her to publish. The police tried to shut down our journalists before the story was released. The open investigation and blah, blah, blah."

I asked, "What happened to freedom of speech?"

"The FBI warned her that other lives were in grave danger. My journalist received a handful of threatening voicemails warning her about publishing the article. When she didn't stop looking for answers, her apartment was ransacked. She was frightened because whoever did it let her cat out. She thought it was dead."

"Was it?" I asked.

"No, the cat came back days later. But by then, my journalist was done with her investigation."

"Who did it?" Jonathon asked.

"She didn't know," Elaine answered. "She reported it to the police who said it looked like a random robbery. The coincidence was too ominous."

"Let's take our story from another angle, then," I said. "Gary stumbled upon something that local businessman, Konstantin Tsezar was involved in," I said. "We think it's why they executed him."

Jonathon added, "The FBI is investigating Tsezar, he's connected to the Russian mafia."

Elaine said, "If what you're saying is true, we need to cover this story. Those men need to be exposed, and I know just the writers to do it. I'll put my best team on it right away."

~45~

I spent a week in Chicago, visiting Traci and diving into work. I avoided Jonathon because I needed time to think things through. Jonathon said he loved me. He'd done everything in his power to help find Traci. Then he donated the one million dollars to the battered women's shelter.

I needed to go to him. I needed to see if he could give me what I wanted.

I stepped into the dimly lit Lake Forest house with my agenda at the forefront of my mind. With the FBI team gone, an unusual sense of quiet had settled over the house. Security guards hung around quietly minding their own business, yet ever watchful.

The scar on my leg ached.

I dropped my things in the bedroom and went to the one place where my dark fantasy could be realized. Where the security guards would *not* be. The dungeon.

In the basement, I pushed open the unlocked door to Jonathon's playroom. As if he'd been expecting me, red nightlights on two walls cast long shadows of the X-rack and a coffin-sized cage. My eyes adjusted, and I stepped inside. Low music played on the sound system. I recognized Carl Orff's *Carmina Burana* from the concert Jonathon had taken me to this summer. The dark oratorio fit my mood.

My knees weakened. The room represented everything I thought I wanted—needed—from him. I thought it assuaged my guilt. But I began to see beyond the veil. In his eyes, I was not the same person who I saw from the inside. In his eyes . . . *He loved me.*

A rustle of cloth behind me caused an icy shudder to ripple across my shoulders. I turned.

"How is Traci?" Jonathon's black silhouette blocked the doorway.

"She's improving but it will take time. Our friends are taking care of her, and I'm helping as much as work will permit."

"Be careful, Janko's still out there."

"I know." I threw the words at him like stones. I didn't want to discuss Traci or Janko or police protection or to be reminded of harsh realities.

He stepped into the room. "I've missed you."

"You've been texting ten or twelve times a day."

"You didn't answer. I had to ask Greg how you're doing."

We were steeped in darkness that blackened my thoughts. "I needed time."

He took another step toward me. "And have you had enough . . . time?"

He expected me to say something. So I put our game back into familiar terms. The peak at Navaho Falls, Arizona. Red clay earth beneath my bare feet. Sun-warmed stones heating the air. Cerulean blue waters of the lake below. I took a big breath, imagined my arms sweeping outward and my knees bent, and asked for what I wanted. "I want—" My gaze swept the red room. "This. I need you and . . ."

Jonathon shifted his weight. I couldn't tell if he reacted favorably or disdainfully.

Did I need to explain?

I said, "I blame myself for what happened. I need to atone—"

"Mina, listen . . ." He shifted his weight again and looked at the floor.

"No, Jonathon. You listen." I placed my hands on my hips. "There was once a promise between us. You even drew up the contract to illustrate all the possibilities. I need something from you now, and you must give it to me."

"I must do nothing," he whispered.

His superiority pissed me off. "Why torture me this way?"

"What way? How am I torturing you?"

"How?" I longed for his anger. His painful slaps. His punishing gaze. I ran at him with my fists flailing. Jonathon caught my wrists as I lunged into him. He let go as I pounded on his chest. The more violent I became, the more rage poured out of me.

"Mina, stop!"

I pushed him away and spat, "Fuck you!"

"Is this how you want it?"

Did he need to ask? "Yes! I'm begging for it!"

Jonathon released me and backed away. "Fine. Take off your clothes." He flicked on some low lighting then closed and locked the door using the interior keypad.

I wouldn't be able to leave if I wanted to, but that was okay with me. Anger had simmered long enough. I reached a boiling point and planned to put up a fight. In my chest, my heart pounded as I kicked my skirt to the floor.

Low music swelled. Jonathon tore a long bullwhip from a hook on the wall and slung it over his shoulder. Lightening shot out of his cold blue eyes. "Climb up on the bed and kneel."

Bitter words erupted from my lips, "As you command, my *master.*" My blouse fell off my shoulders. I knelt on the blood-red satin bedspread.

Unexpectedly, Jonathon came at me. Before I could think to react, he held my wrist twisted in a lock behind my back. "Shall I remind you the meaning of the word submissive?" He pressed my twisted arm into my back and pushed me face first onto the bed. Pinned there, I heard the familiar jingle of hand cuffs. Cold metal zipped closed and locked on my right wrist.

I spun fast, faced him on one hand and my knees. I tried to twist away and swung my left palm to slap him. Jonathon caught my wrist mid-air. I kicked him in the side with all the force of one coiled-up leg.

He huffed a sound like I'd knocked the wind out of him and let go of my free hand. His grip remained tight on the handcuff, but he stopped to stare at me. Never had I seen Jonathon this angry before. He was poised and steady though and seemed not to be breathing.

I, on the other hand, panted with quick shallow breaths.

He said, "You've lost already. Give me your other hand, and I won't hurt you."

"Bullshit." I nodded at the whip, which had fallen on the floor.

His brow creased. "Give me your hand."

"No. Fuck you, Jonathon."

He smiled wickedly. "It's what you wanted. We're doing this *your* way."

My way?

His features relaxed, looking less enraged with each passing moment. He kicked the whip farther away and beckoned me closer. "I'm not going to hurt you. I promise."

I gauged each nuance—the tone of his voice, the crease in his brow, the muscle twitching in his jaw.

"Give me your hand."

Had his anger abated? Mine had not. I wanted his stormy outrage. I wanted to feel his fury and his passion. Hoping to draw more from him, I slapped his smooth cheek. Jonathon caught my wrist on the recoil. His lips pressed together as he pinched the cuff closed, locking my hands together in front of my body.

My slap had drawn a rosy handprint on his cheek and an inward smile from me.

"Now I'll give you what you want." He took the chain between the handcuffs and pulled me forward.

"What are you going to do? Spank me? Whip me? Put me in your cage and tame me? It isn't enough, Jonathon. It will never be enough." The cuffs cut into my wrists.

Jonathon pulled me off the bed. I landed on my feet and followed as he walked around the room. "You're not following the rules outlined by our contract." Sweat began to dampen the armpits of his shirt. It satisfied me to think he was nervous.

"Let me show you around my lair, Mina. In this corner, we have an X rack. See how it tips to the horizontal position and becomes a torture table." He gave the top a push, tipping it back, and it snapped into position.

"Do you think I can't take it?"

Jonathon dragged me a little further. "For very bad girls, we have the cage." The cage was vertical and slender. One would have to stand in it, and it locked tightly around the body giving little room for movement.

A flurry of butterflies disturbed my stomach. "Did Rory ever stand in it? When do you decide your sub needs to be caged?"

"Then lastly—" Jonathon kneeled faster than I could react, forcing me to my knees he locked the hand cuffs to a steel ring bolted to the floor. "—we have cuff-rings. Strategically placed around the room, so I can clip you by the ankle or collar. Or by your handcuffs."

He stood and walked away. Singers' voices chanted in rhythm, as the music grew to a climax then died quickly away. The silence echoed in my ears.

~46~

ostile tears silently slid down my face. Jonathon had left the room. Still in my panties and bra, I pounded my fists against the floor. My handcuffs were padlocked to the steel ring. The ring bolted to the floor.

What next?

Jonathon was gone only long enough for bitter tears to soak my face. He set a tablet on the table near the door, then sat in a chair eight feet away from me.

I kneeled, resting back on my heels—Hero's Pose in yoga—and re-solved to finish this. "Let me go."

"Why would I do that? This is what you asked for. Punishment."

"This isn't punishment. It's restraint."

His hand went to the bright pink cheek where I had slapped him. "You're sexy when you're angry, Mina. I'll give you that." He seemed amused.

"This is not what I want!" I pounded my fists on the slate-colored carpet.

He stood up and walked toward the door, his hand lifted to the key-pad. "I'll come back when you calm down."

"Wait! Don't leave." I hated crying in front of him. The last thing I wanted was for him to think he had weakened me.

He spun on his heel. "Would you prefer a lashing?" His head turned toward the bull whip on the floor beside the bed.

I looked up at him through wet eyes. "Yes. Yes I would. Only, you won't do it will you? I've signed your silly contract and you refuse to punish me. Isn't that right? Well then, let me out. Rip the contract up and let me go. I'll find what I need elsewhere."

He strode toward me with the whip lifted over his head.

I shrank and waited for the blow. After the moment stretched through another refrain of music, I whispered, "You wouldn't."

Jonathon lowered the whip and tossed it away. He was not arguing with me, he was standing his ground. From where I sat on the floor, his ground was firm. What I hadn't understood was the level of dominance he would rise to.

"I told you the contract would change things," he said.

"I was not fully informed of your *room*. Of your . . ."

He shook his head. "I have profound respect for you, Mina, but you can't claim ignorance. Not with me. Our contract is binding. It is a business agreement giving specific advantage to two parties committed to one goal."

The carpet dug little dents into my knees. I somehow deserved that pain. "If we're only going to discuss it, unlock me so we can talk." I rattled the chain.

"Tell me what benefit did you expect to gain?" His smugness nauseated me.

I narrowed my gaze. "You know the answer to that." He was a means to an end. Tears threatened as hot ire built up in my throat. I took a choked breath to calm down.

He said, "The benefit for me is your submission. I control you. Now that you're under contract, I expect things to go according to our agreement." Jonathon paced. "I will not let you out. I will keep you chained to the floor and feed you by hand if I have to."

I pulled violently at the cuffs. "You're as bad as those traffickers."

Jonathon moved quickly. Angrily. Digging into his pocket, he found keys and unlocked the padlock from the floor. He yanked me to my feet and unlocked the cuffs. He picked up my clothes and threw them at me. "Get dressed." He exited the room.

I heard him putting ice in a glass and pouring something to drink. I put on my clothes, smoothed out the wrinkles, and wiped the sticky salt from my cheeks.

This was not going well.

"Sit on the bed, Mina." He returned with two drinks, Scotch or bourbon, strong ones from the looks of it, and he handed me one. "We *are* going to discuss this. Now."

I sat with the drink in my hand.

Jonathon paced. He dragged a hand through his hair. He gulped down his drink—the whole thing—and set the glass down with a crack on the table. "You're trying my patience. Plead your case, counselor." He crossed his arms on his chest.

"I thought we were in a relationship. I thought we could discuss things as adults *often do*."

"What part of dominant/submissive are you not getting?"

"You said you were in love." The word closed up my throat. "I thought . . ." *I thought I was falling, too.*

He shot icicles at me with his gaze.

The smell of the drink in my hand—scotch—assaulted my nostrils and made me sick to my stomach. I put the glass down on a cabinet. "My client would like to review the contract and reassess the situation. She needs more information."

"I'll give permission to read the fine print. Do it now." He handed me the tablet; the contract was already up. I began rereading a document that I'd read several times before signing.

At the top were two definitions. **Dominant**: ruling, governing, or controlling; having or exerting authority of influence: dominant in the chain of command. Also, occupying or being in a commanding or elevated position. **Submissive:** inclined or ready to submit; unresistingly or humbly obedient. Synonyms are tractable, compliant, pliant, amenable, passive, resigned, patient, docile, tame, subdued.

He'd underlined a section within the document where, with the wording, he retained all the rights to make changes and might even refuse to allow cancellation or discontinuation of it.

"Do you understand the rules of the game now?" Agitation still colored his tone.

"In order to reassess the situation, my client requests a recess."

"Denied."

"My client would like to discontinue the contract."

"Denied, Mina."

I didn't know him at all. Anger, love, and hot desire had clouded my judgment. "What are you saying?"

"I will not let you out. I will not tear up the contract. I don't care what misgivings or doubts you have. You will remain under contract with me until I am done. And trust me," his eyes pinched evilly, "I am not done with you."

"Then punish me!"

"No."

Fear. Free fall. I was diving, but there was no water at the bottom. No splash. Only an abyss of darkness. The butterflies flew up again. I thought I was going to throw up.

"I want you, Mina. But not like this. Let's take some time to recover from all that we've been through. I want to get to know you as a friend and a lover. I'm not ready to complicate our relationship with bondage and discipline."

Tears dripped from my chin. I sniffled back the wave of sadness. "Don't you understand? *This is how I recover.*"

Sorrow filled his eyes. I *really* saw him for the first time in weeks. He shook his head—his mop of uncombed black hair—and said, "I can't . . . do it anymore."

I'd misunderstood him from the start.

He said, "Rory was like you in so many ways. The relationship was volatile. Hostile. Like you—today. That's not what I want. I'd do anything to bring you closer. To give you what you need."

I shook my head in disbelief. "Then why not let me out of the contract?"

"Selfish preservation. I can never repeat what happened with Rory. If you want that type of relationship, I need to guard myself—to keep it from happening again." He looked at his knees. "I thought the contract would scare you away. I was dumbfounded when you actually signed it."

"But," I said, "I'm broken." I needed to be strong for what I was about to do. "I'll get what I need by any means."

He said, "I'll be here when you return."

~47~

In the days that followed, I returned to my condo, and focused on work. Greg remained by my side. He escorted me to the pool each afternoon where the rhythmic movements of my daily laps weren't enough to release the tension surrounding all that happened.

Elaine Goodman notified me about the article she printed in the Chicago Tribune. Buried in the pages, it wasn't the feature we hoped for. Her team had received orders from the FBI to stop interfering with an ongoing investigation. The article discussed the likelihood that Chicago's organized crime controlled our local legal system. The author went on to list Gary Underwood's murder with a half dozen others, giving credit to the Russian mafia.

I spoke with Elaine about my client Bohdi Michaels, and she gave the final details to the journalist writing the piece. Although we had no proof, the mere mention of an unnamed US prosecutor's involvement with local organized crime would scare the pants off Slater. His name didn't make it into the story either.

Jonathon texted me a dozen times a day to check on me. He begged me to return to Lake Forest. He asked me to meet him for lunch. For dinner. I needed space to come to terms with my feelings. Though I longed for his warm fingers on my arms. My hips. Or the sharp sting of his hand slapping my ass.

The sound of Jonathon's leather whip slapping my flesh echoed in the everyday sounds all around me. I heard it in the office when Christina slapped down a file folder. I heard it in the coffeeshop when customers patted each other on the back. And I heard it on the television and in the music on Greg's car radio. I thought of its long leather strands biting sharply into my backside. I wanted that stinging heat.

I needed to experience it again.

Instead, I planned a trip to Red Rocks Park, Vermont, where cliffs soared to unverified heights of seventy-six feet. Photos beckoned me to dive into the deep, freezing-cold water. I made airplane reservations and booked a hotel in South Burlington. The cliffs I would dive from were on the eastern shore of Lake Champlain, which stretched 130 miles along the border between Vermont and New York. North of Lake Ontario, and only about thirty miles from the Canadian border, it would be the northernmost cliff that I'd ever jumped from.

Adding to my guilt, I visited Traci daily. My heart ached for her and what she'd been through. She had lost weight, and her eye sockets appeared hollow. She appeared frail.

In her apartment, wearing red striped pajama pants and a T-shirt, Traci sat on her couch sipping hot tea.

Our friend Steph spent nights with her, making sure she took her meds. Traci needed our emotional support to help her recover.

"Have you been eating?" I asked.

"I'm not hungry," Traci answered.

Steph said, "I made an omelet for lunch, but she pushed it away. I think the buprenorphine has taken her appetite but I'm not sure if that's one of the side effects."

I sat on the chair nearest Traci. Jen told me the level of narcotics in Traci's bloodstream could have caused an overdose. Jen, who was an RN at Traci's hospital, had visited Traci's room during her breaks. She also spoke with Traci's nurse and relayed some details to us. But only the things Traci wanted us to know.

"Has your friend David been by to see you?" I asked.

"Not yet," she answered. The life had been sucked out of my friend's beautiful brown eyes.

Across the room, Steph shook her head no. "He doesn't know."

Traci tucked her knees up and lay on her side. "You are so lucky to have Jonathon."

Was I?

I reached for her shoulder and gave her a light massage. Coming up with something positive to say about Jonathon was easy. "He helped orchestrate your rescue."

"Tell him thank you." She sipped tea. "I don't remember much. We were waiting at the intersection to cross."

I had been dying to hear Traci's story. I had to know if I could have done anything differently. I said, "That was the moment I lost you." I imagined the crowded streets that day.

Traci looked down toward the floor as she searched inside for the memory. She caressed her bruised cheek, and a semi-smile lit her eyes. "I hope I kicked their butts all the way to China, but I just don't remember."

"I'm so sorry. Traci, they meant to take me. I wish they had. I would give everything to take your place."

"We switched shirts. They thought I was you."

"I know."

"I think there was a woman with them."

Angelique? "What did she look like?"

Traci thought for a moment. "She had sun-streaked, long hair and she spoke to them in some form of Russian, I think."

Angelique did not have long sun-streaked hair.

Rory.

Traci reached for her teacup and finding it empty, set it down on the coffee table again.

Steph patted Traci's leg. "You should get some rest."

"I know. I'm tired." Traci handed the empty cup to Steph.

I pulled a light throw over Traci's legs, then Steph and I went to the kitchen.

Steph's pale blue eyes saddened. "She's changed. I don't know what they took from her, but Traci isn't the same."

"They scared her, Steph. All we can do is be with her and help her get back on her feet."

Steph said, "Wil, I'm worried about *you*. What kind of people are you involved with? Is this a client?"

"Yes. It's a client." I told an updated version of the lie. The story I told everyone. My private life had turned my friends into pawns in an international game of chess. It wasn't Jonathon's fault I got drawn into his spider web. I had lusted after him. Like a female cheetah in heat, I stalked him, wanting him for my own. And when he took me, I asked him for something he couldn't give me.

I've fallen for you in every way.

"Steph, I'm going to make them pay for this, I promise." I didn't have the slightest inkling how. First, there was something I needed to do.

$$-48-$$

He said he'd be there for me when I returned.

Since the weekend trip was short, I packed a small bag that included a bathing suit, change of clothes and one sheath dress for dinner the night before my dive.

On the late-night two-hour flight from Chicago to Burlington, Vermont, I perused Google's list of top sights near Lake Champlain. I'd never before been to South Burlington, where American history and museums abounded. My finger hovered over the link to the Church Street Marketplace—an outdoor shopping mall that stretched four blocks. It brought to mind the horrific day Traci was kidnapped.

I shut my laptop and lay my head back on the headrest. I envied the woman sleeping across the aisle from me. Her deep breathing sounded peaceful. That kind of contentment felt out of my reach.

At seven-thirty last night, Greg had driven me to The Office Bar, where I met with Charlie Reid for a much needed pep-talk. She walked me through a plan to help Bohdi Michaels avoid the twenty-year prison sentence for which he seemed destined. Her shrewd advice helped me understand why she was so successful. She'd given me hope.

Waiting at the bar for me to exit the bathroom, Greg was none-the-wiser when I changed into jeans, Sketchers, and a Nike athletic top. He'd be furious when he learned about my escape. So Charlie waited, and once she was sure I'd gone, she told Greg. Greg would tell Jonathon. By then it would be too late for either of them to follow me.

The airplane touched down at 4:16 AM. Sleepy passengers followed me out of the first-class seat. I hurried across the tarmac to the exit and caught another cab. It was after five-thirty in the morning before I dropped my bags on the floor of the king-bed corner room of the South Burlington Hilton.

An ashen sofa, grey carpet, and stainless steel accents fit my dreary mood. I sank onto the bed and wearily gazed at the room. Outside of the wall-to-wall windows, pale blue striations in the brightening sky caught my attention. I pulled the curtains aside and stared at the surface of Lake Champlain. The corner windows allowed me to see a huge swath of the sixth largest lake in the United States. Situated near the shore, the Hilton occupied a central location along the lake's shore. Water reflecting the morning sky attracted me like an early bird to a worm.

From this height . . .

Hotel noises—sounds of pipes and running water, doors closing and people chatting in the hallway—reminded me I didn't have much time. I needed rest. Tonight, I'd take myself out to dinner and then hike to the jump site.

Sleep evaded me. Muffled sounds of a one-way cell phone conversation hummed through the walls. Doors slammed and people laughed in the hallway. At one point I dreamed of Jonathon.

The lighting throughout the dream made me think I was deep under water, where in a windowless blue and green room a collar at my throat chained me to a wall. In front of me, locked iron manacles bound my wrists. The dungeon-like room contained a large bed and a carved wooden medieval chair with a high back. I was naked, and the short chain of the metal neck collar held my back and butt cheeks pressed against the cold stone wall.

Jonathon entered with a woman. I found her highlighted, long brunette hair attractive. A tattoo of cherry tree branches blossomed above her tight fitting, low-cut trousers. Though I'd never seen her, Jonathon had described her tattoo to me in detail.

Rory.

With a cunning look in her eye, she said something in Russian and slapped a leather paddle against one hand.

I awoke craving punishment again.

With hours to kill before my middle-of-the-night dive, I made reservations at local eatery, Bistro de Margot. The artistic plates in their online photos reminded me of someplace Jonathon would have taken me. I told the host to reserve me an extremely pricy bottle of Chardonnay from South Africa.

Tonight was a new moon. In the pitch black of a moonless sky, it would be difficult to find my way. So I spent the rest of the afternoon on my laptop, memorizing trails and looking at maps of Red Rocks Park.

Before I turned off my cell phone at the airport last night, I checked it for messages. At about the time I ditched Greg, he began calling and texting.

I replied, *Don't keep looking for me, I'm out of Illinois till tomorrow.*

He notified Jonathon—as I suspected he would—who called eight times and left a dozen or so duplicate text messages.

Where are you?

Why don't you answer?

Please answer the text, or I'll report you missing to the FBI.

The last one gave me pause. I thought of his furrowed, wrinkled brow and imagined him clenching his fists. I typed:

I'm fine, I'll be back on Sunday.

I hit send and turned off my cell phone again.

At the restaurant, the sommelier brought my hundred dollar wine and poured a glass. As he did, I gazed at the other diners in the low-lit room. White tablecloths and dark carpeting absorbed the typical restaurant sounds—flatware clinking against china, people conversing, laughing.

Perhaps I was searching the room for Jonathon. I wondered if he knew where I was. Soon the waiter set the colorful *salade lyonnaisse* with split snow peas and radish sprouts in front of me. I picked at it with the three-tined fork. The peas tasted delicious, but I had no appetite. Next came lamb chops ratatouille with fingerling potatoes. The rich sauce and beautifully roasted lamb melted in my mouth. It was far more than I could eat.

Though recent events were in the past, and Chicago a fair distance away, none of them left my thoughts. I kept a watchful eye on every person who came and went. I missed Greg's watchful, reassuring presence.

It was after midnight before I dressed in my neoprene wetsuit and cargo pants. The tips of the trees in Vermont had already turned fiery red. The water temperature would have dropped below sixty degrees by now.

Warming up in the hotel room, I recalled my competitive days in college when I performed an inward dive with two and a half somersaults. I lately practiced this dive at the gym. Since an inward dive begins with the diver's back facing the pool, it was too risky to consider when diving from a rock-face cliff. My blue ribbon dive had been the twist with two and a half somersaults. Three judges ranked my dive ten of ten total points. They gave my approach and flight top marks. The other three gave me nine-point-fives because my take-off was slightly less than ideal.

That competition was years ago, before law school. I still practiced those winning dives. Over time, my form had suffered very little. From the seventy-foot cliffs on Lake Champlain, I planned a twist with a single flip. I knew the peak I'd dive from, and knew the water there was very deep. The only trouble would be locating it in the dark.

An Uber driver took me to the trail head. I tipped him twice the fare to return in three hours and then took off down the dark trail with my flashlight illuminating the way. I found my way through cedars and oaks. Crickets and cicadas sang with tree frogs and other night creatures. A cool breeze off the lake pulled me in the right direction about a mile from the road.

At the edge of the cliff, I paused to breathe the night air. City lights from South Burlington lit a few low lying clouds over the water that partially covered the black, star-specked sky. Twinkling below me, the dark water rippled and glistened. The cry of a raptor screeched in the trees. Here, I sat on the jagged rocks and listened to my inner demons. Nature touched me in ways nothing else could.

When I was ready, I stripped my pants off and left them where I could find them in the morning. I zipped my cell phone into a plastic baggie and tucked it into the wetsuit. The sun began to lighten the eastern horizon. The crickets stopped chirping. My toes curled over the edge of the rocky face, and I bent my knees.

My take-off was perfect. In flight, I swiftly twisted and tucked into the somersault. Air rushed past my ears for what seemed like minutes. Straightened legs and pointed toes. Fingertips broke the water's surface and I curled with the impact. I went in clean and deep. At the surface, I emerged with a sharp inhale of fresh thoughts.

~49~

Greg picked me up from Chicago O'Hare. "Jonathon's expecting you in Lake Forest." His hands held the steering wheel of his Santa Fe, but his displeased, rutted brow was aimed at me in the passenger seat.

I still hadn't called Jonathon but noticed three more texts.

I'm worried about you.

Don't do anything foolish.

Lake Champlain? Be careful.

The last was sent at the exact same time I had been standing on the edge of that cliff.

"I can't go there."

Greg said, "Dammit, Ms. Green."

"I'm Ms. Green now?"

"Where the hell did you go? I looked for you for two hours Friday night. Jonathon was worried about you."

Though the dive went well, new-found shame strangled me. "I needed to escape."

"You should have told us. I would have gone with you."

"Don't you get it? I needed a break from all this."

Greg's charged silence didn't last long. "Janko Vorobiev is still out there."

"So what, Greg? I work with rapists and murders. I'm used the facing dangerous men head on."

"With shackles on."

Did he refer to them, or me?

"What did you think I do for a living, Greg?"

His knuckles had turned white, and his left leg bounced up and down. "I assume that you have some way to screen out the crazies and protect yourself?"

"I've protected myself in the past."

"Damn it. Your filter is broken. Jonathon is not the enemy." He was driving too fast and turned off the highway. The wheels of his SUV squealed on the exit ramp.

Your filter is broken.

My filter *was* broken. Greg's outburst was a wakeup call. To what though? My choice of clients? My choice of lover? Since I'd met Jonathon so many dreadful things had happened.

He cursed under his breath. "I won't be here forever, Mina."

"Jonathon's paying you. I don't expect you to stay."

Greg exited the highway and drove about a mile to a park. He stopped the car in a parking lot that faced a children's playground where a half-dozen grade school kids played on the equipment, sliding down a yellow plastic slide and climbing monkey bars.

"Why are we stopping?"

Greg shook his head. "I thought you were pretty sick, Mina. I thought you were smart and had your shit together. I thought you were cool. It turns out you aren't."

He got out of the car and slammed the door. Nearby, a trail led to forest preserve. Greg took off toward the woods.

I opened the car door. "Why the hell are you so angry?"

He turned abruptly. "Don't follow me. Go back to your condo. The key fob is in the car."

"I'm not leaving you here." Lamely, I apologized. "I'm sorry. I don't know how to convey my appreciation. Your help—your protection—has meant a lot to me, Greg. As you and Jonathon have both said, Janko is—"

"You work with murderers and rapists. You'll be fine."

He turned my words against me. I followed from a distance, allowing him space. Once the road and car couldn't be seen any more, I asked, "Greg, where are you going? Would you please stop and talk to me?"

He spun on his heel. The set in his jaw and his narrowed gaze scared me. "If you don't see it, then you're blind."

"See what?"

He ran a hand through his chin-length blond hair. "You've fucking ruined him."

"What do you mean?" I rubbed the backs of my arms with opposite hands. Self-soothing wasn't working.

"I did this as a favor for my friend. For Jonathon. He never paid me. But you know what? I'm done. He is clearly out of his mind. And I'm going to tell him so."

Jonathon had sway with his friends. He was the kind of person who engendered devotion for life. I'd seen it with his partners Jake and Darren. *My filter was broken.*

"What are you going to tell him?"

Greg said, "Don't you see? Since you came into his life, he walks, talks, and eats Wilhelmina Green. The man is madly in love." Greg turned his back on me and took off walking again.

"Where are you going?"

He said, "I quit. Go home, Mina. Go back to your condo." He disappeared into the woods.

Soberly I walked back to the car and sat in the driver's seat.

Had I lived with the angst for so long that I couldn't see what was right in front of me? Self-sabotage had caused this. I'd become a serial tryst terminator. I'd pushed away every man who tried to date me. I saw fault lines in each of them. No one could be who I wanted them to be.

Jonathon had shown up for me in more ways than I could count. He did everything in his power to keep me safe. To do as I asked. Even if my cravings for punishment scared him.

Jonathon was kind and caring and . . . If I wasn't doomed to repeat the past by ending yet another relationship, then I had to see this through. *I loved him.*

Greg's outburst awakened me. The next thing I knew, I'd started the car and was headed back to Lake Forest.

-50-

No longer wearing a sling on his arm, Erik stopped me in the cavernous entryway. "Nice to have you back, Ms. Green."

"Please call me Mina. Is Jonathon in his office?"

"Something came up at PPS. He'll be back in a short while." He asked how I'd managed to ditch Greg a second time.

I dropped my gaze and said, "Text Greg for me, would you please? He's angry with me."

Erik nodded solemnly, as if he knew why.

I left Erik in the entryway and dragged my carry-on luggage to the bedroom where I changed into my bathing suit. A brisk swim would help clear my head. I had much to discuss with Jonathon when he returned. Weary, I walked down the steep flagstone steps to the pool on the shore of Lake Michigan.

What have I become?

For an hour, I lay on the deck in the low afternoon sun and replayed the conversation with Greg. I had approached the relationship with Jonathon like a business partnership. Knowing what Jonathon could deliver drove me toward him like a hungry lioness to her prey.

My motives had been narcissistic and self-serving. Tig Wallace and some of the lawyers I worked with—and against—came to mind. Greedy, uncaring, and shameless. Myopic.

I'll be here for you when you return.

I hoped he meant it. When Jonathon returned, I would tell him how I felt. For better or for worse.

The light of hope at the end of the tunnel set my wheels in motion. I wet my goggles and spit in them. I dragged the elastic band over my head and secured them to my face. Tucking my head, I dove off the diving board and sank into the cool water. Methodically, rhythmically,

I swam laps across the smooth pool water. Each ripple I made caused another and another, until the surface was no longer smooth.

As I came up from a flip turn, I caught the reflection of someone standing near the pool's edge.

Jonathon.

I swam toward the edge of the pool. Once I'd taken off my goggles, I realized my mistake.

"Hello, Mina." Janko squatted on his heels and set a compact semi-automatic rifle on the tile near the pool's edge.

The pool was too deep to stand in at this end. I hung by fingertips and planted my feet on the inside wall. "What do you want, Janko?"

"I'm here to visit my old friend."

My gaze shot from the gun to Janko. "Jonathon is not your friend," I said darkly.

"Let's talk." He reached out a hand to help me out of the water.

"What could you possibly have to say to me?" I set my goggles on the side of the pool.

Janko flicked his hand. Instinct told me not to take it.

My filter isn't broken. It just needed a clean lens.

Janko sensed my hesitation and brutally grabbed me by the hair. I cried out and placed my hands tightly over his hand in my hair—like they taught in self-defense. He yanked me out of the pool in one swift move, set me dripping on the concrete deck and kicked his gun out of reach.

"There. I hear that you are the perfect submissive. Perhaps you'd like to show me now. Be submissive, and I will not hurt you . . . much." He laughed and moved to retrieve the semi-automatic weapon. Janko leveled it at me. Wet red blood soaked the top of Janko's Italian leather shoes.

"Who?" I prayed Jonathon hadn't returned home.

"The guy at the end of the driveway. The man on the patio. The Black man in the Foyer."

I gasped. "Erik?"

"They will not interrupt us. Jonathon's security are all dead."

"How can you be sure. There were a half dozen—"

"I. Am. Certain."

Breath caught in my chest. Inadvertently, I glanced at the bench behind him where my cell phone rested on a towel. He noticed and backed toward it.

"Looking for this?" He picked up my cell phone and threw it into the pool. "There. Now you don't have to worry about calls from your lover." He tossed the towel at me. "Dry off, I'll take you up to see Erik."

I covered my body with the towel. In the back of my mind, I wondered if Greg would return to the house. I hoped he wouldn't walk in on Janko holding the gun.

"Are you alone?" I asked. I wanted to know if his gangsters were stationed around the house, if they'd helped him take out an entire team of security men and women. Had he set a trap for Jonathon who'd return from Chicago soon?

"Do you think you can fight me?" An explosion of gunfire and shattering glass ripped through the pool house as Janko shot out windows on one side of the room.

I shrank beneath the towel. It wouldn't protect me against his rifle.

Aiming the gun at me, Janko encouraged me to climb the steps to the back door of the house. We passed through the kitchen to the foyer where Erik lay on the floor. A poke in my backside nudged me forward. "When will Jon return?" he asked.

"Why would I tell you?"

"Because I asked you a question." He spun me around and backhanded me across the face.

The blow knocked me to the cold marble foyer floor.

"Tell me!"

I shrank from the butt of the gun poised above my head. If Janko didn't know . . . "He won't be back for days," I lied.

"Ah, but there is another here, isn't there?"

I shook my head.

"Already, I searched the house. Where is he?"

"I don't know what you're talking about."

Janko kneeled beside me. "The other bodyguard will be back. Won't he." He grasped my chin and turned my face toward Erik's body. "Look at him. If the other comes here, I will kill him, too. Do you understand?" He shoved my head to the floor. "Do. You. Understand?"

Between clenched teeth, I said, "Yes. I understand."

Janko pulled me up by the arm and marched me forward. Throwing me into the bedroom, he barked, "Put some clothes on. Brush your fucking hair and make yourself look nice. We will wait for this *other* like civilized people."

~51~

orobiev sat on the bed and leveled the rifle at me while I got a pair of jeans and a shirt out of my suitcase. He ripped them from my hand and threw them into the closet. "Where is the dress I sent to you? The one you wore at the fundraiser."

I snarled, "I threw it in the trash."

"A shame. Find something else. Something nice!"

I held up a sleeveless black dress and he seemed satisfied. I dressed behind the closed bathroom door then put on a pair of black high heels.

Janko's beady eyes followed me like a coyote seeking fresh prey. "Where is your diamond collar?"

I'd left it here the last time I returned to Chicago. The black velvet box sat on top of the dresser still.

Janko saw where my gaze landed and prodded me with the rifle. "Wear it."

I clipped the necklace around my throat as Janko came to my side to examine the jeweled collar. My shoulder. My hair. His touch sickened me.

He clasped his hand around my throat and squeezed. "He marked you with this. He thinks he owns you. We'll see who owns you now."

"No one *owns* me."

He laughed then dragged me by my wrist through the house and down to the basement. Janko flicked on the torch lights and punched in the code for the dungeon. As he opened the doors wide, cold fear settled into my belly.

"How did you know the code?"

"It was easy. I typed your name."

Janko had known Jonathon cared for me before I did. But did he know Jonathon would make him pay for this?

"We'll drink while we wait, no?" Janko set his weapon down out of my reach. He took a bottle of expensive vodka out of the freezer, placed two glasses on the bar and poured. Raising his glass high, he said, "*Na zdravie.*" He downed it in one gulp, slammed the glass down, and poured another. "Drink. It is unlucky to refuse when someone toasts to your health."

I pushed the glass away.

"Drink or I will force you." He reached across the bar and grabbed a fistful of my hair.

I glared at the sinewy man and drank the fucking vodka.

He finished his second and poured more into each glass. Janko sat casually on the stool next to me. As if we were friends, he said, "I want to get to know you, Ms. Green. Tell me about yourself."

I narrowed my gaze. "I have nothing to say to you. You're the worst kind of criminal. You've preyed on innocent people and victimized them. You targeted Jonathon, and now you think you can walk away with whatever you want. I'll make sure you don't ever go home to Croatia or whatever rock you crawled out from under."

Janko grinned like I amused him.

I said, "The FBI knows you're working for Tsezar."

"They have it wrong. Tsezar works for me."

My mouth went slack.

"You think it's an accident Angelique got caught? Or that Bohdi Michaels hired you?"

"What do you have to do with my client?"

He sipped, an arrogant lift in his brow.

"Bohdi and I work for the same crime family. Though he left Paris, he is chained to the organization. Shackles, you know? Everyone is submissive to something. I too am bound to the family. My love for them is great. They have done much for me and I . . . have killed for them.

"Bohdi's sister and his parents."

He lifted his chin. "This conversation bores me." He set the rifle on his lap. "Let me tell you about your lover."

"I know everything I need to know about Jonathon." I didn't want to hear any more.

"Not everything. We made a bet once. Did he tell you?"

He did.

Janko kept talking. "The bet was to find a true submissive. Not some sociopath, mind you. But a woman who is a genuine servant. And to collar her."

Janko touched the collar around my neck, and I grimaced and recoiled.

"I see that he won the wager."

Greg thought Jonathon was in love. *If so, how could Janko be telling the truth?* Before our contract, Jonathon had written on a card, *I love you,* and signed it. He admitted to me that Janko knew his weakness—he'd fallen for me.

I've been so blind.

A cell phone vibrated in Janko's pocket. He looked at it, then dismissed the call and set it on the bar. "The dead man's phone. I hoped your lover would let him know when he's returning."

"Jonathon probably called me first. But you threw my phone in the pool."

"Perhaps. You think you know Jonathon? Drink and I'll tell you about your lover."

I sipped. Janko poured another for himself.

"I have known Jonathon a long time." He chuckled. "A very long time. We met in Dubai five . . . or was it ten years ago. He was a kid back then, a kid with grandiose ideas. Even then, Jonathon knew what he wanted in a woman. And look at him now. He has done well for himself." Janko nodded his approval as his gaze appraised me. "I was there the day he met you, do you remember?"

"Of course I do."

"Fate is interesting, don't you think?"

Janko wasn't seeking an answer from me. "Like a woman, fate is fickle as the wind. But also like a woman, once she has made up her mind, there is no challenging her. She is watching us all the time. Fate put you two together for a reason. You must have wanted it, too."

The vodka did little to help my dry throat.

"Tell me, I've never been too sure of Jonathon's style, did he move in slowly to ensnare you with his charm and good looks? Or did he allow you to make the first move? I imagine he seduced you with good wine and beautiful jewels." His hand touched my necklace.

I slapped Vorobiev in the face.

He caught my wrist and laughed. "I see you aren't too sure either. You believe he loves you?" Grinning as if he'd won the round, he let my hand go.

"Mina." He seemed to savor the sound, to taste it on his foul, putrid tongue. "Your name is like a Russian name. Pretty, like you. Drink." Vorobiev insisted on clinking his glass against mine and refilled his again.

I hoped the alcohol would affect his judgment in my favor. It certainly took the edge off my fear.

"You are the bargaining chip. Angelique was collateral damage. Bohdi Michaels is the scapegoat." He downed another shot and turned on me. "I *will* get the money. If I don't, then someone else will come. And someone else. This is not a game."

My eyebrows pulled together involuntarily. I refused to believe it. "You're bluffing."

Up on the ground floor, a floorboard creaked, or a door shut.

"Ah, the guardian has returned." Janko set his drink down and picked up the rifle. He aimed it at the stairway.

I jumped off the stool, but Janko was faster than me. He wrapped an arm around my neck and firmly placed a hand over my mouth.

I hummed through his fingers, "Don't come down here! Janko's here!"

A sincere warning lit Janko's eyes. "Shut the fuck up."

Several too-quiet minutes passed before we saw Greg inching down the stairs. He held his gun out in front, aimed at Janko. "Mina, are you all right?"

Janko pulled me in front of him. "Ah, look. It is Robin Hood come to save the damsel in distress. Where is your bow and arrow?" Janko took his hand from my mouth and aimed his semi-automatic rifle at Greg.

"Be careful, Greg." I warned.

Janko jabbed me in the throat. I coughed.

"Mina?" Greg said. "It's all right. We'll get you out of this."

"Welcome. Greg, is it? Please join us," Janko said with irritating calm.

"I called the police as soon as I saw what you'd done to Erik.

"I'm glad," Janko said.

"Drop the weapon." Greg demanded. He didn't have a shot. I was between them.

"It will take the police seventeen minutes to respond to the call. Are you prepared to see what can happen in seventeen minutes?"

I felt the gun move away from my back as Janko buried his face in my hair and sniffed. "Mmm, I like her. If I decide to keep her, what can you do about it?"

A single shot rang in my ears. I flinched and tried to knock the gun away from Janko at the same time Greg collapsed down the last few steps. The unsettling bend in his knee told me the shot had broken his leg.

Using me as a shield, Janko inched his way toward Greg with the rifle pointed at my head. To Greg, he said, "Give me the gun."

Shiny fresh blood soaked Greg's black slacks. With one hand he put pressure on his broken knee. Greg groaned and handed over his weapon. "The police are on their way," he grunted.

Janko uncocked Greg's Walther and shoved it into his belt. "Get up. Help him up." He pushed me forward.

I helped Greg to his feet, but color drained from his face, and he groaned with pain.

Janko frisked Greg and took his cell phone. "Move. In there," Janko said. He forced us into the dungeon room.

Greg's face paled as I helped him walk. Twice, he nearly collapsed.

"Take what you want and let us go," I pleaded.

In the red room, Janko seemed to know where to find things. Keeping the gun pointed on us, he opened a drawer and threw handcuffs to me. "Put these on him then kneel on the floor," he ordered.

Undeniably, Janko would use the gun if provoked again. I kicked off the high heels and followed instructions, cuffing Greg behind his back then helping him into a chair near the door.

I kneeled on the floor beside him. I said, "He's hurt. He needs a doctor."

"So cute. She cares about you, Greg." Janko kicked Greg in his bleeding leg.

Greg bent over, writhing in pain.

"Leave him alone," I said. I searched for a clock. How much time had passed? Would the police arrive soon enough?

Janko hit Greg in the face with the butt of his rifle. Greg sagged in the chair, unconscious.

I stood and quietly said, "What do you want?"

Fire lit Janko's eyes and he came toward me. I took a wide, fighting stance welcoming his attack and preparing to use his momentum against him.

Janko swiftly grabbed my arm dragged me toward the bed. Powerless against his strength, I clawed at him with my free hand, digging my thumbnail into the soft tissue below his jaw.

Janko punched me in the gut.

I doubled over, trying to catch my breath.

"Remember your place!" He swiftly wrapped a length of rope around my wrists and lifted my arms to a bolt loop on a soffit overhead. With a clip ready, he fastened my arms high above my head.

"Tell me what you want," I said.

When Janko finished locking me in place, he stood back and grinned. "I want you, Ms. Green."

-52-

Hanging from my wrists—a dive in reverse—I balanced on my toes. Janko traced the barrel of his gun from my belly to my chin.

"Don't touch her," Greg coughed.

Janko snaked a fist through my still-damp hair. "You don't seem to be in a position of power."

Greg rasped, "When Jonathon comes for you, I'll be right beside him, fucking you up."

"Jonathon will watch me take what's most precious to him. I'm going to leave him with nothing." Janko tugged one last time on my hair then let go and turned to Greg. Janko pulled him to his feet and pushed the barrel of the gun to Greg's lower jaw. "Is today a good day to die? Get up!"

Pink spittle flew from Greg's mouth to the floor. His face, where Janko delivered the blow to his jaw, colored red and purple. Balanced on one leg, Greg stumbled and crumpled to the floor.

Janko kicked him. "Where is Jonathon?"

"I don't know," Greg coughed.

"Leave him alone." I struggled to pull out of the handcuffs cutting into my wrists. "The police will be here in minutes."

Greg's face whitened as he leveraged his good knee under his body and tried to get up. Janko struck Greg in the back of the head with the gun. My bodyguard collapsed on the rug.

"Janko Vorobiev." A deep voice sounded from outside the room. Jonathon stood in the doorway looking like a man ready to wage war. In his hands a Japanese sword gleamed in the light. The sight of him filled me with hope. Yet dread poured over me like smoke from a brushfire.

"Finally." Janko opened his arms wide. "Here is the man of the hour. I wondered how many of your men I would kill before your grand entrance."

"You're fucking with the wrong man." Jonathon assessed the situation, his gaze flying from Greg—unconscious on the floor—to me. I saw traces of remorse wash over him before he faced his enemy with bloodlust in his eyes.

Janko pointed the gun at Jonathon, daring him to enter. Jonathon pointed the sword. "Only a fool would bring a sword to a gun fight, Jon."

"Guns are for cowards."

Janko laughed. "So you say."

"Are you man enough to fight me with your bare hands, Janko?" Jonathon asked.

"Happy to." Janko's self-assured voice frightened me. He lowered the weapon and placed it on a nearby dresser. Let's make it fair. As fair as it can be. Ha, you know I am the better fighter."

Jonathon placed the sword on the floor. Janko didn't wait for Jonathon to stand. He charged across the room and leveled a kick to his head. Prepared for it, Jonathon caught Janko's leg under his arm and rose abruptly, twisting the leg. Janko flopped backward but caught himself on his hands. He righted himself and the men faced off in squatting stances with one arm and one leg forward. In Warrior Two yoga position, they circled.

"I want the money."

"Did you think you could threaten me and get away with it?" Jonathon asked.

Janko lunged forward, throwing punches.

Jonathon expertly blocked the attack then caught the second thrust in his hand. He turned Janko's arm underneath his own arm and twisted. The action lifted Janko up on his toes and turned him, his back toward Jonathon. Jonathon dug his fingers into the man's upper lip, his thumb under Janko's jaw.

Janko managed to twist out of the hold and somersault away, landing on his feet. His grin was forced. He seemed afraid.

Jonathon followed and jabbed Janko in his ribcage with fingers straightened into a pike. He knocked the wind out of Janko then took his rival's arm. Rolling his shoulder over, Jonathon stepped in between Janko's legs and flipped Janko onto his back on the floor. Then he pulled Janko's arm behind him and rolled his opponent onto his belly. Jonathon pinned him there with his knee on Janko's neck.

Janko choked a laugh. "Very good!"

"He has another gun," I warned.

"Did you think you could come into my home kill my entire security team and expect to get out alive?" Jonathon rumbled the throaty threat. He frisked Janko and found the second gun holstered under his arm, then cocked and thrust it onto Janko's temple.

"Get up!" he demanded.

Janko rose to his feet with his hands in the air.

"You'll never get that money," Jonathon said.

Janko shrugged. "It's okay. I was paid in advance."

"For what?" Jonathon bared his teeth.

"To take your woman."

"Who paid you?"

Janko didn't answer. He dove and somersaulted toward Jonathon then launched himself upward. He struck Jonathon's jaw and snaked his arm around Jonathon's. Janko attempted to disarm him. Both men had a hand on the pistol.

As Jonathon swung his free hand underneath and knocked the gun in the air, Janko let go, and the weapon fell to the floor. Jonathon somersaulted backward and mid-roll, he picked up his sword. He landed on his feet as Janko reached for the semi-automatic on the dresser.

Jonathon was faster. The blade of the sword sliced into Janko's outstretched arm, drawing blood. "Don't," he threatened.

Janko seemed to consider it, hesitating momentarily to look Jonathon in the eyes. "I was wrong. You are the better fighter. You win."

I held my breath at the pause in the action.

Then Janko twitched. At the same time he grasped the gun, Jonathon drew the sword across his opponent's arm.

I closed my eyes at Janko's scream. He collapsed on one knee, gripping his dismembered arm as Jonathon positioned the blade over the back of Janko's neck.

"Who paid you?" Jonathon asked.

"Who do you think?" Blood soaked the carpet beneath Janko.

Jonathon's gaze turned inward as his cheeks colored. "Not—"

"She despises you."

~53~

Jonathon's home crawled with cops, FBI investigators, and medics. The EMTs took Greg to the nearest hospital for emergency knee replacement surgery. He would be in recovery and physical therapy for months to come. Janko's severed hand was put on ice. He and the cooler rode with two police officers to the hospital. The county coroner pronounced poor loyal Erik dead. An ambulance drove off with his body.

Agent Curbelo queried Jonathon and me for hours. About Janko's threats. About Janko. Though emergency responders entered the room where the fight happened with the whites of their eyes all aglow, no investigator questioned Jonathon about his *lifestyle* or about our relationship.

When the house cleared, Jonathon and I moved to the deck outside his swimming pool. Dawn painted the eastern sky pink and orange. We gazed out at the shimmering lake, listening to the rhythmic shush of waves hitting the shore. Behind me Jonathon rested his hands on my waist.

A few things stood out in my mind, things that Janko said. I asked, "Did you make a bet with Janko?"

"A bet?"

"About finding a *true submissive.*"

"Janko thought he could gain rapport with me by talking about dominance and submission. He must have known Rory and I had a relationship. He didn't know that by then, I shied away from that side of myself." He nuzzled my neck. His end-of-day stubble tickled, and I leaned away from him. He said, "I did look you up when I returned to Chicago. I wanted to make sure Janko didn't follow you."

"Then when you became a person of interest in Kymani's murder?"

"I knew you were the best woman for the job. I couldn't have known you would want a sexual relationship. But I fell for you on our first meeting."

"Love at first sight?"

"It was."

"Being with you, Jonathon . . . it's changed me."

He tilted his head to one side. "Do *you* think you are a true submissive?" As if he had already decided.

"I like it when you're cruel. I like punishment because it makes the rest so much sweeter."

"I'm too hard on you."

I smiled. If I hadn't been so exhausted, so sleepy, I would have laughed. "I asked for it."

"I'm sorry for not being there for you. I'm sorry Janko got into the house."

I held him. "Jonathon, you *were* there. You were there for me when I needed you most. Don't you see that?"

"You must understand. I'd do anything for you."

He returned my kisses in the most gentle, compassionate way.

-54-

Summer was ending. Cooler air promised that a change of seasons wasn't out of reach.

During the jury selection for Bohdi Michaels's trial, I stared at the pen in my hand. At the notes I'd made about each prospective juror.

Seems honest.

Deemed trustworthy.

Family man.

Professional and courteous.

Soft spoken.

Unpretentious and frank.

Each trait could also describe the man I loved.

Since that awful day, Jonathon often checked on me with text messages. We spoke on the phone—sometimes several times a day—and Jonathon frequently took me to dinner. Since his house was still considered a crime scene, we both stayed in Chicago. Sometimes at his Waldorf Astoria Condo, sometimes at my Lincoln Park apartment.

Almost two weeks afterward, I sank into a hot tub in my bathroom. Candlelight from four white pillars flickered across the wall. Lilac and lavender soothed my nerves and my body. Bubble bergs floated in the hot fragrant water as I drifted through memories of the last month. When my NIN ringtone roused me from silent reverie, I patted my fingers dry on a clean purple washcloth and answered Jonathon's call.

"How are you?" I asked.

"Okay. Investigators are still asking questions about how Janko got into the house. The working theory is that he hacked into my security system and disabled the alarm. I'm having my security team look into it."

All Jonathon's security systems connected to an app on his cell phone. I'd seen him check his for issues. "Didn't the app alert you?"

He said, "No. That's not all. The police found evidence that he was inside the house for several hours before shooting Erik."

He'd triggered a memory. "How did Janko know the entry code to your red room?"

Jonathon sniffed. I imagined he rubbed the back of his neck or clenched his fists. "He must have hacked passwords from my computer."

My skin crawled at the thought that he'd been lurking somewhere as I changed into a swimsuit. But I had more questions. "At the end, Janko mentioned a woman. It was Rory Bradford, wasn't it. She orchestrated this whole thing. She paid Janko."

He said in a hushed voice, "She'll get what's coming to her. I'll make sure of it."

I wanted to be there for him. "Jonathon—"

"I'm going out of town tomorrow."

The tub water had grown cold. I flipped the drain lever and stood up. Wrapped in a burgundy bath sheet, I asked, "Can I see you before you go?"

"Of course."

Jonathon arrived within moments. I wondered how he'd gotten to my condo so quickly. His idiosyncratic ways, his inscrutable nature where what I loved most about him.

I asked, "Are you really leaving?"

"I have to. She won't stop until . . ." He crossed the room in a few strides and wrapped his arms around my waist. With our lips locked in a fiery kiss, he swept me off my feet—like the old cliché—and carried me into my bedroom. And this time, it felt like our first encounter. Like we'd never before touched or explored each other's bodies.

This time, love was present in each action. Each stroke. Each kiss.

I helped him strip off his T-shirt. Tonight, I wanted him to know how much I loved him. I pushed him back on the bed and ran my fingers through his soft black hair. His strong shoulder muscles glistened in the low light as I crawled over him like a proud, hungry lioness. As I eased my body over his, I kissed his face with a fervor as if it were dialogue and unspoken words that I needed to give to him.

Indeed, I had not given enough of myself.

While I straddled him on my knees, Jonathon peeled the camisole straps off my shoulders. My hard nipples stood erect. Eager. I took them between fingers in both hands and pinched them. I rolled and massaged them as Jonathon's warm hands overlapped mine. I leaned into his caress. Into his firm lips and rough, end-of-day whiskers brushing my skin.

He admired my breasts while cupping them in his hands, then he took my nipples between his fingers. I let him twist and knead them until the intensity grew, fanning the coals of a deeper, inner fire.

My hand floated beneath my panties and pulled them away. As I dragged two fingers through my wet sex, my aroma rose.

"Make yourself come, Mina."

"Whatever you desire," I said. With my gaze locked on his, I fingered myself. Arching with the lovely feelings I provoked, I moaned. "Is this what you want?"

"Yes. Come for me. Make yourself come."

Faster and faster, I flicked my clit with one hand while the other pinched a nipple. My breathing slowed and I looked into Jonathon's eyes. My breath caught in my throat as sensation took control.

"Beautiful, Mina. You are beautiful. Give me your hand." Jonathon grasped my wrist. He sucked my fingers, one by one, until they were clean.

Gripping my waist, he slid his leg out from under me. In a moment, he flipped me on my back—crouching over me with ravenous desire in his eyes.

I peeled the panties off, and he lowered his mouth to my vulva. His hot breath set me ablaze. Tucking my hips, I pressed into him.

"I want you, Jonathon. I need you," I whispered.

He stroked my flat, smooth belly. "You are everything I want, too, Mina."

"Promise. Don't ever leave me," I said.

"I promise." He lowered his mouth to my sex. His tongue flicking and caressing as one hand found my wrist and pinned it to the mattress.

I tugged to get away—to free my arm from his unyielding grip—but the powerlessness I felt fed the flame. I melted into his grip. To his touch. To his passion. I wanted to be here with him. Beneath Jonathon. Submitting to his fervent, loving kisses. The bed rocked with my shuddering body.

When Jonathon sat up, I helped lower his jeans over his erection. I pressed on his shoulder, and he rolled to his back.

"Now let me please you," I said. "I want to show you how much I love you because you deserve everything I can give."

Kneeling atop him, I took his stiff erection into my mouth. His fresh beach scent—sea spray and sandalwood—reminded me of so many tombstoning dives. I dragged my lips and tongue along his shaft. I slid a hand beneath his buttocks and squeezed his firm cheek.

Jonathon let out a euphoric moan. When I released him, I straddled his narrow hips and sank onto him. He pulled my hips close to meet his own. His cock filled me and with each thrust, I met him halfway.

Jonathon took my hands. With his arms bent at the elbow, he entwined his fingers with mine. I leaned into his support, using the leverage to glide up and down. He matched my rhythm with equal drive. Waves of pleasure rolled through my body as he swelled and released. He gasped and cried, "Mina!"

I rode him long past his peak, relishing in the feel of his arms around me. His abdomen against me. His warm breath at my neck. When the waves took me, Jonathon held me closer.

~55~

The bed was still warm where Jonathon's body had lain, but my lover was gone. In bare feet, I padded to the kitchen and found a pile of torn paper on the counter. Our dominant/submissive contract, in pieces. Beside it, a bright pink sticky-note—a love-note with his handwriting—stuck to the black granite counter.

As a submissive, you have all the control. Love, Jonathon.

He'd told me that before, and I never grasped the meaning. Yet when I thought of our relationship as a whole, I realized Jonathon gave me everything I ever needed. He gave me punishment when I asked for it. He gave me space when I—like a child having a temper tantrum—walked away from him. Through it all, he had been there for me in every way I needed. He loved me. And I loved him.

Where do we go from here?

I pulled up his number on my cell phone and dialed. The call went to voicemail, but I left a message. "Hey. Thanks for stopping by last night." I didn't know what to say. "I . . . uh, I wanted to see if you'll go on a date with me. I had an enjoyable time last night and—hell, I had a wonderful time. I love being with you, Jonathon. I love you. Call me when you get a chance. I'd like to take you out to dinner."

With a silent click, I hung up and smiled. I pushed the torn up contract into the recycle bin and flicked on the television. It was a new day.

A new beginning.

I boiled hot water for a cup of pour-over coffee and scooped Fair Trade Guatemalan roast into the coffee maker. The local news team babbled about three new shootings in Chicago. They discussed protesters marching at the courthouse. I made a mental note to avoid that area when I went to Bohdi Michaels' hearing today. I had just begun to pour boiling water over the coffee grounds when the news team mentioned Jonathon's company, Prevail Pharmaceutical Software Corporation.

"Co-presidents Jake Barnes and Darren Ward of the Chicago-based Fortune Five-hundred corporation, Prevail Pharmaceutical Software, are scrambling to elect a new CEO. Jonathon Thomas Heun announced his sudden retirement yesterday, to everyone's utter shock that the founder had stepped down."

My gaze locked on the screen, and I nodded. As we lay in bed last night, Jonathon told me of his plans, so I knew this was coming.

The video switched to live footage in downtown Chicago near the PPS building. Reporter Jill Anders scurried after Jake Barnes with her microphone out. "Mr. Barnes, why didn't Mr. Heun give advance notice of his retirement? What will you do now? Do you have someone in mind for his replacement?" She fired off the questions too fast for Jake to answer as he marched toward the glass doors of the building.

The sound of water splashing on the counter caught my attention, and I set the kettle down. I had over-poured water into the strainer. Grounds and a hot puddle spread across the granite.

The spill could wait. I wanted to hear Jake's reaction.

"Ms. Anders, we don't know what prompted Jon's sudden retirement." Jake had stopped with his hand on the chrome door handle. Gray circles bagged under his eyes. I wondered if he'd slept all night. "But be assured, we're moving as quickly as we can to fill his shoes. Jonathon was a skilled leader. We're looking for someone with his talent and knowledge of the pharmaceutical industry."

"Do you think he left because of the recent murder at his Lake Forest home?" Jill asked.

"He is not implicated in that crime, Ms. Anders."

"Does Attorney Wil Green have anything to do with his decision? Does he have future plans?"

Captivated, I sat on a kitchen stool.

Jake said, "I don't think she has anything to do with his decision to step down."

"Then why, in your opinion did he do it?"

"Jonathon is a private man, Ms. Anders. Let's keep it that way." Jake then ducked into the PPS building.

The smell of coffee and the tap-tap on the floor drew my attention from the screen. I tossed a kitchen towel on the spill and reached for my ringing phone.

"Nice to hear your voice, Mina."

"You certainly rocked the tower. Jake looked upset on the news."

"I saw. He and I reached an understanding, though. He has someone in mind for my replacement."

I smiled. Jonathon had cooked up a plan that I could get behind. "Where are you?"

"Sitting at some bar in terminal D. I miss you already."

"The bed was still warm this morning. I miss you too. How long . . ."

An announcement to begin boarding the flight to Heathrow cut him off. Jonathon waited a moment.

"I don't know yet. I'll be in touch. I'll let you know when you can join me."

"In Greece?" I walked to my bedroom and began dressing for the gym. "It sounds so romantic."

"I hear Santorini Bay has a few nice cliffs to dive from."

"How will we get there?"

"I'll buy a yacht."

"You will?" I thrust one leg into a pair of khakis, then the other.

"I need to be ready."

"For what?"

"Not what. Whom."

I knew he meant Rory Bradford.

~56~

The obligation of Bohdi's trial kept me in Chicago for the next few months. Labor Day had come and gone, and cooler, autumn air blew in from Canada, promising an early onset of winter the day that jurors deliberated. They took only four hours to come up with verdicts for Bohdi's five charges.

Not guilty of laundering.

Not guilty of solicitation.

Not guilty of terrorist financing.

Guilty of theft.

Guilty of accepting bribes.

Bohdi and I considered it a win. His sentence was reduced to five years in prison and a fine. Charlie's advice had been great, but I pulled out a few tricks of my own.

When I shook hands with Slater, he said with a false grin, "You're a worthy opponent, Ms. Green." Then he turned on his heel and stalked out of the courtroom.

Six weeks had passed since Jonathon left. Now that Bohdi's trial was over, I focused my attention on my lover and recalled the last days before he stepped down as CEO and disappeared. Words still batted like the wings of a trapped butterfly through my mind.

Greg: *"Your filter is broken, Mina."*

Janko: *"I've never been too sure of Jonathon's style. Did he move in slowly to ensnare you with his charm and good looks? Or did he seduce you with good wine and jewels?"*

Jonathon: *"I've fallen for you. In every way."*

Greg: *"Don't you see? He cares deeply for you."*

Janko: *"I hear that you are the perfect submissive."*

Jonathon: *"For you, Mina. I'm doing this for you."*

Janko: *"I was paid well in advance."*
Greg: *"If you don't go to him, I quit."*
Me: *"I love you, Jonathon."*

In the interim, I returned to the Lake Shore Women's shelter to see if I could volunteer. Wendy, the woman who turned me away months ago was speaking on the phone when I entered. When she hung up, she looked my way and stood. "How may I help you—wait, I've seen you before."

"I'm Wilhelmina Green, and last time I was here, you turned me away."

Her mouth pinched to one side, making a big dimple in that cheek. "I remember now. You're that lawyer."

"I am, Wendy. It's Wendy, right? Do you mind if I call you by your first name?" I asked as politely as I could.

"That's fine. What can I do for you?"

"It's not what you can do for me, Wendy. It's what I want to do for you. I'd like to set up a weekly donation, a direct withdrawal from my account. I'd like to volunteer my time, but I may have to travel in the next few weeks and don't want to leave any loose ends." I pulled my checkbook from my purse.

"Okay," Wendy sat down at the desk. "I can help you with that."

"Thank you." I wrote out the four figure amount of my weekly withdrawal on the check and handed it to her.

"Thank you Ms. Green, your donation is greatly appreciated."

I stuffed the checkbook back inside my purse. "When I return from my trip, I'd like to join your mentor program. Is there a number I can call to set that up?"

"Absolutely. We need all the help we can get." Wendy reached for a business card. "This is Avril Devonte's number. She's the one in charge of the mentor program. She'll help you get started when you're ready. We can always use volunteers."

I told her how much I appreciated her help.

That week, I got a new tattoo. The flowering rosemary branches with their narrow evergreen-like leaves and tiny white and sky-blue flowers bloomed bright red on my tender skin. Green, branches wrapped around my belly button then continued down my outer thigh past the scar from my Croatia dive. At my hip, the woody stem of the plant turned to a waterfall cascading down my leg to inches above my knee. The waterfall reminded me of so many tombstoning dives. The rosemary reminded me of Mana island near Stiniva Beach in Croatia. Of the day I first met Jonathon.

The tattoo had taken eight hours to complete. I had the work done in one sitting on a Saturday, while I held my phone and talked to Jonathon.

"I miss you," I said to him.

"I can't come back to the States yet. I'm working on something here."

"Can you tell me what?"

"My money and influence must account for some good. I'm working on a way to stop the drug trafficking ring. I'm going to cut the head off the proverbial beast."

Jonathon had asked me not to come. He told me how dangerous it was.

Leaving Chicago was easier than I thought. I sublet my condo to Traci and David. Their budding romance filled my heart with joy. When David learned about what she'd been through during the kidnapping, he vowed to help her get past it. They had become inseparable. Seeing that my bestie had met a man who loved her as I did and more, gratified me. They were partners, like a perfect pairing in a rom-com movie.

Were Jonathon and I like them? Could he be my modern-day hero?

I thought so.

Though we talked as often as he could—lack of cell phone service in the Grecian Islands prohibited daily, or even weekly calls—I missed him. I craved his touch like an addict longing for her next fix. I dreamed of the slap of his hand. Even his tenderness.

During our conversations, Jonathon told me little about where he was or what he was up to. He said my ignorance protected me. He should have known curiosity tickled my brain and would soon spur me into action.

Rory Bradford lived in Greece. Though not much was available about her personal life online, I knew of the international company she worked for. When Jonathon spoke of the "beast," he referred to her. She was deeply entrenched with Transnational Organized Crime and the Russian mafia.

When two weeks passed without hearing from my lover, I packed my bags. Everything I wanted to keep, I put in a storage pod. The rest, I distributed to friends and family. Assad Ridhwaan arrived at my doorstep as if Jonathon and I hadn't skipped a beat. As if Jonathon hadn't been gone for almost two months. He took me without any questions to Jonathon's Waldorf Astoria condo.

I asked, "Have you heard from Jonathon? Do you know where I can find him?" Though I knew Jonathon had chartered a yacht, I didn't know his most recent anchorage.

"He misses you a lot."

"That wasn't an answer."

"I know, Ms. Green."

"Assad, please call me Mina."

He nodded in the rear view mirror. "Ms. Mina, Grant and I want to let you know, we think you're doing the right thing."

On my last night in Chicago, I poured a glass of crisp white wine and sat on Jonathon's long black couch in the condo high above Lake Michigan. I thought of the Michael Endara painting of Benjamin Kyle that hung in a bedroom of Jonathon's mansion. Jonathon once told me he never wanted to end up like Kyle, who woke up one morning without his wallet and without any inkling of who he was. It took ten years for Kyle's family to find him.

I'd be damned if I'd let the same happen to Jonathon.

My fully charged phone rang on the cushion beside my sensitive—now peeling—tattoo. I answered. "Greg Hauser. So good to hear your voice."

"Therapy has gone well, and the new knee performs like a champ. I'm jogging eight miles on the treadmill and using the Nautilus again."

"I'm so glad." I stood slightly and slid out of my cotton skirt so I could examine my new tattoo in its full, scabby glory.

"I want to come with you," he said.

"But your knee. Doesn't it take six months to fully recover?"

"Eleven months for one-hundred-ten percent. At nearly three months, I'm doing great. My physical therapist says so. But I'm determined to recover faster, and *you* can't do this alone."

"You can't come with me, Greg. I'll be happy to know you've got my back. And if I don't return . . . I emailed you my reservation information. I'll make sure you hear from me every day. I promise."

"And if I don't?"

"I'll expect to see you in Greece." My fingers delicately traced the rough rosemary stem from my bellybutton to my hipbone where it morphed into the image of a waterfall.

"When do you leave?"

"Tomorrow. I'm going to find Jonathon. you can count on it."

Alone, I looked out the massive windows to the streets below. To the distant watery horizon.

From this height . . .

THE END

Acknowledgements

There was a time that I thought I'd never publish this series. But thanks to a healthy support system of friends and family who believe in me, I have all the tools at hand. First, I want to thank all my friends at Blackbird Writers who gave me the encouragement, the confidence, and the tools to make this happen. Many thanks to my editor Stacey Donovan at Book Editing Associates. You pushed me in all the best ways to make this story better and I'm grateful for your thoughtful criticism of the first drafts. Valerie Biel, I'm so happy to have you on my team. You've taken on the jobs that I'm worst at and brought me so much joy. Most heartfelt thanks to my critique group for putting up with my first drafts. I'm sorry to have punished you so. Thank you expert reader Sharon Michalove for your Chicago insider notes.

Most of all, thank you readers for deciding to read Mina's Choice Books. I'm forever grateful.

—1—

MINA

"I will possess your heart."

Ben Gibbard, Death Cab for Cutie's singer, calmed me with his lyric voice as the buzz of the tattooist's electric needle grated like a dentist's drill. I tried to focus on the words and the rhythmic bass guitar humming in the background.

Lo Rain, a purple-haired artist, bent over my hip and thigh. Nag Champa incense filled the air. She drew wild lavender and a waterfall that reminded me of several cliffs I'd tombstoned. The waterfall would circle past the scar on my leg. Once, in Croatia, I'd made a bad judgment. When I plunged into the water, I hit coral, and it tore my leg wide open. The tattoo would always remind me that the choices I made were mine to own.

With my cell phone pressed to my ear, I lay back on the narrow padded table, my gaze locked on the painted ceiling above me. Gray clouds swirled around Greek gods, demons, and cartoon characters all peering down as if laughing at my pain.

"How's it feel?" Jonathon asked. He would have sat in on the session if he could.

"Can't you guess?" My teeth ground together. I tried not to think about the burning sensation from the needle pressed into my skin.

"Tell me." His deep voice resonated with me. I missed him.

"She's drawing a lavender flower with the fine needle tool."

"And?"

"It stings. But I'm tough."

"You're the toughest woman I know, Mina."

"I miss you. When are you coming home?" Jonathon was in an undisclosed location in Greece. He could have been on one of the thousands of islands or on the mainland. I had no idea.

"I don't know," he said. "I haven't been able to find her."

Three weeks earlier, he had stepped down as CEO of Prevail Pharmaceutical Software to follow a lead. The woman he'd dated years ago had orchestrated an elaborate plan to kidnap me and extort millions from Jonathon. He had traveled to Greece to find her—Rory Bradford, his ex-girlfriend. She was the mastermind behind the extortion plan orchestrated by Janko Vorobiev less than a month ago.

Her heart must have been shattered when Jonathon left her. When their love turned sour. Her revenge was cruel and unforgiving. Her thugs killed Jonathon's personal bodyguard and ruined my best friend Traci Lambert's life.

Jonathon wasn't out for revenge. He planned to stop her reign of terror.

Though I longed for him to hold my hand during this self-imposed ordeal, the pain of the tattoo artist's needle was nothing compared to the thought of losing him. "Are you being careful?" I asked.

"Of course." It was a throwaway answer and one I didn't believe. He refused to tell me what plans he had to ruin Rory.

"Tell me about Greece," I said.

"I haven't had much time to enjoy it."

"You must be joking. The cerulean blue sky and Mediterranean Sea? I've been there and smelled the salty air. You *must* have found something to enjoy."

"It would be so much better if you were here."

"I miss you too." I missed his stormy gaze and the smooth tone of voice. I missed the sting of his studded paddle on my ass. "Where are you now?"

"I'm drinking iced coffee at a small table on a busy street—"

"Paved or brick?"

"The street is paved with stones. Nearby, there's a statue of Poseidon holding his staff. There's a Mythos beer umbrella above me with the name in bold green cursive. It's so hot, I'm trying to stay in the shade, even though the sun's setting."

"Are you in Athens?"

"No."

"Mykonos?"

"No."

"Chalcis?"

"Stop. You know I can't tell you where I am. She could be listening."

"But you're using a burner phone."

"You know her reach is far and wide." He'd told me about how insanely controlling Rory was. Though she claimed to be a submissive, she worked hard to fill that role and to deserve Jonathon's punishment. She taught him how to be a dominant in the bedroom.

"I want to see you," I said. "I could be there this weekend—"

"No. It's too dangerous, Mina. Erik Edwards gave his life. Janko almost killed Greg. If I hadn't come home in time, he would have killed you."

When Rory paid Janko Vorobiev to extort a seven-figure sum from Jonathon, the plan failed, so Janko came after Jonathon. He killed Jonathon's personal bodyguard, Erik, and shot Greg Hauser, a good friend and confidant, in the knee. Luckily, Jonathon came home in time. He fought Janko, who got what he deserved, and now that man was serving time in federal prison.

"I won't put you in danger ever again," Jonathon said.

"I'd like to get my hands on Rory. I can hold my own. You know I'm a black belt."

"Martial arts won't protect you against semi-automatic weapons," he said.

The needle dug into the flesh above my hip bone. I sucked air through my teeth. "What have you learned about Rory?"

"I've hired mercenaries to fight her. I've got to be strategic and calculating. And ...I'm worried she knows I'm here."

Rory's far-reaching influence was deadly. I'd be devastated if I lost him.

Our relationship began early last summer when he hired me to represent him. Jonathon had become a person of interest in the murder of his personal assistant. When I learned that he was into a certain lifestyle, I became a person interested in him.

Lo Rain turned the tattoo pen off. "I need you to roll onto your side."

"Hold on." I situated myself on the narrow padded table with my left arm raised up under my head, I pressed the phone to my right ear.

"Are you getting close to finding Rory?"

"There's so much I can't tell you over the phone."

I noted the fear in his voice. "How much longer?"

Lo Rain answered, "About an hour. I'm filling in the waterfall with color now." She started up the pen again. The needle dug into my flesh, and I grimaced.

"There's no telling," Jonathon said. "It could be weeks or months before I locate her. I wish it were over and I could come home. I love you, Mina."

"I love you too."

$-2-$

JONATHON

The hardest part of being in Greece was being a half a world away from Mina. I missed her more than anything. I missed her sass, and her soft lips. I missed her brilliant conversation and her long, graceful arms. Last month we became closer than I ever dreamed possible. In all the ways no one ever understood me before, Mina got *me*. She saw *me*.

I looked out across the street at pedestrians hurrying to evening meetups, couples hand in hand, peering into shop windows, a young mother pushing a stroller. It had been a week since I called Mina. I thought of her and smoothed the beard I'd grown since I arrived in Greece.

Mina cried when she heard I was leaving. But when I explained I needed to find Rory—to stop her—Mina understood. All her work defending sociopaths, felons, and psychotic scumbags had taught her something about the criminal mind. Mina understood Rory would never let up. In fact, it was her idea to dismantle Rory's scaffolding. To infect Rory's tower of power and bring her to the ground.

The rest came easily. Rory and I went to college together. We'd had a very dysfunctional relationship and when we parted ways, she returned to Europe. To her crime-boss father. She told me once that she was born in Europe when I questioned her ability to speak Italian. But I didn't know she also spoke Russian. Or that Russian was her first language.

Rory Bradford, the woman I dated for four years, was actually Rory Protsenko, the daughter of Artur Protsenko, king of a well-known Russian crime syndicate. More recently she tried to extort money from me. And worse, she sicced her thug Janko Vorobiev on the woman I loved. To get her revenge, Rory tried to ruin the best thing I had going.

Now it was my turn. I could never let Rory get away with what she'd done. I needed to put an end to this before she became even more desperate.

In the last month, I'd learned Rory oversaw production of fentanyl from her factory near Izmir, Turkey. Though her father was the leader of a criminal empire, Rory had branched out on her own. She was power hungry and hated being under anyone's thumb—including her father's. She sold the deadly drugs to criminals and mercenaries from all over the world. For various reasons, most of them would rather do business with her than the Chinese.

Stan Moorlehem and I staked out the fentanyl plant one night while they loaded crates into the backs of four Sprinter vans. Mayhem—Stan's nickname—and I followed the vans to the port in Izmir. I alerted Nico Fortunato—a Navy SEAL I met through Bujinkan training—and his team tracked the shipment. Nico commanded a team of highly trained men and women who intercepted a small freighter headed toward Bari, Italy. PHMSA, the Pipeline and Hazardous Materials Safety Administration, confiscated three tons of the deadly drug made by Rory's company.

While sipping iced coffee, I made notes about what happened on a Chromebook, then sent them to Mayhem. "Rory seems undaunted by our attempts to destroy her. When PHMSA officials traced the shipment back to one of her factories, they found it had been burned to the ground. No trace of that operation was left. She had many, though, so we move to phase two. Find Rory's headquarters. Find her other manufacturing locations. And find Sotoris."

I hit send, then transferred the communication and all my notes to a thumb drive.

Across the road, a fifteen-foot metal statue of Poseidon towered above the stone circle. His fish tail swept waves made of aging blue iron. Brightly colored compact cars drove around the circle past the café—a blue and white Twizy, a red Mini Cooper, a yellow Mercedes-Benz MB Smart Coupe—so close, I could almost touch them. The road was too narrow for more than one at a time.

I looked at each driver, trying to see if they made the briefest eye contact. If so, I would leave. I would hide and cover my tracks. Rory's people were everywhere.

Javier Garrido, my new personal bodyguard, stood against the patio entrance in the shade of the setting sun. Javier had only been working for me for about a month. I'd selected him from a handful of well-trained bodyguards after Janko Vorobiev killed my right-hand man, Erik Edwards. I signaled for him to join me.

"Sir?"

"Sit down, Javier." I dragged the metal chair away from the table for him. Javier previously worked for a former governor of Illinois. He managed difficult scenarios and bomb threats. Originally trained in the Army, his transition to protective services earned him high scores. More than that, he was fiercely loyal. He stayed with the past governor until he died of old age.

"Sir?"

"We need to talk, Javier." I was still getting to know him.

He unbuttoned his black suit jacket and sat beside me. It might have been the heat, but he looked uncomfortable. This was never going to work between us if he couldn't relax with me.

"Have I done something wrong, sir?"

"No. Of course not." I finished the iced espresso and signaled the waitress to bring two more. *"Ena akomi, parakalo."*

She nodded and went back inside.

"Javier, what did you expect to get out of this job?"

"What do you mean, sir?"

"And stop calling me sir. It gives me a superiority complex. Besides, I think we're about the same age."

"Yes, si—" Javier nodded.

"Just Jonathon."

Javier lowered his head.

He was trained to be respectful. I had to respect that. "Mr. Heun, then."

"Mr. Heun." He nodded.

The waitress set two iced espressos on paper napkins. I handed her the cash payment and a tip in euros.

"Tell me something about yourself. Where did you grow up?" My track record this year with personal bodyguards was not good. My last personal bodyguard was a close friend. The one before that betrayed me and tried to kill Mina. Though I debated the wisdom of befriending Javier, it was important to learn about the people working for me. I never wanted to take them for granted. Especially when their lives were on the line.

Javier cleared his throat. His eyes were hidden behind slim, dark sunglasses. "I immigrated from Mexico to the U.S. with my family about twenty years ago. My father and mother gained citizenship after living and working in Chicago for ten years."

"Where did you go to school?"

"Phoenix Military Academy in Chicago. After that, I enrolled in the Army."

"Where were you stationed?"

"I was never deployed to the front lines." Javier downed a big swallow of the iced coffee.

"How do you feel about that?"

Javier looked at the table. "I'm not sure."

"Look, I have some hand-to-hand combat skills. I'm a twelfth-degree black-belt in Kendo martial arts." Sword fighting was more than a hobby of mine. It was an obsession. I collected rare katanas and when I was home, I trained daily. "I'm telling you this so you know I can hold my own in the right circumstances."

"Forgive me for saying so, but you're a legend among my colleagues. How you stopped that international criminal—I mean—you cut off his hand!" His eyes lit up, but he quickly stifled the emotion and composed himself.

Legend? "I'm not proud of it." It had taken every ounce of restraint to keep from killing Janko.

He squinted at the setting sun. "If I may, si—ah, Mr. Heun—I'm happy to be working for you. I believe in what you're doing here. It's the work of a saint. If you know what I mean."

"Javier, you think too highly of me. I'm not a saint . . . or a super-hero. I'm a man risking my life to hopefully save others' lives. That includes my fiancée." Technically, I hadn't asked Mina to marry me yet. I didn't want her to make plans that may or may not become reality. I knew the deadly risks I faced here.

Javier fidgeted with a white-gold ring on his left hand. I'd noticed it before.

"Are you married?" I asked.

His eyes lit briefly. "Her name is Rachel."

I could see it in the way he caressed the ring. Javier would never tell me he was afraid he wouldn't make it back to Chicago.

"The men working for me are professionals. They have experience with the Russian mob and have helped police track and kill terrorist cells of ISIS and other groups. I don't want you to worry that we won't make it home."

Javier looked down at his shoes and gave a slight nod.

"I will make sure you get home." I reached across the table and gripped his arm. I understood his fear.

Beginning to doubt Javier had the balls for this job, I finished the last of my coffee. "Let's get back to the villa where it's more private."

Javier nodded. "No disrespect, Mr. Heun, I'd like to spar with you someday."

As I pushed the metal chair away from the table, I saw an orange Ford Fiesta rounding the curve and coming for us. Javier leapt at me and shoved the table out of the way.

Javier thrust me into the building as the Fiesta crashed into our table, just missing us. The car hit the building. With a blinding flash, an explosion deafened me. The force of the bomb threw me into the wall. I fell to the ground.

Hot flames licked my hands as I rolled on top of Javier. He seemed to be unconscious and as I tried to get up, a second explosion knocked me to the sidewalk. My cheek lay against hard pavement. Before my eyes fluttered closed, I saw burning bodies lying on the ground, tables overturned, and linen on fire. Smoke poured out of the blackened shell of the orange car.

I woke with the taste of blood on my teeth and my ears ringing a high-pitched *shree*. The space was pitch-black around me, not even the night sky glowed through a window. Yet somehow I knew it was past midnight. The last thing I remembered was Javier lunging for me as a car careened toward us.

I was sitting upright in a wooden chair. When I hitched my shoulder, pain shot through my arm. It was dislocated. I tried to adjust myself in the seat and quickly learned my ankles were bound to the chair legs. My arms were tied behind my back and ropes held me to the chair. My shirt and shoes had been removed. I assessed other body parts. My teeth were intact, but my lip had split. My cheekbone, knuckles, and elbows felt bruised. The back of one hand burned with extreme pain. I tried to feel the injury and touched an open wound.

There could only be one person who would want to do this to me.

Beyond the intense ringing in my ears, I heard someone breathing. I wasn't alone. "Javier?" I croaked.

A blinding spotlight came on and I squinted. "What do you want from me?"

"In time, my friend. In time."

I heard the strike of a match and through the glare of the spotlight, the coal of a cigarette glowed orange.